FORGET
ME NOT

OTHER BOOKS AND AUDIO BOOKS
BY MICHELE ASHMAN BELL:

A Candle in the Window

An Enduring Love

An Unexpected Love

Finding Paradise

A Forever Love

Latter-day Spies: Spyhunt

Love Lights the Way

Pathway Home

Timeless Moments

Without a Flaw

Yesterday's Love

FORGET ME NOT

a novel

MICHELE ASHMAN BELL

Covenant Communications, Inc.

Covenant.

Published by Covenant Communications, Inc.
American Fork, Utah

Printed in the United States
First Printing: January 2005

11 10 09 08 07 06 05   10 9 8 7 6 5 4 3 2 1

ISBN 1-59156-730-0

This book is dedicated to my
dear friend, Shelley Thompson,
who inspired me to write it.
I'd also like to dedicate this book to the
memory of the soldier whose bracelet I wore as a
young girl in 1971, Lieutenant Commander Gordon Paige,
who died in Vietnam, and to the
The National League of Families of American Prisoners
and Missing in Southeast Asia for helping me
in my search for Lcdr Paige.

*Thus saith the Lord; Refrain thy voice from weeping,
and thine eyes from tears: for thy work shall be rewarded,
saith the Lord; and they shall come again from the
land of the enemy. And there is hope in thine end,
saith the Lord, that thy children shall come again
to their own border.*
Jeremiah 31:16–17

CHAPTER ONE

"Di di di!" the Vietnamese guards shouted as the emaciated soldiers scrambled toward the dense jungle growth. Moving quickly to escape the pointed jabs of the guards' bayonettes, the men scurried toward the shroud of palms and ferns as the *whup-whup-whup* of U.S. helicopters overhead drew nearer. Huey slicks and gunships, Chinooks, Cobra gunships, and OH-58 and OH-6 observation helicopters spiraled downward and appeared to be on the verge of landing in the compound of the prisoner-of-war camp.

"Di di, di di mau," the captors shouted to the gaunt-faced soldiers cowering under the hateful glare of the North Vietnamese Army guards. This wasn't the first time American helicopters had come close to discovering the camp. But somehow, the NVA seemed to stay one jump ahead of them.

Hope of rescue. This was what the prisoners dreamed of, lived for. This was what kept them alive—hope that the choppers would swoop down in a blaze of glory and take them from this cesspool of filth and torture.

Bringing up the rear, Dalton "Mac" McNamara was one of the last men to join his fellow prisoners, and just before the jungle growth swallowed him, he turned and looked up through the palm fronds dancing beneath the wafting air of the chopper blades barely forty feet above him, the skids nearly touching the thatched roof of the prisoners' living hooch.

There, peering back at him, was an infantry captain, perched in the open door at the rear of the chopper. The man was so close that

Dalton saw his rank and branch insignia on his camouflage uniform. In one of his hands was a pistol, in the other, a pair of binoculars. As their eyes met, Dalton felt the stabbing pain of the bayonet in his back. *"Di di di!"*

Then, the world suddenly seemed to move in slow motion, and the choppers turned and began to leave. Dalton's hundred-and-forty-pound body, frail and weak from chronic dysentery and malaria, was unable to respond quickly enough to his mind's command to break free from his captors and spring onto the roof of the hooch to grab freedom aboard the helicopter—freedom that was merely forty feet away.

The window of opportunity lasted a mere second, and Dalton's slow thinking caused him to lose his chance. It was too late.

The sound of the departing rotor blades took Dalton's last hope of rescue, leaving him and the other men devastated in spirit. After the starvation, the sickness, and the misery, after burying almost half of their fellow prisoners, hope for life faded into a numbness that had become their miserable existence.

"I saw his eyes," Dalton mumbled to a fellow prisoner, a marine named Wilson. "He knows we're here."

"Then they'll come back," Wilson whispered, knowing that the guards were agitated and jittery from the close call. Past experience told them to not anger their captors.

Dalton shook his head. He knew the drill by now. "No, they'll move us before they return. They had their chance."

After trudging back to camp in the sweltering heat, the lifeless men fell through the door of the hooch, their minds filled with questions of what if. *What if the choppers would have landed?* The NVA guards would have been outnumbered. They could have taken them. *What if they would have been rescued?* By now they would be on their way back to Saigon, back to real beds, real food, real lives.

What if?

The remaining hours of day blurred into darkness, and before falling asleep that night, Dalton thought about his capture. He had never figured out why some men lived, some men died, and some men were captured. He wondered, as he'd wondered hundreds of times before, if this would be the place he died.

Just as Dalton had predicted, the next day the prisoners were roused from their sleep and moved to a new camp. Many of the men had difficulty making the long journey through the jungle. Most had been injured before or during their capture and had received only primitive medical care. Wilson had arrived in Dalton's camp with a wounded hand that had turned black. The NVA medic told him the arm would have to be amputated. Wilson wasn't about to let the heartless medic chop off his hand, so Wilson told him he had a heart condition, which persuaded the medic to treat the wound with penicillin instead.

Dalton and another man, Ron Sherman, who'd had some medical training prior to his tour of duty in Vietnam, had removed Wilson's filthy, stinking bandages and washed them in a nearby creek, then hung them to dry. Several days later, maggots invaded the wound and, after devouring every bit of dead, infected flesh, disappeared as quickly as they'd arrived and never returned again. Dalton had never seen anything like it.

Wilson's hand had survived amputation, but would his body survive the effects of imprisonment?

The men had no shoes; walking was painful on their bony, bleeding, and infected feet. They received no mercy, no compassion for their condition. If they fell behind, they received a bayonet in the back. Dalton had lost count of how many stab wounds he had.

The new camp was no better than their other camp, except for a stream nearby where they could get water and wash themselves.

They moved into their new hooch with their few belongings and their blankets that were no more than discarded rice sacks sewn together. Ironically, printed on the sacks were the words *Donated by the People of the USA*. The blankets did nothing to ward off the rain-drenched chill of the mountains. All they wore were the same flimsy black pajamas worn by the Vietnamese, given to the soldiers once their fatigues eventually rotted from their bodies due to the extreme humidity.

With the close proximity of water came swarms of huge mosquitos. Because of the lack of mosquito nets, every prisoner suffered from malaria. They were also afflicted with acute and chronic dysentery, which made them run for the latrine far too many times a day. Their clothes became detestable and the compound was like a barnyard, but the men were too sick to do anything about it. Having a stream nearby would hopefully help this matter.

The deficiency of vitamins in their diets caused them to suffer from scurvy, osteomalacia, bleeding gums, and edema. They also lost teeth. Dalton wondered, if they were eventually rescued, if their health would ever return to normal. Somehow he doubted it.

The North Vietnamese withheld quinine until a soldier was in serious danger of dying. Even then, the quantities of the medicine were inadequate to make a substantial improvement in one's condition. Watching a man die was heartwrenching, but when his spirit departed, there was an enviable expression of peace on the face of the lifeless corpse. Yet no man was in a hurry to find peace that way.

Dalton did his best to keep up his spirits and the morale of the men around him, but conditions like these, day after day, pulled each of them further and further down to despair and hopelessness.

Each day the men gathered firewood and as many edible plants as they could find. The rest of the day they talked of home, girlfriends, family, and what they would do when they were rescued. At night they escaped into their dreams, their only reprieve from misery. Unless they were awakened by one of the rats. Dalton had kicked many a hungry rat across the room during the night. It was just one more thing they had to endure.

With the new camp came several new guards and a new commander.

One young guard named Trang actually showed a hint of humanity to the prisoners and pestered them to help him learn English. His true loyalties were questionable, since he was fascinated with anything regarding the American way of life. He asked about automobiles, movie stars, and living conditions in America. Dalton felt that if an American chopper had landed in the middle of the compound that very day, Trang would be the first one aboard, begging to go to America with the soldiers.

The other new guard, named Sy, treated the prisoners with contempt. He seemed to be happiest when the prisoners were miserable. None of the prisoners liked him, but then again, none of the NVA guards seemed to like him either.

Then there was the camp commander, who never cracked a smile, rarely spoke a word directly to the prisoners, and mostly stayed inside his thatched hooch. The prisoners nicknamed him "Godzilla" because of the stiff, bowlegged way he walked, the stern, angry expression on his face, and the way he scowled at his surroundings as if waiting for an attack.

Yet as grouchy as he seemed, Dalton noticed occasional glimmers of kindness about him. Without warning he would allow the men extra rations of rice, or some days he would even provide chicken or pork from the livestock kept by the camp cadre. It was when he gave the prisoners a few chickens to raise that Dalton realized the man had a modicum of humanity inside and under different circumstances was probably a decent human being. Dalton wondered if the man had a wife and family. Did he hate the war as much as they did?

The constant companionship of fear and discomfort made dying seem easier than living in the jungle, but day after day the men survived. Days blurred into weeks, weeks into months.

Among themselves, the prisoners discussed the war, its possible outcome and the effect it had on their future. Even though none of them wanted to be there, many disagreements erupted over the politics of it all, and often the discussion became heated until finally one of the guards had to break it up.

One thing all the soldiers did agree on was the amazing effectiveness the NVA troops had with the most rudimentary of devices. They were masters of booby traps, and all of the men had stories to share of their experiences with one type or another. The most basic NVA booby trap was the excrement-smeared spike located in a concealed pit or hole. The victim would either fall into the pit or step into the hole and be pierced by the spike. There was also the method of attaching spikes to bamboo whips or rocks, which were released by a trip wire. The victim would almost always contract blood poisoning if the skin was broken by one of these spikes.

The Vietcong guerrillas also buried bullets in the ground, right up to their tips, with the primer sitting on a nail as a firing pin. The Americans called these "toe-poppers" because the bullets would go off if stepped on. There was also an abundance of land mines planted throughout grassy areas.

The booby traps had a huge demoralizing effect on the U.S. troops because men were lost to booby traps without even encountering a single Vietcong soldier in combat. The traps were deliberately constructed to maim rather than kill, and when a patrol operated in an area likely to contain booby traps, the psychological effects were as effective as normal combat. Several of the men in the camp suffered the effects of an encounter with one of these traps, and many had died in the camps from the wounds inflicted by them.

As the months passed, the prisoners survived the monsoon season, which turned the ground into a foot of mud. The stream became a treacherous outlet for flash floods and mudslides, which had washed several men to their deaths.

Morale was low, the level of misery high. If it wasn't the ninety-percent humidity making life unbearable, it was the threat of poisonous snakes and scorpions and the continual stinging of mosquitos and ants.

Through it all, Dalton vowed to not let the Vietcong break his spirit. He was determined not to let the detestable conditions rob him of his will to live. He never went to sleep without saying a prayer and finding something to be grateful for. Some days it was nearly impossible to do, and prayer was the only thing that got him through. He refused to believe God had forgotten about him, as so many of the men claimed.

Upon rising, he always mumbled a plea for help for himself and the other men. He prayed for rescue and to someday be able to return home to his family. His faith prevented the flicker of hope inside from being extinguished by the feelings of defeat and helplessness. But it seemed as though each day, when they thought it couldn't get any worse, something would happen to show them that it could. And each night, when the men went to bed, they wondered if it would be their last night on earth.

CHAPTER TWO

Newport Beach, California, thirty years later

Paige McNamara opened the suitcase she'd just pulled out of storage and discovered a plastic flower lei inside.

She smiled. Memories of her honeymoon with Dalton flooded her mind. Their trip to Kauai had been better than perfect. Both of them longed to return to the lush island, bask on the beach in the sun, dine on fresh seafood in a restaurant overlooking the ocean, and hike the trails along the breathtaking Na Pali Coast.

But Kauai would have to come later. Right now they were packing for another trip, a trip that had sounded wonderful in the beginning but had become increasingly difficult to prepare for. A trip to Vietnam.

The purpose of this trip was to find answers and, more importantly, closure for both Dalton and his daughter, Skyler, whose mother was a Vietnamese woman Dalton had met while serving during the war.

Paige knew the trip would be physically difficult and emotionally draining, but they all believed it would also bring peace, something both Dalton and Skyler needed in their lives. Dalton had struggled greatly with the things he'd witnessed and experienced during the war. Most of it he couldn't—no, wouldn't—talk about. But nights of restless sleep and long, extended moments of solitude and silence proved to Paige he was still haunted by the war.

In her own way, Skyler was also haunted by the war. Not first-hand, but secondhand, through her father and mother. Soon Lee had

been a lost and desperate young woman when Dalton found her. He
helped provide a way for her to leave Vietnam and make a better life
for herself in the United States. She'd lived with Dalton's family and
adapted quickly to an American way of life. Yet her own life was
haunted by the war. She'd lost her father, brothers, and husband in
battle. But worse was the child whose life was lost to protect an entire
village of women and children. While hiding from North Vietnamese
soldiers, her baby had started to cry, and she knew that the soldiers
would find her and the others if he didn't stop. So she held the baby
to her chest, trying to smother his cries. The infant's cries had
stopped then, never to be heard again.

Soon Lee never recovered from the guilt. Her dreams were filled
with her baby's cries. After Dalton returned from the prisoner-of-war
camps, he and Soon Lee fell in love and got married. Dalton had
hoped that after they'd had a child of their own, Soon Lee would be
able to move on and that the nightmares would stop. But the guilt
never ceased. Finally, Soon Lee couldn't go on. Using the sleeping
pills that were necessary for any sleep she got, Soon Lee went to sleep
permanently, to escape her pain. But that pain lived on, through
Skyler.

Answers. Dalton and his daughter both needed answers. And
somehow they believed those answers were in Vietnam.

Paige was willing to do whatever it took to help these two people
she'd grown to love and care for deeply. Dalton was her soul mate, her
other half. Skyler was the daughter she'd never had. And with Paige's
son Jared home from his mission, her life was complete.

Jared had planned on going to Vietnam with them, but before
Christmas he had started dating the sister of one of his former
mission companions, and the two had since become inseparable. He'd
already informed his mother and stepdad that he wasn't going to be
able to go on the trip with them. His list of reasons included school,
basketball, and his job, but they all knew it was Nicole who made
leaving for three weeks harder than when he'd left for two years on his
mission.

Paige knew it would only be a matter of time before the two
became engaged. Jared had already started looking for a ring and
working extra hours with a landscaping company to save enough

money for it. She wasn't ready for him to take this next big step in his life, but she'd learned long ago that he was no longer her little boy. He was a grown man, and he was ready to move on with his life.

The sound of the front door opening and then slamming shut reverberated through the house. It was too early for Dalton to be home from work, which meant it had to be Sky.

Paige shut her eyes and prayed that she would be able to say the right things so Sky wouldn't get upset with her. The change in her relationship with her stepdaughter concerned her. When she and Dalton had first gotten married, Paige and Sky had been close, more than friends, almost as close as a mother and daughter. But within the last few months, Sky had grown agitated, and at times seemed annoyed with Paige. Dalton noticed it too but didn't know what to think of the change in her behavior. He wondered if maybe the pressure of graduating from high school and having to make so many important decisions about her future was making his daughter so unpleasant. Paige, on the other hand, thought it had something to do with this trip to Vietnam. She felt Sky needed to find out about her mother to complete herself. It was something Paige understood because she had never had a good relationship with her own mother. She'd always wished she could have had heart-to-heart talks with her mother about her parents' divorce, her mother's bitterness and unhappiness, and her distance from her children, especially from Paige. Slowly, over time, Paige's heart had softened and healed.

If going to Vietnam would give Sky the things she needed to be whole, then Paige supported it completely. She just wished Sky wouldn't take her frustrations and anxiety out on her. But she did. And it was to the point that Paige wondered if maybe it would be better for her to stay home and let Sky and Dalton go without her. With everything going on in her own life, she had plenty to stay home for. But she felt a great need to go with them so she could understand both of them better. Soon Lee was also a part of her life.

"Sky, is that you?" Paige called.

"Yeah, what's for dinner?" Sky answered from the kitchen.

Paige hesitated to answer, never knowing if what she'd prepared for dinner would be something Sky would be in the mood to eat. Still, trying to prepare her stepdaughter's favorites didn't seem to make the evening meal any more pleasant. Sky seemed to make a point of being difficult and picky. For Paige, it was a no-win situation no matter what she did.

"Your dad said he'd pick up something on the way home. I've been over at Bryant's all day, so I haven't had a chance to make anything."

"What's he getting?"

"I don't know," Paige replied. "Call him on his cell and talk to him. I'm sure he'll get whatever you want."

Paige wasn't up to putting up with Sky's testiness. She'd had a particularly difficult day herself. After her friend Lou passed away from breast cancer, she'd felt a need to step up and help Bryant out with the house and their two children. It was hard enough to deal with the loss of her best friend, but to see the struggle Bryant and the kids had without Lou made it even harder. Bryant was a shell of a man, going through the motions of daily life but completely empty inside. The children still seemed to be in shock over the death of their mother. Neither of them said much about it, but Paige sensed their pain. Each time she hugged them good-bye, they clung to her with desperation.

Bryant had a part-time nanny who was there when the kids got home from school, did light housework, made them a home-cooked meal each night, and helped the children get their homework done before Bryant got home from work. But Paige felt like there was so much more that needed to be done for the family. She changed sheets, caught up on the laundry, and did a lot of the deep cleaning around the house. But most important, she offered hugs and love and sometimes a shoulder to cry on.

Bryant offered to pay her for her full day of work, but Paige wouldn't hear of it. They were like family to her, and it was her way of doing something to help. In some ways it helped her feel close to Lou.

She still worked at Lou's interior design store, Louisa's, a few days a week, but it wasn't the same with Lou gone. One of the managers had offered to buy out the Newport Beach store, and Bryant thought it best to sell. He couldn't run the store, and Paige didn't feel qualified nor did she possess the desire to take over Lou's position as owner, so the decision was made. For the time being, Paige would stay on as a buyer and part-time help.

All of it was much more emotionally than physically draining.

Plopping the suitcase onto her bed, Paige began the arduous task of packing. Most of her things would be carried in a backpack. The suitcase would contain gifts for Soon Lee's family and school supplies for the children in their village.

She and Dalton had come up with a list of items to take on the trip, both of them deciding to pack light and wash clothes along the way. Sky thought it was "gross" to have to wear the same clothes over and over, but when they asked her if she was willing to haul a huge suitcase all over the country, her attitude had changed.

Paige went to the laundry room, where she started the last load of laundry and folded a batch of whites from the dryer. While folding T-shirts into a pile, Paige felt a pair of hands slip around her waist.

Dalton kissed her on the neck. "Hello, beautiful," he said.

Paige closed her eyes as his kisses trailed up her neck to her earlobe. He pulled her into a warm hug and held her. She doubted she would ever take for granted the tenderness and displays of affection he showed her. Her first husband, Mark, hadn't been the type to show affection toward her. Dalton was the loving, caring husband she'd always dreamed of but never thought she'd have.

"How was your day?" Paige asked, snuggling close to him.

"Long. I looked forward to coming home to a nice, quiet evening with you."

"Dad," Sky hollered from the kitchen. "Did you remember to get the salad dressing? I wanted the creamy tomatillo."

"Uh-oh," Dalton said.

"Dad?" the impatient voice came again.

"I don't think I got the right dressing," Dalton confessed.

Paige kissed her husband and said, "Don't worry, dear. I think I have some in the fridge. I'll go see."

With luck, Paige found some of Sky's favorite salad dressing from the last time they had eaten at that particular restaurant.

"How's your packing going, Sky?" Dalton asked his daughter.

The girl shrugged. "I haven't done it yet."

"Honey, we leave the day after tomorrow."

"I know, Dad."

Sky's attitude puzzled both Dalton and Paige. The girl had seemed so excited about the trip in the beginning, but as it got closer, she'd gotten more and more agitated about it. Yet she wouldn't say what was bothering her.

"You need to get packed so we have time to get anything you might need," he told her.

"Okay, I'll do it," Sky answered.

"I can help you, if you'd like," Paige offered.

"I can do it," Sky said, then she mumbled something else under her breath. Paige wasn't sure, but it sounded like "Quit acting like you're my mother."

The comment stung like a slap in the face. She and Sky had been so close after the wedding and throughout Sky's senior year in high school. Sky had worked hard in her studies and her dancing and had received several dance scholarships to schools in California and even one to the University of Utah in Salt Lake City, the school she'd finally chosen to attend in the fall. Things had been going so well, the two families had meshed together, and Paige had never known such contentment in her life. Until Sky's recent behavior change.

This trip. Paige couldn't help but wonder if all of this had something to do with this trip. Was it a sign? Were they not supposed to go? Paige suddenly felt uneasy about going to Vietnam. Perhaps it was because Jared wasn't going. She'd always thought of the family going together, but he had other things to do.

Maybe I should stay home, she thought again. She knew Bryant could use the help with the kids, the house, and the ownership changeover for Lou's business. And Jared was about to take one of the most important steps of his life. That was something she definitely didn't want to miss out on. She had plenty of reasons to stay, but deep in her heart she still wanted to be there with Dalton and Sky.

* * *

"What do you mean you think you shouldn't go on this trip?" Dalton's arms paused in midair as he pulled off his T-shirt. Then, slowly, he pulled the shirt over his head and tossed it onto the bed.

"I think that's what's bothering Sky. I think she wants this trip to be just you and her."

"Paige . . ."

"No, Dalton, think about it. This trip is going to be very emotional for both of you. She's going back to meet her mother's family, to see where her mother grew up and lived. This is about her bonding with her mom and hopefully making some good memories, finding some closure. She doesn't want me to get in the way of that. I can accept that."

Dalton's expression was one of hurt.

She walked over to him and slid her arms around his waist, but he stood stiff, unyielding.

"Honey, I just want to do what's best for her."

"*I* need you there with me, Paige," he said. "I can't do it without you. I'm . . ."

She looked up into his face, waiting for him to continue.

He swallowed.

"What is it?" she asked.

"I just don't know what to expect, going back there. Maybe this whole idea was a mistake."

Paige shut her eyes and hugged him to her chest. She'd known it was going to be difficult for him to return to a place that had caused him so much pain and agony. A place that had turned his dreams into nightmares for over thirty years. A place where he'd suffered and nearly died.

"I know," she said, stroking his neck. "I can't imagine how hard it's going to be. But it's going to be hard for Sky too. If I'm making it worse, then I shouldn't go. You've seen how she's changed toward me. I don't want to ruin what's left of our relationship."

Dalton held her tightly in his arms, staying silent for a moment. Then he said, "I'll talk to her. We aren't making any decisions until I talk to her."

With their trip in two days, they needed to decide right away. Paige still felt torn between the decision to stay or to go. Part of her desperately wanted to be there with Dalton and Sky as they faced reminders of their pasts and moved on to their futures. But part of her wanted to stay behind because, deep in her heart, something told her they shouldn't go. None of them.

Maybe that was why she didn't push Jared to join them. That feeling of foreboding made her uneasy. She knew it was silly, but nevertheless, it was there.

* * *

"Sky, we need to talk," Dalton said as he entered his daughter's room. He'd waited until the next day and had let her sleep in so she wouldn't be tired and grouchy when they talked.

"What?" Sky said flatly.

Dalton sat down on the side of the bed.

"What is it, Dad?"

Dalton cleared his throat, then said, "Paige is thinking about staying home from the trip."

Sky's eyebrows lifted, and she nodded slowly, thoughtfully.

"What do you think?"

"Honestly?"

Dalton nodded.

"Well, I've been thinking about this for a while now."

Finally, Dalton thought, *she's going to open up.*

"I mean, this is *our* trip and I think having her along will change it. I guess . . ." She looked down at the silky ribbon on her pajamas and fingered it for a moment. "I'm sure I sound really selfish and bratty and immature, but everything we're going to do over there is centered around Mom, and I guess . . ." She paused for a moment, looking down at the ribbon again. "I guess I don't want to share Mom with her."

Dalton remained quiet. He was afraid to interrupt for fear she would clam up and then he'd never know what was going on inside his daughter's mind.

"I don't want to worry about how Paige is feeling, like if she's feeling left out or awkward or something. Plus, Mom's family might feel uncomfortable having her there. Gosh Dad, I don't know. I mean, I love Paige and everything, I just think it will be weird to have her there." She looked at her father with brows lifted in question. "Does that make sense?"

"Sure it does, sweetie. I'm just surprised, that's all. You've been so close to Paige."

"We're still going to be close, and I'm glad you married Paige. It's all been really great, but she's not my mother. She never will be. And right now . . ." Sky paused again, this time shutting her eyes and swallowing hard before going on. "Right now I want to know about my mother. I *need* to know about her, Dad. I feel like part of me is missing, and I think it's because I don't know who my mother is."

Dalton sighed, slowly nodding his head. Soon Lee's death had left so many loose ends, and he feared that Sky would be troubled because of it. Paige treated Sky with as much love and devotion as she would her own child, but until Sky came to terms with her mother's death and found closure, she would never be able to move on.

"So you're saying you don't want her to come with us?" For him the trip wouldn't be as good if Paige wasn't there, but he understood Sky's feelings. It was a difficult situation. Obviously Sky didn't want Paige to go, but he didn't want to go if Paige didn't.

"Yes . . . No . . . I don't know," Sky said, her confusion obvious. "I guess I just think it would be better if all we had to concentrate on was Mom."

Dalton quickly reminded himself of the purpose of the trip: to introduce Sky to her mother's family. To show her where her mother grew up. To give Sky a chance to know all she could about who her mother was and where she came from so she could understand more about herself and her cultural heritage.

This trip was for Sky.

"I guess I need to have a talk with Paige," he said.

She looked away as she said, "As much as I don't want to hurt Paige, I feel like it would be better this way."

"Okay," he said, "I'll talk to her." He wished that they could postpone the trip. Maybe if Sky had more time she would feel different about Paige coming along. Sharing the experience with Paige was important to him. But with only two days until they left, he knew they couldn't back out now. Sky would continue her struggle to find out who she was, and without the closure this trip would provide, he was afraid that struggle would lead her to make bad choices, to follow paths that would give her a life of heartache and sadness.

"Thanks, Dad." Sky gave her father a hug. "I guess I'd better get packed then."

Dalton left his daughter's room distraught. This trip was not turning out at all like he'd thought it would—not only for the problems it was causing within his family, but for other reasons.

He wasn't sure if he could face the ghosts from his own past.

CHAPTER THREE

Dalton found Paige in the kitchen, just as she was hanging up the phone. She'd been talking to Bryant, and she couldn't stop the tears from trickling down her cheeks. She missed Lou. With all her heart she missed her best friend, the person who was like a sister to her. Lou's death had left a giant hole in her heart.

"Paige, what's wrong?"

Paige let Dalton hold her as she sobbed.

"Honey, talk to me," Dalton coaxed gently. "What's the matter?"

"Oh, Dalton," Paige cried as Dalton led her to the living room where they sat down on the couch. "I feel so bad for Bryant. He's having such a hard time himself, but Carter and Maddie aren't doing well at all. They both stayed home from school because they were just too upset to go. Maddie's having trouble because every time one of the kids' moms show up to help the teacher, she misses her mom that much more. And Carter's birthday is tomorrow, and he doesn't want to even have his party because his mom isn't going to be there."

Dalton shook his head and leaned back as Paige rested her head on his shoulder and wiped at her eyes.

"I know this probably sounds really dumb to you, but I just don't understand why Lou had to die. I had breast cancer too. Why did I live and she die?" she tearfully asked. "Why?"

"I don't know," he said. "We may never know." He held her close, sharing her pain. Then he offered this thought, "It's like that scripture in Proverbs that says, 'Trust in the Lord with all thine heart; and lean not unto thine own understanding. In all thy ways acknowledge him, and he shall direct thy paths.' God is aware of them. That's what I had to remember when Soon Lee died. I just had to have faith in the Lord that Skyler and I would be okay. Then you came into my life," he said, kissing her on the forehead. "I can't imagine not having you in my life, Paige."

Dalton's words were like a soothing balm to her heart. She felt peace replace the turmoil she'd felt moments earlier.

"I still feel guilty though. Is that weird to feel guilty to be alive?" she asked her husband.

"Not at all," Dalton said. "I've lived with that guilt for over thirty years. I saw my own men brutally killed right before my eyes. I saw men in the jungle camps die from diseases, and I've wondered every day of my life since then why I survived and they didn't. But for some reason, God gave you and me a second chance, and what we do with that chance is our gift back to Him. Bryant and the kids will hurt for a long time, and they will always feel Lou's loss, but they'll be stronger. Things will work out. You'll see."

Paige snuggled close to her husband's chest, thanking God at that very moment for this wonderful man in her life. She didn't know what she'd done to deserve such an amazing husband, but a day didn't go by that she didn't express her gratitude to her Father in Heaven for him and for Sky.

"So," she asked, "did you get a chance to talk to Sky?"

Dalton didn't answer right away.

"Dalton?" Paige asked, wondering if he'd heard her.

"Yeah. We talked."

Paige sat up and turned to look at him. "So, what did she say?"

"Well," he paused. "She's really struggling with her mother's death. I think she's trying to make sense of it and gain some understanding. She's not sure what to expect on this trip and it's causing her a lot of anxiety. She feels like she and I just need to focus on Soon Lee and meeting her family."

Paige felt a tightening in her chest as disappointment set in, yet she understood Sky's feelings. She just wished it made it easier.

"We need to respect her feelings then. If it will make it easier for her to not have me around, then I love her enough to stay home so she can deal with all of this the way she needs to. I know how it is to have confusing feelings about your mother. I still don't have answers I wish I had about my own. I want Sky to find the answers she needs so she can be at peace."

Dalton hugged Paige, kissing her forehead. "Do you know how much I love you?"

Paige shut her eyes and nodded. "Almost as much as I love you."

Dalton chuckled and kissed her again. Then he sat back and looked at her, his expression solemn. "I want you to know something, Paige. There is nothing in Vietnam I need to see again without you there. But I believe Skyler needs to find closure with her mother. She needs to know who she is and where she came from."

Paige nodded in complete agreement, then thought about Dalton. He didn't think he needed closure, but truth be known, he did. He'd been having more trouble than he usually did sleeping. And she believed that this trip would bring peace for him.

"I'll tell you what I think," Dalton offered, lowering his voice so just the two of them could hear. "I think she's mad that you're here and her mother's not. That's why she's been treating you so bad lately, I'm sure of it. She told me she loved you, but she just needs space to deal with her mother's past."

Paige felt hurt inside but she didn't want to cry. The trip was going to be difficult for both Sky and Dalton, and she didn't want to add to the difficulty. Determined to stay strong, she pulled in several breaths.

"Then it's decided. I'll stay home," Paige said. "It's probably for the best anyway. This way I can help Bryant and the kids, and I can spend time with Jared and Nicole. I have a feeling they're close to getting engaged. I want to be here for it if it happens."

"Yeah, you should be here, I guess," Dalton said. "This sure isn't how I had it planned."

"It's okay, really. I'll be fine. And you can e-mail me and tell me everything that's going on each day. That will be fun to look forward to." She gave him a brave smile.

"It won't be the same without you. I don't want to go if you're not going," he told her. "I don't know how I can do it without you."

Paige kissed her husband and held him tight. "It'll be okay. You'll be in my prayers."

Dalton nodded but didn't speak.

"Maybe sometime we can go together if you ever want to go back," she told him.

Dalton cleared his throat the way he usually did when he got emotional. He held her close a minute longer, then stood. "I guess I'd better get showered. I have a few errands to run before we leave tomorrow."

Paige watched him leave the room. When he was gone, she broke down and cried.

* * *

"Thanks for the delicious dinner, Mrs. McNamara," Jared's girl-friend, Nicole, said. She was a petite girl with long, brown, naturally curly hair and thickly lashed brown eyes. Nicole was also sweet, intelligent, and worshiped the ground Jared walked on. Paige didn't blame her son for flipping over this girl. She was a treasure, and Paige couldn't have handpicked a better match for him herself.

"You're welcome, Nicole."

"Yeah, thanks, Mom. You've sure gotten to be a better cook since you married Dalton," Jared observed.

"Well, thank you," Paige told her son. "I think." It was true, though. Paige hadn't always felt like cooking when it was just her and Jared at home. He was content with take-out or something simple at home, like microwave dinners. Dalton made it easy for her to cook because he was so much help in the kitchen. He did all of the barbecuing, fully appreciated a nice dinner, and helped clean up the dishes afterward. How could she not cook?

"So what time do you guys leave in the morning?" Jared asked Dalton.

"We have to leave the house at four A.M. to get to the airport and get checked in," Dalton answered. He reached for several plates while refusing Paige's and Nicole's offers to help clear the table.

"Are you excited, Skyler?" Nicole asked the girl, who'd been silent most of the meal.

Paige wondered what was going on inside Sky's head. She wished she would open up and talk to her like she used to. They would stay up nights after Sky had been on a date or out with friends and talk about every detail. It was the kind of relationship Paige had always wanted with a daughter, but somehow they'd lost that closeness.

Sky shrugged. "Yeah," she said.

Nicole's gaze slipped to Paige for a moment before looking back at Sky, who offered no further comment.

Paige had told Jared and Nicole that she'd be staying home from the trip, and they'd tried to understand the importance and difficulty of this trip for Dalton and Sky. It made it easier for Paige to stay home knowing that Jared and Nicole would be here. Plus, she had commitments to help Bryant and the kids, so she would stay busy while Dalton and Sky were gone.

Dalton returned from the kitchen with a homemade German chocolate cake and a container of ice cream. "I'll finish clearing the dishes if you want to serve the dessert," he told Paige after planting a kiss on her forehead.

Always the doting husband, Dalton had been even more attentive to his wife since they decided she wouldn't be accompanying them on the trip. They hadn't been separated even one night since they'd gotten married. When he traveled out of town for work, he was either able to get home the same night or Paige went with him. Neither of them looked forward to the three weeks apart.

After dishing up slices of cake oozing with gooey coconut-pecan frosting, Paige handed the plates to Nicole, who placed generous scoops of ice cream beside each slice.

Jared launched into his enormous piece without waiting for the others. "Mom," he mumbled with his mouth full, "this is incredible."

"Thanks, honey. It's Sky's favorite." Paige looked at her step-daughter for approval, but Sky didn't meet her gaze.

"I think it's now my favorite too," Jared said, then licked his lips.

The group enjoyed their dessert as Dalton answered questions about their itinerary and some of the stops he and Sky had planned for their trip.

"Wow," Jared remarked when he heard about Dalton's plans to try to visit one of the jungle prisons where he was held captive as a prisoner of war before he was moved to the prison in Hanoi. "That could be rough."

Dalton nodded. "I'm trying to prepare myself for it, but I still think it will be harder when we visit the spot where I was captured. I'm determined to do it, though. I think it's time to face the past." He glanced over to Sky, who seemed lost in thought. He then looked at Paige. She knew what he was thinking. They both wondered if the prospect of actually meeting her mother's family had triggered all the pain Sky had kept inside after her mother died. They both agreed that Sky needed to work through her mother's passing and accept it. She carried a lot of anger inside of her, questions about her mother's decision to leave this earth. They both hoped that somewhere in Vietnam, she would find the answers she needed. They were a family now, and they all needed to let go of the pain from the past and move forward together.

"Well," Jared said, "good luck with your trip. We're going to miss you."

Dalton didn't answer. He reached for Paige's hand and gave it a squeeze.

* * *

None of them slept much that night. They were finally in bed around midnight then back up at three A.M. While Dalton and Sky showered and changed, Paige packed them some food to eat at the airport while they waited for their flight.

Placing bagels spread with cream cheese, yogurt, bananas, and bottles of juice into a bag, Paige found herself fighting the emotion that swelled inside of her. She wanted to be by Dalton's side as he stood in the spots that had altered who he was and had changed his entire life, places where he'd seen life-and-death struggles, where he'd experienced the worst forms of torture and deprivation.

He'd given her so much strength ever since she'd met him, and she wanted to give some of that strength back to him. But all she could do was pray for him and for Sky.

The clatter of suitcase wheels sounded in the hallway. Paige quickly dabbed at the tears in her eyes with a napkin and put on a cheerful face.

She expected Dalton, but it was Sky.

"So," Paige said brightly, "are you ready? Do you need any help?"

"No," Sky replied, her tone more humble than Paige had heard lately.

"I packed you and your dad a lunch. A breakfast, actually," Paige said with a laugh, hoping to keep the tone light. "They don't feed you much on airplanes anymore. I hate to send you off with an empty stomach."

"Thanks, Paige," Sky answered.

"Also." Paige reached into the pocket of her robe. "I got you a little bon voyage gift. It's actually something my grandmother gave me. I've been saving it all these years, hoping that I'd have a daughter to give it to."

Paige handed her the small jewelry box tied with a red ribbon.

Sky looked at the box, then up at Paige before she opened it. She untied the ribbon and lifted the lid. From the box she lifted a silver chain on which hung an oval locket made of brushed silver. On the front, etched in the metal, was the image of an angel with wings.

Sky stared at the locket in her hand for a moment.

"It opens," Paige told her, dying to know if the girl liked it. She didn't wonder for long. Sky opened the locket and remained quiet.

She looked down at the picture of her mother inside, then up at Paige with tears in her eyes.

"It's beautiful," she said. "Thank you."

To Paige's surprise, Sky approached her and gave her a hug.

"I'm glad you like it," Paige told her. "I wanted to give you something to remember this trip by."

Sky nodded. Looking down at the locket again, she said, "I love it."

"I think your mom is a guardian angel for you, you know?" Paige said. The picture of Soon Lee reminded Paige of Sky. Soon Lee had a lovely smile and porcelain skin, her features fine and delicate. But it was Soon Lee's eyes that got to Paige's heart every time she looked at the picture. Even though she smiled in the picture, Soon Lee's eyes seemed sad, full of longing. Paige saw that look in Sky's eyes now and prayed that this trip would bring peace and happiness to Sky's soul and joy, once again, to her eyes.

"Will you help me put it on?" Sky asked her.

Sky lifted her long, silky black locks of hair while Paige fastened the locket around her neck.

The sight of Sky wearing the locket warmed Paige's heart. She truly loved Sky as much as she could love a child of her own. Paige felt a kinship with Soon Lee, and she felt that somehow she had Soon Lee's blessing to be a part of Sky's life. She wanted to be the best mother she could to this young woman who was trying to sort out her life, discover who she was, what her roots were, and how it all fit together.

Paige never wanted to let Soon Lee down, but sometimes she wondered if Soon Lee couldn't be a little more help on the other side.

"Good morning," Dalton said cheerfully as he entered the kitchen. He stopped when he saw the two before him. "What's going on?"

"Look what Paige gave me, Dad."

Sky showed him the locket and opened it so he could see the picture inside. "It was her grandmother's. Isn't it awesome?"

Dalton looked at Paige with lifted eyebrows. Paige hadn't told him what she was going to do, so it was a surprise to him also.

"Well," Paige said, noticing the lateness of the hour. "You two had better hit the road. Here's some food for you." She handed the bag to Dalton.

"Thanks, honey." Dalton's voice broke as he spoke. They had both avoided the subject of saying good-bye. It was just too painful.

"I'll be watching my e-mail, so let me know as soon as you get there. I want details too," she told her husband firmly. "Not just facts. I want to know how it smells, how the food tastes, what it's like. And pictures—take lots of pictures. Make sure he does that for me, okay, Sky?"

Sky nodded.

"I guess we'd better get going," Dalton said. He looked at his wife and shook his head. "I'm going to miss you." He took her into his arms and gave her a tight squeeze.

"You'll be so busy, you'll be home before you know it," Paige answered, fighting back tears with every ounce of strength she possessed.

She returned Dalton's hug and kissed him one last time.

Then she turned to Sky. "You two have lots of fun and stay together," she warned.

"We will," Sky answered, looking away.

"Can I have a hug?" Paige asked.

Sky nodded and then threw herself into Paige's arms. Paige looked at Dalton with surprise. She didn't know what to make of Sky's sudden show of emotion toward her.

"Paige, I . . ." Sky began. "I . . ."

Paige waited for the girl to finish, but Sky didn't say anymore. She patted Sky's back and held her close for another moment.

Finally, Sky stepped back. "Thank you for the locket."

Paige's resolve to stay strong was starting to crumble. "You're welcome." She swallowed and forced a smile. "Now, you two get out of here. It's after four."

Dalton and Sky moved out of the kitchen, both grabbing the handles of their rolling suitcases that also be could worn as backpacks. Dalton also pulled the larger suitcase, full of gifts and school supplies.

Dalton opened the door, then turned back, giving Paige one last look.

Reminding herself to stay strong, Paige smiled and said, "I expect you to bring me back something really awesome. Jewelry would be fine," she teased. "Something sparkly and exotic and rare. And expensive."

Dalton gave her one last look, then wheeled the suitcases out the door.

Paige watched them leave and felt the slam of the door echo painfully through the chambers of her heart. She braced herself, knowing that she was in for a good, long cry, when suddenly the front door opened again. Dalton rushed inside and raced to her, giving her a crushing hug. "I almost forgot to tell you I love you."

"I love you too," she replied.

"I'd give anything if you were coming with us."

"Me too."

"I gotta go."

"I know."

He kissed her one last time then raced back outside and was gone.

Paige locked the door behind them, then started for her bedroom to go back to bed but broke down before she could make it. She ended up on the couch, crying herself back to sleep.

CHAPTER FOUR

Vietnam jungle, 1972

"Hey, man," a voice came through the thick fog filling Dalton's head. "You gotta wake up."

"Leave me alone, Wilson," Dalton said, the words taking every effort to mutter.

"You're gonna die if we don't do something."

"That's okay," Dalton's reply was slurred and weak. "I'm ready to go."

"No, you're not, man," Wilson said, shaking Dalton's shoulder, causing him to cry out in pain. He was feverish, dehydrated, and knew that this was what it felt like just before dying. And he was at peace with it. He knew it would be hard on his family—his mother especially—but he wasn't afraid.

"Go get Godzilla," Wilson barked to one of the other men. "Now!"

Dalton drifted in and out of consciousness. His dreams took him back to Chicago with his family. It was Thanksgiving. All of his family was there, even his grandfather who had passed away. He felt so much joy being back with his loved ones. He'd missed them. He'd thought he'd never see them again. And then there was the food—so much delicious food. It was the turkey that made his mouth water. A large, golden turkey, fragrant and dripping with juices. He could almost taste it.

His father offered a prayer, pleading for their health and praying that they wouldn't die. Dalton wondered why his father was saying such things in the prayer.

Then, as always, his mother offered Dalton a leg from the turkey. Even as a child, he'd always gotten one of the drumsticks and his brother had gotten the other.

His mother grabbed hold of the drumstick, but when she tried to cut if off of the turkey, a searing hot pain shot through Dalton's own leg. He cried out in agony, but she kept sawing at the leg. The pain was more than he could bear. He tried to get up from the table but couldn't. He couldn't stand, couldn't move.

"Stop," he screamed. But she continued cutting at the drumstick until, finally, she removed it.

Collapsing in exhaustion, Dalton escaped the dream that had turned into a painful nightmare.

And when he awoke, he realized that his nightmare had just begun.

* * *

"Come on, man. Just try it. We worked hard on that crutch." Wilson and the other men presented Dalton with a homemade crutch that was no more than bamboo poles lashed together with vines and a rice sack wrapped around the top to cushion his armpit.

After the amputation, Dalton had remained unconscious for several days. If the men hadn't forced some broth and liquid down his throat, along with some quinine, he surely would have died.

He didn't know whether to thank them or not.

The camp commander had performed the task of removing Dalton's gangrened leg just below the knee. Dalton was grateful he'd been unconscious, knowing that the pain was too much to bear, and in God's way, he'd been spared having to deal with that much pain. But the throbbing still continued, and as he tried to sit up, he felt the throbbing increase in his stump of a leg.

"I can't," Dalton said, collapsing back.

"You gotta do it," Wilson encouraged. "If we have to move suddenly, and you can't walk, they'll leave you behind, man. You gotta try."

Feeling defeated, Dalton couldn't find the will inside to try. The pain was just too great.

"Listen, man, I'm not letting you give up. Before I came to Nam, my old man told me something. He said, 'Courage is not the absence of fear, but the ability to press on in spite of it.' I know it's hard, but I also know you can do it."

Wilson's words somehow managed to break through the barrier of pain and pierce Dalton's soul. Giving up wasn't an option.

Dalton attempted to sit up, but his head spun and his leg throbbed mercilessly.

"That's good," Wilson encouraged. "Now at least you're trying. Take it easy now. We'll try again later."

Each day after that, the men tried to help Dalton build his strength by feeding him extra rations from their own plates and helping him to sit up, then stand, then finally take small steps, one at a time. It took weeks of pain and rubbing his armpit raw to get used to having the crutch dig into the flesh under his arm. But finally he got to where he could get around and keep his balance without much assistance from the other prisoners. Even Godzilla seemed to be impressed with his determination.

* * *

"We're moving," Wilson whispered to Dalton, waking him from a deep sleep.

"What?"

"They're moving us somewhere. The guards are breaking camp."

Dalton groaned. Even hobbling to the latrine was a chore for him. How could he make the trek to another camp?

The guards soon roused them, gave them each their pitiful bowl of rice with chunks of pig fat, and soon had them ready to march.

From what the men could gather, they were somewhere near the Laotian border. The prisoners marched in groups of seven or eight and left camp on different days to avoid losing all the prisoners at once in the event of an air strike or American ambush.

The sickly group struggled through the thick jungle growth, trying to negotiate the ferns and vines that made each step difficult. The high humidity and heat zapped every ounce of energy they possessed. Sheer willpower kept their bodies moving.

Dalton did his best to keep up, since lagging behind wasn't an option, and to his surprise, he fared better than some of the other men who were suffering from horrible edema in their feet, ankles, and legs. By the end of some days, their lower extremities were huge, painful masses. Wilson was one of the men with severe swelling.

"Look at that!" Wilson complained as he pushed on the top of his right foot. His finger sank nearly two inches into the flesh, the depression remaining for two or three minutes. Each step he'd taken that day brought a searing pain that shot through his entire body.

But the men helped each other, and even though Dalton's situation with just one leg made trekking through jungle growth and steep terrain difficult, he saw men suffering worse maladies and knew his own situation wasn't as bad as it could be.

On the trail, the guards showed their impatience with the weak and sick prisoners by yelling at them and jabbing them to keep them moving. Eventually even the guards began to realize the men did the best they could. But Wilson's condition grew worse every day.

Early each morning, after a meal of watery rice soup, the men began their daily trek toward some unknown destination. Dalton was almost always at the rear of the pack, but soon Wilson dropped back to join him.

"I'm not gonna make it, man," Wilson groaned, grimacing with each step.

"No way, Wilson," Dalton said. "We're in this together. You can't let them win."

"But they already have," Wilson said through gritted teeth. "They're going to win this war, and we will die for nothing."

"We don't have much farther," Dalton said, even though he had no clue how many more torturous days they had ahead of them. "You gotta hang in there."

Wilson continued to walk slower and slower until Dalton was ahead of him. The guard at the rear yelled for Wilson to get moving, and Dalton turned back to help his friend. Wilson had stopped, his head hanging, his shoulders shaking as he began to sob.

The guard yelled again and lifted his bayonet.

Then, with an unexpected surge of strength, Wilson straightened his back, lifted his head, and shouted at the guard, "Kill me. Just kill me, man."

Dalton hobbled back to his friend and put an arm around him. Defeated and still crying, Wilson took one step, then another, and the procession continued.

The trek was hard enough, but it was also the rainy season, and when they weren't being blasted by the oppressive heat, the men were being drenched with rain that soaked them to the bone, chilling them to their very core.

As the men trudged through the low, muddy areas, they would find leeches four to five inches long attached to their bodies. The leeches were hard to get off and, when removed, usually took the skin with them, the sores remaining open and painful, unable to heal because of the men's malnourished state.

Wilson spoke less and less each day, turning almost zombielike, walking as though he was no longer inside the swollen, miserable body that bore his name.

"Hey, Wilson," Dalton said, as they bedded down one night, "do you remember how pizza tastes?"

"No, man. I don't remember nothin' anymore."

"When we get home, we're going out for pizza. I know a place that has the best pizza in Chicago."

"Sounds good, Mac."

Dalton heard a weariness in his friend's voice that alarmed him.

"You okay, bud?" Dalton asked.

"Yeah."

"Hey." Dalton propped himself up on one elbow and leaned close to his friend. "You hang in there. Remember what you told me one time?"

"No, man. I told you, I don't remember nothin'."

Dalton chuckled. "You said, 'Courage is not the absence of fear, but the ability to press on in spite of it.' You gotta press on. Okay?"

"Okay."

Dalton let his friend drift off to sleep, but he watched the rising and falling of his chest for several minutes before lying down himself. Dalton feared for his friend's life and wondered if he'd make it one more day.

* * *

It was usually Wilson who woke Dalton up in the morning. But this morning Dalton woke up before his friend.

"Hey, Wilson. What happened to my human alarm clock?" Dalton joked, giving his sleeping friend a poke.

When he got no response, Dalton poked him again, and before he even checked for a pulse, he knew his friend had finally been freed from the torment he'd suffered right up until his very last breath.

Ironically, it was that same day, the ninth day of their trek, that the group reached what appeared to be a hospital. Had Wilson hung on for just a few more hours, he might have been saved. Dalton's heart ached for the loss of his friend, but he knew God was merciful to take him. The man had been in so much pain.

The men were checked and given large portions of rice and some meat and vegetables. Dalton remained at the hospital, along with several of the other men with Wilson's same condition, while the rest of their group continued on. The sick would stay there until the next group of prisoners from their camp came through.

The Vietnamese played propaganda broadcasts for the prisoners on the radio. Several American pilots at the Hoa Lo prison in Hanoi told about the good treatment they received and how they were given ham and other good food at Christmastime. Dalton and the other men learned that this was where they were headed—Hoa Lo prison, also called the "Hanoi Hilton."

When the next group arrived, Dalton's small group, which had improved substantially in just a few days, joined them on the next leg of their journey. After another ten days on the trail, this time without the challenge of such steep terrain, they arrived in Ky Son, where they were met by another set of guards who loaded the prisoners into trucks.

They were on their way to Hanoi.

* * *

Rules were strict at the new prison. The guards demanded absolute obedience and silence. There was to be no talking among the prisoners, not even inside their cells. And if any of the men tried to communicate, they soon regretted it. The guards looked for excuses to punish them.

The menu was different at the prison than it had been in the jungle. Instead of vermin-infested rice, they had vermin-infested boiled pumpkin or cabbage soup.

Dalton found the rooms to be every bit as intolerable as the jungle. The cells stank of unspeakable odors and ran rampant with mice, rats, cockroaches, ants, spiders, and, of course, mosquitos.

Since the men couldn't speak to each other, Dalton and his group of prisoners didn't know what was in store for them. But they soon found out.

Soon after their arrival, Dalton was taken to a red-tiled cell known as Room 18. His hands were bound tight together. They would have bound his feet but had to settle for tying his knees together. The guard then barked an order at Dalton that he didn't understand. He was shoved toward a foot-high stool, where he sat down.

The interrogator sat behind a small table and began to speak in broken English.

"You are war criminal. You have no rights under Geneva Convention. Your country did not declare war, so you have no protection."

Dalton knew that wasn't true, because the Geneva Convention referred not just to declared wars but to any armed conflict.

"When you were captured, what was your mission?"

Dalton supplied his name, rank, serial number, and date of birth as required by the Geneva Convention.

"What was your target?"

Dalton repeated the same information.

He had barely recited his date of birth when he received an unexpected, sharp blow to the side of his head from the guard standing directly behind him.

Dalton fell to the floor, writhing in pain. Several kicks to his ribs and back left him gasping for air. Then, before he could catch his breath, the guards pulled at Dalton's arms, rotated his palms upward, twisting his arms, and put manacles on his wrists so tight that his arms felt as though they would snap out of their shoulder sockets.

The guard bound his elbows together with a tourniquetlike loop, slipped the rope through the wrist manacles, and then yanked Dalton into a sitting position on the floor. Dalton bent forward until he was completely bowed over. The guard put the rope over a hook in the ceiling and pulled it taut until Dalton's arms were raised up behind his back to the point he was certain his shoulders would pop out of their joints at any moment.

"You think about your war crimes. When you are ready to talk, you yell 'Bao Cao' and we will remove the ropes."

Dalton was then left alone.

Night fell.

The dull ache in his arms had long since turned into a throbbing and had then escalated into a white-hot, excruciating pain. His sternum felt as though it would split in two. He wondered how long he could endure this and if his arms, which had turned black, would also have to be amputated.

This was the first time Dalton was put on the ropes, but it wasn't the last. In fact, all the men received such treatment until they finally broke. Some held out only a few hours. Some a few days. Very few made it a week. But they all submitted. They were then forced to write propaganda statements to their government, giving information that was dated or inaccurate.

Day after day, Dalton lay in his cell, physically broken, weak, and weary, but he vowed not to let the North Vietnamese get to him. They had practically destroyed him physically, but he wouldn't allow them to break him mentally.

To keep his wits about him, he reviewed math skills, tried to spell every word he could think of, conjugated German verbs from his two years of classes in college. He thought of favorite authors and tried to remember all of their works. He recalled as many scriptures as he could. One scripture in particular that he'd drawn strength from was from the twenty-seventh Psalm. *Deliver me not over unto the will of mine enemies: for false witnesses are risen up against me, and such as breathe out cruelty. I had fainted, unless I had believed to see the goodness of the Lord in the land of the living. Wait on the Lord: be of good courage, and he shall strengthen thine heart: wait, I say, on the Lord.*

Using a small, bent nail he'd found in the corner of his cell, Dalton carved the words *Wait on the Lord* to help him remember to not lose hope, to not give in or give up. He didn't know if he would survive the ordeal, but he knew the Lord was with him. And even when he was on the ropes praying that he would just pass out so he wouldn't have to feel the pain anymore, he knew he couldn't lose faith. Because once that was gone, he would die.

And he knew there was still much to live for.

CHAPTER FIVE

Sky smiled with excitement as the landing gear dropped and the announcement came over the loudspeaker that they were about to land in Ho Chi Minh City, Vietnam.

Dalton's stomach turned.

During the war, the city was known as Saigon, but it had been renamed after the war. Either way, Dalton remembered it as being big, ugly, dirty, polluted, noisy, and hot.

Sky gave her father's arm a squeeze. "Can you believe we're almost there, Dad?"

Dalton shook his head, not having a lot to say. He wasn't sure how he was going to react to returning to this place that only held painful memories for him. Most of all, he missed Paige. This whole experience would mean so much more if she could be there with them.

"Kinda weird, huh?" Sky said.

"Very weird," he replied.

"Can I ask you something, Dad?"

"Sure, honey. What is it?"

"When you were a soldier and you first came to Vietnam, what did it feel like?"

"Well, it's been such a long time, I can't really remember. I know I was apprehensive about what we were about to do."

"You mean shooting at people and stuff?"

He might not have put it quite so bluntly, but the fact of the matter was, she was right. "Yeah," he said, "but remember, they were shooting at me too. It was my job. I had to follow my orders."

"Is this going to be hard for you?" she asked.

"I imagine so. But I'm also hoping it's good for me to come back here. And for you."

"I'm nervous to meet Mom's family. What if they don't like Americans? What if they don't like me?"

Dalton gave his daughter's hand a squeeze. "They're going to love you, sweetie. Don't you worry."

"I hope so," she answered, nervously fingering the locket around her neck.

Seeing the locket made Dalton think of Paige. More than ever he wanted her—needed her—by his side. He was afraid this journey was going to be difficult and emotionally draining. She had a way of lifting him, strengthening him, and encouraging him just by her presence.

The descent began, and as the plane dropped, so did Dalton's stomach. What could possibly lay in store for them?

* * *

Skyler screamed as the cyclo driver weaved in and out of traffic with amazing speed.

"I am like speeding bullet," the man pedaling the triwheeled contraption said. "No one can keep up with me."

"And live to tell about it," Dalton murmured to Sky, who laughed.

Traveling by cyclo was one of the main modes of transportation for tourists. It was relatively cheap, depending on bartering skills, and it was one of the fastest ways to get through the traffic of motorbikes and bicycles clogging every city street. The cyclo had three wheels, with the back part a bicycle and a cart on the front for passengers or cargo.

Dalton fought the wave of memories that suddenly surrounded him. The smells, the sights, the time-warp of feelings all collided, creating an overwhelming surge of remembrances. It would take time to process all the feelings that were coming back to him. They were feelings he'd kept suppressed for years, feelings he wasn't sure he ever wanted to remember or revisit but would now be impossible to ignore.

Their "speeding bullet" driver pulled up to the front of their hotel, which looked as run-down and shabby as the rest of the buildings along the street. Still, Dalton and Sky were both so exhausted they didn't care where they stayed as long as there were beds and bathrooms.

Once they checked in and were shown to their room they both dropped into bed as quickly as their luggage hit the floor.

* * *

When Dalton awoke, it was late afternoon. Stifling heat inside the room made his head ache. He remembered the heat and the energy-zapping humidity.

He got up to find some Tylenol in his bag, then went out on the lanai that overlooked the throngs on the crowded street below. He knew Paige would've been amazed at the sight. She had the ability to adapt and adjust to her surroundings, appreciating the differences of new people, their culture, and their lifestyles.

It was all too real now. Thirty years hadn't dulled his memory. He was here, back in the country where he'd almost lost his life.

Tears stung his eyes, and he pinched the bridge of his nose to stop them.

"Hey." Sky appeared in the doorway. "It's cooler out here." She stepped outside and looked down at the street below. "This place is a madhouse. It's worse than the hallways in high school." She stopped and looked closely at her father. "Dad, what's wrong?"

Dalton cleared his throat and blinked to clear his vision. "Nothing, I'm fine."

"Dad?" Sky put her hand on his arm. "Is this a little harder than you thought it would be?"

"Uh, yeah," he answered emptily. It didn't do any good to bring up the issue of leaving Paige home now.

Sky studied him for a second, then said, "That's not it, is it?"

"I don't really feel like talking about it. Besides, it doesn't really matter." He straightened his back, ready to go back inside.

Sky shrugged and looked out at the masses. "How do they live like this? There are bodies everywhere, fighting to get to where they need to go. They're like ants scurrying around in chaos."

"It's all they know," Dalton explained. "They do what they have to in order to survive. Their lives and the lives of their families depend on the small amount of money they make and the little bit of food they can buy each day. It's a hard life, but it's the only life they know."

Sky shook her head slowly, still taking it all in.

Dalton stood. "I think I'll take a shower, then maybe we can go find something to eat."

"Dad?" Sky said.

Dalton turned.

Sky opened her mouth to speak, but only said, "Never mind."

Leaving her outside, Dalton went in, hoping to drown his sorrows in the refreshment of a cool shower.

* * *

Sky opened her locket and looked at the picture of Mother, trying to envision her when she was a young girl living somewhere in this city, working here, scrambling to make a living for herself.

It seemed unreal. It seemed impossible.

Then Sky wondered what things would have been like for her had she been born in this country instead of in the United States. She shuddered.

Her father often told her how much she reminded him of her mother. Now that Sky was older, out of high school, ready to take the next big step in life, she wished her mother were there helping her, giving her advice, sharing all the wonderful, exciting experiences of her life.

A mixture of sadness and anger filled her.

Her mother had given up.

She wished she could understand why her mother did what she did. Her father seemed to. He knew what her mother had been through—her secret, private thoughts and feelings. But Sky didn't. She'd been too young to understand when her mother had died, and she had forgotten so much since then. She knew her mother had been depressed, and at times she had seemed preoccupied and distant, but her mother was also warm, loving, and tender. Those were the times

Sky remembered. Those were the things that kept her mother's memory alive. Those were the things that made Sky want to come here to this country—so she could understand her mother and get to know her better. She knew it would be difficult and painful for her and her father, but they were also convinced it was important to confront their pasts.

She thought about her father and all this country meant to him. She thought about the sadness in his eyes earlier, and her own heart ached.

"Hope you don't mind a cold shower," Dalton said from the doorway.

"It'll feel great. I'm so hot and sticky."

"The bathroom's all yours," Dalton said.

Sky went inside and gathered the things from her suitcase that she would need, then headed for the bathroom. After a refreshing shower in a filthy stall, she got dressed and found her father at the small table in the room, looking over a map. He'd been trying to figure out the areas where he'd been captured and taken to the jungle prison.

"Any luck, Dad?" she asked.

"I have a general idea, but I hope we can find a guide who knows the area and the history behind it." He made a note on the map with a pen and continued studying the south part of the country.

"Dad," Sky said.

"Yes, honey?" Dalton answered without looking up.

"Are you okay?"

"I'm fine," he replied.

Sky knew he wasn't, and she wanted to know why. She walked over and knelt down by him.

"Are you nervous to go to some of these places?" she asked.

"Oh, I suppose a little," he answered.

"Is that all it is?"

"Honey, it doesn't really matter. I'd rather not talk about it."

"But I can tell something's bugging you. Why won't you tell me?"

"Like I said, it doesn't really matter."

He got up and folded the map and slid it into the pocket of his backpack, then checked his wallet. He took out some of the bills and put them in the pouch he wore around his neck that contained his

passport, credit cards, and other money. He only kept enough money
in his wallet to take care of their immediate needs.

"It's Paige, isn't it?" Sky asked.

"What do you mean?" Dalton replied, returning his wallet to his
back pocket.

"You're distracted, and you seem kind of upset. Is it because Paige
didn't come?"

Dalton didn't answer right off, so Sky knew she'd finally touched
on the right subject.

"Honey, it doesn't matter. It's too late anyway."

Sitting down on the chair her father had vacated, Sky released a
slow breath. She'd been feeling guilty about being the cause of Paige
not coming. But she had felt so strongly about having her father to
herself during this time when they were going to focus on her mother.
It was selfish on her part, she knew. Now that they were there in
Vietnam and her father was missing Paige—and even she was missing
Paige—she wondered if it had been such a good idea.

She just didn't know. Would it be weird with Paige around, or
would she help them with this emotional journey? Would it be hard
for Paige?

At that moment, the questions didn't really seem to matter. What
mattered was that Paige was back in California, and Sky wished she
were in Vietnam with them.

She felt like a royal jerk for what she'd done.

"Dad," Sky said.

"Yes, hon?"

"I think I made a huge mistake."

"A mistake? What do you mean?"

"I mean . . ." She shut her eyes. "I wish Paige were here with us."

Dalton heaved a weary sigh.

"I thought this was what I wanted. I thought this was something
we needed to do by ourselves. I didn't want to share it with anyone. I
wanted it to be about Mom and us. Now I see that having Paige
around really wouldn't change that. And maybe it would be good for
her to get to know Mom like this too."

"She certainly was excited about the trip," Dalton said. "But she
understood you needed your space. She loves you very much, Sky."

"I love her too, Dad. That's why I want her to come and meet us."

"What?" Dalton's expression registered surprise.

"Can't she just fly over and meet us here? You want her here too, don't you?"

"Well of course I do, but . . . but," he stammered, "we changed all the plans, the flights and everything."

"But it's not too late, is it? Can't we have her come?"

Part of Dalton wanted to pull his hair out, and the other part wanted to hug his daughter.

"Well, I guess we can call and see if she's willing to come by herself. And we can see what it would take to get her here. I don't know what sort of last-minute flight she could catch."

"Can we, Dad?" Sky bounced in her chair. "Can we call and talk to her?"

"If you're sure that's what you want."

"I am. And I want to tell her I'm sorry. Even if it is weird, we'll work it out, right?"

Dalton gave his daughter an appreciative smile, making Sky feel happy inside.

Sky jumped to her feet. "Come on, let's go find a phone."

"All right, wait up," Dalton said, grabbing his sunglasses and camera, then following her out the door.

* * *

After stepping onto the sidewalk with caution, Dalton and Sky turned left and began looking for the phone booth the man at the hotel had told them about. The hotel phone couldn't be used with a calling card. Fortunately, the desk clerk's English had seemed good enough to give out simple directions.

"Didn't he say to cross the street and go around the corner?" Sky said as they came to the end of the block.

"Yeah, but I don't know how we're going to get across alive."

They watched as several other pedestrians stepped precariously into the steady flow of traffic going both ways. Like choreographed dancers, they wove back and forth, trying to avoid accidents and injury in order to arrive safely on the other side.

Dalton and Sky looked at each other, neither of them feeling confident in their chances to do the same.

"You go across street?" A boy, maybe fourteen years old, approached them. He was barefoot and dirty but had a broad, toothy grin. "I help you."

"How much?" Dalton asked before agreeing to anything.

"You have American dollars?"

"Yes."

"Five, then."

"Five dollars? I don't think so," Dalton said, turning away.

"Okay, then three."

"Still too much," Dalton replied, keeping his head turned.

"Two? Two dollars?"

Dalton could see the kid was desperate. "Okay, two dollars."

The boy's face lit up. "Good. Two dollars." He held out his hand.

"I'll give it to you on the other side," Dalton told him.

"Yes, okay." The boy nodded. "We go." He reached for Sky's hand, but Dalton offered his instead. "Okay, mister. You hold onto her. Don't stop, don't look at driver. Okay?"

Dalton and Sky nodded, and before they knew it, they were on the street, getting screamed at and having horns honked and bicycle bells rung at them by angry cyclists.

"Hurry," the boy yelled at his cargo in tow.

Dalton didn't have time to look back to check on Sky but kept a firm hold on her hand. The loud blast from a small truck startled them, but they continued on until finally, out of breath and shaking with fear, they arrived on the other side, and Dalton paid the boy.

"How will we ever get back?" Dalton asked his daughter.

"I help you," the boy offered. "Five dollars."

Dalton scowled at him.

"Okay, two," the boy said.

"Do you know where a phone is?" Dalton asked him.

"Yes."

"How much?"

The boy laughed and waved away Dalton's comment. "Free for you. Come, this way."

They followed the boy past several stores before finally ducking inside a door into a small café. Several tables were situated out front, with people eating and enjoying the shade from the building.

A woman behind a counter looked up and began scolding the boy, but he held up two dollars and she began to smile and speak in happier tones. The boy gave her the money and turned to Dalton. "You hungry?"

Dalton was famished, and by the look on Sky's face, so was she.

"What do you have?" Dalton asked.

"Is called Pho," he said. "Noodles with vegetables and meat."

"Please, Dad, I'm starving."

"We'll take two," Dalton answered. "But where's the phone?"

"We have phone."

"How much to use it?"

"Twenty dollars."

Here we go again, Dalton thought. They finally agreed on a lower price, and as Dalton dialed the numbers on his long-distance phone card and placed the call, the boy's mother prepared their meal.

Dalton had to dial several times before he finally got the number to work, and when the ringing began, he felt his heartbeat speed up.

"Hello?" Paige's voice came.

"Paige, honey, this is Dalton."

"Oh my goodness, I didn't expect you to call so soon. How are you? How's Sky?"

"We're fine. We're in Ho Chi Minh City, and we're getting a bite to eat."

"How are you doing?"

"It's been kind of surreal in some ways. Bizarre, really. But I think it's going to be good."

"I'm glad," Paige said, her voice not sounding as enthused as her reply.

"Hey, speaking of bizarre, I have a weird question for you."

"What's that?"

"How would you like to come and join us?"

"What?" she exclaimed.

"How would you like to fly over and join us?"

"Why, what's going on?"

"Sky's decided she made a mistake and wants to apologize. She wants you over here with us, and of course I do too."

"She does?"

"Yeah, we need you here, Paige. It won't be the same without you. It's pretty crazy here, but I think you'd like it."

"I can't believe you're calling and asking me this."

"What do you say, honey? Will you come?"

"Dad," Sky's voice interrupted him. "Can I talk to her?"

Dalton turned to his daughter, whose expression was anxious.

"Sure," he answered. "Hold on, Paige," he said into the phone, "Sky wants to talk to you."

Sky grabbed the phone. "Paige, this place is nuts! You have to see it. Will you please come? I am so sorry I was such a brat. Please come join us. Please?"

Paige laughed. "Are you sure, Sky? I know how important this trip is to you."

"It is important, and that's why you should be here."

"Wow," Paige said. "How can I resist an invitation like that? Okay, I'll see what I can do. I don't know what kind of flights there are or anything."

"I know, I know, but try, okay? I saw some places to shop while we were walking down the street. You have to come."

"Put your father back on the phone."

Sky handed him the phone and gave him a thumbs-up. She raced to their table and the steaming bowls of food waiting for them.

"So, what do you think? Will you come?"

"I don't know how I could resist you two. But I'm scared to come alone, and I don't know how to do the flights and stuff."

"Just call Ron Jenkins at the travel office. He'll help you. And you'll be fine, honey. The flight is long, but you won't have any trouble."

"You make it sound so easy."

"It is. Just call Ron, and I'll call you in a few hours to see what you've found out."

"Okay," Paige answered. Then she added, "I love you."

"I love you too. I'm glad Sky came to her senses because, honey, I really need you here with me."

"I'll do everything I can to get there," she replied.

They said their good-byes with reluctance, both of them hoping the change in the plan would work out.

Dalton joined his daughter at the table. Next to her bowl was a small pile of cubed tofu chunks.

"How is it?" he asked, picking up a pair of chopsticks, which neither he nor Sky were very adept at using.

"I haven't tried it yet. I had to get rid of the tofu first." Sky took a taste of the noodles and pulled a face. "Eww! Tastes like fish."

Dalton remembered the fish sauce the Vietnamese used on everything. "You're going to have to get used to it," he said, "or you're going to starve."

"I'd kill for a Wendy's," Sky said.

Dalton took a taste of the soup. The fishy taste was mild compared to what he remembered. "It's *nuoc mam*. They preserve fish in salt, then after a few months they pour off the liquid and use it to flavor foods. Try it again. I think you'll get used to it."

Realizing it was this or nothing, Sky took another chopstickful of noodles and let as much of the juice drain off as she could, then took a bite.

"Well?" Dalton asked.

Sky shrugged and finished chewing. "I guess it's okay. Hey, I have an idea. Let's have Paige bring some food with her. I'd love a Snickers right now."

Dalton laughed. That sounded pretty good to him too. "Good idea." He had feared he would have trouble eating since he'd only been fed slop as a prisoner here, but after the first bite, he knew he'd be fine. This food was nothing like the food he'd had at the camps.

As they ate, the front door burst open and two young children charged inside, laughing and chatting. They raced behind the counter and found the boy who'd helped Dalton and Sky across the street, continuing their high-speed chatter while he joined in and helped them take off their backpacks. Dalton assumed they were his younger brother and sister, because the boy took the two children off to a table at the back of the room and served them each a bowl of noodles. The boy then began to clear tables from other customers who'd finished with their meals. As he walked by their table, Dalton stopped him.

"Everything okay?" the boy asked them. "You like?"

"Yes, it's very good," Dalton answered. "By the way, what is your name, son?"

"I am Quat," he answered.

Dalton nodded. "Well, Quat, do you think it would be okay if we were to come back soon and use your phone again?"

Quat nodded, smiling. "Yes, is good. You use for free, okay?"

Dalton smiled back at the boy, his heart warming at the smiling faces of this boy and his younger brother and sister. He'd worried before coming that after the severe torture he'd received at their hands, he wouldn't know how to react to the Vietnamese people. But these people before him were hardworking, gentle, and kind. He had no feelings of animosity toward them at all.

"Thank you," Dalton said. "Very delicious."

Quat nodded and smiled. "You be back later?"

"Yes, in a few hours."

"Okey-dokey," Quat replied.

"By the way, where did you learn such good English?" Sky asked him.

"My brother. He know much English. He teach me," Quat told them. "He say we all should learn English."

"That's wonderful, Quat," Dalton replied as he and Skyler got up to leave. "We'll be back later. Will you be here?"

"Yes. I will help you cross street again."

"That would be wonderful," Dalton said to their new friend. "Thank you."

With a wave of his hand, Quat left them so he could gather more dishes.

Leaving the café, Dalton and Sky made their way down the crowded sidewalk, amused and amazed at the chaotic busyness of the city.

Sky pointed out the different types of clothes she noticed the people wearing. Some of the youth on motorized scooters were dressed in clothes that looked quite American, with jeans and stylish shirts, but then there were the elderly who wore loose-fitting cotton pants and shirts that looked more like pajamas than clothes.

"Look, Dad," Sky said as she pointed to two young women on bicycles, stopped at an intersection. The girls had their hair pulled back and pinned up off their necks. They each wore long pants in startling white and a long, fitted tunic top with slits up to the waist. The top had a mandarin collar and long sleeves. On their feet were high-heeled wooden sandals.

"They look like china dolls," Sky said.

Dalton caught his breath. Seeing these young women dressed in the traditional Vietnamese clothing reminded him of Soon Lee, who wore outfits exactly like the ones these girls wore.

"Hey, look," Sky said as the street opened onto an open market packed with peddlers selling their goods—everything from flowers to jewelry, luggage, and beautiful silk clothing—in roughshod stalls.

"Wait a minute, didn't that movie just barely come out back home?" Skyler asked as she saw a vendor with movie DVDs and videos. "How did it get out on DVD so soon?"

"That's the black market for you," Dalton said. "Those are pirated copies of the movie. Not the real thing," he explained. "You can get pretty much anything on the black market, but you can't always be sure it's legal."

They walked past a stand where vintage clothes, books, and odds and ends were being sold. Dalton stopped to browse through the old books, and Sky looked at some of the pieces of jewelry for sale. She noticed several dog tags on chains in a basket of tangled, beaded necklaces and bracelets.

"Dad, look at this," she said, untangling the chains from the rest of the mess.

After she handed him the necklaces, Dalton stopped and stared for a moment at the metal tags in his hand. He read the information on the tags but didn't recognize the names of the soldiers they'd belonged to.

"Are those from the war?" she asked.

"Yeah, I've heard there's a lot of war memorabilia on the black market," he answered, still looking at the tags. It had been a while since he'd seen a pair of these, and he immediately wondered about the soldiers they belonged to.

Digging some bills out of his pocket, he motioned to the woman in charge of the booth.

"You want?" she asked, giving them a grin that displayed brown-stained teeth. The woman turned and spat on the ground, then returned with a smile.

Dalton noticed Sky's repulsed reaction and quickly asked the woman, "How much?"

The two haggled back and forth, then once they agreed on a fair price, Dalton handed her the money and took the set of tags.

"Those tags are so cool. Do you think there's any way we could find their owners?" Sky asked.

"Sure, we could try. I just felt they'd be better off in my hands than rusting away in some outdoor market. Who knows, maybe the guys they belong to are still alive."

"That's pretty cool, Dad," she said, looping her arm through his. "By the way, what in the world is wrong with that woman's teeth? Don't they believe in toothbrushes over here?"

"It's beetle nut."

"What's that?"

"It's a nut that comes from an evergreen tree."

"Why do they chew it?"

"It has a stimulant effect—makes them feel good."

"And it makes their teeth disgusting. Plus all that spitting. Sick!"

"It's their culture, honey. Things are a lot different over here."

"Pretty much everything is different. It seems like a different planet to me."

Dalton laughed and slipped his arm around his daughter's shoulders. "I guess it does, but somehow I think we're the ones who look like aliens, not them."

CHAPTER SIX

"Bry, are you sure you're going to be okay? I'm sorry I keep changing my plans on you at the last minute," Paige said over the phone to Lou's husband.

"We're going to be fine, Paige. You've done enough for us. Go and enjoy your vacation. I'm thrilled you're able to go after all."

"Thanks, Bry. Tell the kids I'll bring them home a surprise."

They said good-bye, and Paige hung up the phone as guilt flooded her. She felt so awful leaving that poor man and his two children alone for three weeks. Nothing was the same for any of them without Lou.

An ache stabbed her heart, and she clutched her chest as a wave of sadness hit her. There was never any warning. Something random like a song on the radio, a certain perfume fragrance, or restaurants that were Lou's favorites would trigger an onset of emotions that were overpowering. Just when Paige thought she was handling her friend's death okay, she would burst into tears and be sad for days. Bryant said the same thing happened to him, but he rarely had a good day between the bad ones.

The doorbell rang just as she hung up the phone, and Paige knew it was Jared, picking her up to take her to the airport.

"Hey, Mom. You ready?" Jared stepped inside the house, walked straight into the kitchen, and opened the fridge.

"Sorry, hon, there's nothing to eat. I didn't want to leave food in the fridge until we got home."

Jared shifted to the pantry, where he found a couple of granola bars and a juice box. "I didn't get any breakfast. Maybe I can grab something on the way to the airport."

"Hand me a couple of those," Paige said. "I may want them on the plane."

She stuffed the granola bars into her purse, then grabbed her backpack while Jared got her extra bag. "Geez, Mom, what have you got in here?"

"Food and treats, a few extra toys, school supplies, gifts."

"That's all?" he teased.

"Dalton took most of the stuff with him, but I decided to grab a few more things. Plus, Sky says she needs some American food."

"I'm glad you get to go."

"Me too, but I wish I didn't have to go alone. I'm a little nervous."

"Dalton and Sky will be there to meet you, won't they?"

"Yes. It'll be fine. I just haven't ever traveled alone internationally."

"Just don't take anything from anyone."

"I won't."

"And be careful."

"I will," she answered with a chuckle. "Look who's playing parent now."

"I can't help it. I don't want anything to happen to you. I want you to get home safely, because I'll have a big surprise waiting for you when you do."

Paige let out a little squeal. "Jared, are you—"

"Asking Nicole to marry me," he finished for her.

Paige dropped her bag and gave her son a giant hug. "I'm so happy for you, sweetie. Nicole is a wonderful girl. I couldn't have handpicked a better wife for you myself."

"Thanks, Mom. I'm glad you approve."

"This is so exciting. Oh my goodness." She glanced at the clock over the mantle as it chimed the time. "We'd better get going. The traffic is horrible this time of day."

"I'll get the door," Jared said.

The two carried the luggage out to the car and were soon on their way. Inside Paige's stomach, tension rose. She didn't know why she was so nervous, but she figured it was probably just all the excitement of Jared's engagement news and going to a foreign country.

* * *

Paige emerged from the tunnel leading from the plane into the terminal and froze. The airport was crowded, noisy, and smelly. And worse, there was no sign of Dalton or Sky anywhere.

People pushed her from behind, and Paige quickly stepped out of their way.

Exhausted from the long trip, Paige spied an empty chair near the gate and grabbed it. It felt good to be out of the cramped airplane seats and somewhere she could stretch out. The first part of the trip from California to Tokyo had taken close to eleven hours. The second part, from Tokyo to Ho Chi Minh City, had only taken six and a half hours, yet it had seemed twice as long as the first flight.

Paige held her backpack close and kept watch for Dalton and Skyler. Right now she felt overwhelmed and intimidated by the strange surroundings, but once they showed up, she knew everything would be fine.

* * *

Paige awoke with a jerk as the small Vietnamese woman next to her tried to pacify her screaming baby by nursing her, with no regard for modesty or effort to be discreet.

Paige turned her head and looked around, then glanced at her watch. She'd dozed for nearly an hour. Her neck ached from sleeping with her head cocked to the side, resting on her backpack.

Where are they? she wondered. Had there been some miscommunication about the time her flight arrived?

Then she remembered that she had the number to the hotel. She could call their room and find out what was going on.

Using a phone card, she dialed the series of numbers and waited anxiously inside the rank-smelling phone booth for an answer.

An older man missing half his teeth eyed her as he walked by several times. His gap-filled grin made Paige shiver. She turned away.

A man answered the phone, speaking quickly in his foreign tongue.

"Do you speak English?" she asked.

"Yes," the man replied.

Thank goodness, Paige thought. "Could you give me the room for Dalton McNamara, please?"

"Hello?" came the reply.

Paige tried again. "Dalton McNamara. An American staying at your hotel."

"American? Oh yes. We welcome you."

Paige tried not to panic. How was she ever going to get him to understand? "Please," she said, speaking slowly in the hopes that it would help. "Dalton McNamara and his daughter, Skyler. They are staying at your hotel."

"No, they are not here."

"They aren't staying there?"

"Yes."

Paige's head began to ache.

"They are staying there?"

"Yes. But they are gone."

"Gone?"

"Maybe shopping? Or to get food?"

Paige began to breathe again. "Did they go to the airport?"

"Yes, maybe. I don't know. Mr. Dalton did not say."

Hope rose in her heart. Surely that meant they were on their way. "Okay, well, thank you."

"You leave message?" the man asked.

"Oh, yes, please tell him his wife called. I'm at the airport."

"You are wife?" the man asked. "Very good. I tell him."

"That I'm at the airport."

"Yes, airport. I got it."

She hung up the phone and peeked out to see if the toothless man was still there before she stepped out of the booth.

After returning to the gate, she paced back and forth and began to wonder if they were waiting for her at the baggage claim. She told Dalton she was checking one piece of luggage. Maybe they were down there.

Bravely she made her way through the terminal, taking in the sights and smells around her. It seemed as though people made themselves at home wherever they were inclined, and several times she had to step over or walk around a sleeping body or a cluster of people sitting and eating bowls of rice with chopsticks.

Her presence seemed to garner a lot of staring, which she tried to ignore. She wasn't the only Caucasian in the place, but a white woman alone probably made them wonder who she was and what she was doing there.

With some luck, she found the baggage claim, which had long since stopped turning and was clear of luggage except for her one suitcase. With a heaving tug, she pulled the bag from the conveyor belt, and it landed on the floor with a loud bang.

Pulling up the handle, she placed her backpack on top and wheeled her luggage off to the side, where she found another seat. She scanned the terminal in each direction, looking for any sign of Dalton or Skyler and praying they would show up any minute. She hadn't liked the idea of flying alone, and this was one of the reasons. The more she thought about it, the more nervous she got. Then it occurred to her that maybe they were waiting outside the customs area. Perhaps they couldn't get to the gates and baggage claim and had to wait for her until after she cleared customs.

That was it!

Relief filled her. How silly of her not to think of that right away. They would be tired of waiting and probably worried themselves, but Dalton and Sky would be on the other side of the customs counter. With that encouraging thought, Paige jumped to her feet and headed that direction.

But when she got through customs, they were nowhere to be found. Now what should she do? Paige had been in the country over two hours now, and for some reason Dalton and Sky had either forgotten the time or couldn't get to the airport.

She called the hotel one last time, hoping they'd come back to their rooms, but once again, the man said they were still gone.

"No sign of them yet, lady," he told her.

So, digging deep for what was left of her courage, Paige decided to take a taxi into town. She'd changed a fifty dollar traveler's check into dong, receiving nearly 14,900 dong per dollar, and ended up with a brick-sized handful of cash.

Sticking the strange-looking money into her waist pack where she stored her travel visa, passport, and airplane ticket, she straightened her shoulders and strode to the curb, but she found no taxi waiting.

With the help of a skycap who spoke very rough, broken English, she found that the fastest way to town was a bus that was due to arrive any minute. The thought of taking a bus didn't appeal to her, but it beat waiting around the airport all day. When the bus pulled up, she was flooded with apprehension. It was already filled to capacity. As soon as the doors opened, a rush of people collided as those hurrying to get out fought against those trying to get in.

Paige shied back from the chaos, bumping back against her baggage. The thought of squeezing her luggage and herself onto a bus and trying to communicate her desired destination to the driver was too much to fathom.

Then, out of the corner of her eye, she saw a flash of yellow. A taxi. An actual taxi pulled up to the curb. Without a second thought, she dashed for the taxi and ripped open the door, startling the driver.

"Rex Hotel, please," Paige said.

The man nodded. "Okay, lady."

Paige waited for some indication that he was going to open the trunk for her and put in her luggage, but no such luck. With all of her might, she lifted the two bags and shoved them into the backseat beside her.

"Excuse me," she asked, pulling the door shut behind her. "How much is it?"

"You have dong?" he responded.

"Yes."

"Good, then we go."

Paige looked for a seat belt, but the buckles were either missing or broken. She grabbed onto the seat and braced herself, not knowing what kind of ride to expect.

Wondering what Dalton and Skyler were doing, Paige gazed outside at the landscape from the busy highway filled with odd makes of cars, mostly broken down and held together by rust and luck. Several small pickup trucks whizzed by, the truck beds filled to capacity with field workers. Marshy green fields and clusters of palm trees stretched out as far as she could see. Except for a few rolling hills, the land was flat.

Twenty minutes later, as they neared the city, traffic slowed, becoming congested and noisy as horns were honked in a futile effort to hurry the vehicles along. Paige fanned herself and rolled down the window. The heat was stifling, and rivulets of sweat ran between her shoulder blades and down her neck.

Looking out at the lanes of oncoming traffic, she noticed a broken-down bus, similar to the one she'd nearly boarded at the airport. The passengers were gathering their belongings and walking down the road, most of them wearing conical-shaped hats to protect them from the blazing sun.

The driver suddenly slammed on his brakes, throwing Paige forward and then back hard against her seat. A motorcycle had cut in front of them, and the taxi driver had barely missed him.

Shaking her head, Paige prayed for safety as the stop-and-go traffic wound its way into the vast expanse of the outskirts of the city, which was filled with run-down buildings made colorful by lines of laundry stretching across the streets.

Once they got off the highway and onto the city streets, the traffic began to flow at a slower pace since the streets were filled with bicycles and pedestrians. Some of the bike riders peered in at her sitting in the backseat of the taxi, and Paige shrank back to avoid their gaze. She would be happy when they got to her hotel so she could see Dalton and Skyler.

Blasting his horn, the taxi driver swerved in and out of bicycles with amazing skill. Then, with a sudden turn, he cut across traffic and pulled up with a screech in front of an old, gray-brick building.

"Hotel Rex," he announced.

It didn't look like a hotel, but on a sign in front were the words *Hotel Rex*.

Paige mustered a smile and said thank you. She wasn't sure what bills to give him from the handful of dong she held in her hand.

He had obviously worked with foreigners before, and the next thing she knew, he'd rifled through the stack, taking several large bills. He bowed his head and said, "Thank you."

He helped her remove her luggage from the car, and with her and her belongings out of the taxi, he was gone.

Wondering how much she'd paid him and if she was even at the right place, she realized there was only one way to find out. She pulled her suitcase behind her and walked inside the hotel, where a short, middle-aged man who could barely see over the counter greeted her.

"Hello," he said with a smile.

In the background, the sound of a crying child could be heard, and an odor like cooked cabbage wafted on the hot, humid air.

Paige appreciated his smile. "Hello, I am Mrs. Dalton McNamara."

"Oh, Mrs. Dalton. Welcome. Mr. Dalton not here."

She didn't know if that meant he and Sky were out for a while or gone for good. "Are they coming back?"

"Yes," he said.

"Could I go up to the room and wait for them?"

The man asked to check her passport and I.D., and once he was satisfied, he showed her to the room.

The moment she stepped inside, relief filled her. The room was small and humble, but there on the bed were some of Dalton's clothes, and on a chair were Skyler's things.

The sight of something familiar in such a foreign place was like a cold drink of water on a hot day—something she would have paid dearly for. But at that moment she just wanted to find the bathroom. She'd needed to go since getting off the plane, but after one look at the grungy restrooms at the airport, she'd decided to wait until she got to the hotel.

After glancing at the bathroom in their room, Paige realized she'd made a mistake. The airport toilets were much cleaner than the one in her room, but she had no choice. The only good thing was that she'd brought along a supply of toilet paper with her.

She walked over to the open window and glanced outside, studying the people below. Watching them in constant repetitive motion with sullen looks on their faces, she somehow sensed a collective feeling of frustration in the lives of these people. They were poor and had basically nothing. They worked hard but barely earned enough to survive. Their lives were filled with challenges.

The endless stream of bicycles caught her attention. Some carried loads of straw, others stacks of baskets. She was amazed at the strength and balance these people had with their oversized loads on their small bikes.

The street was also filled with cyclo drivers clamoring for passengers. Some cyclos were also loaded with goods. One man she saw had six mattresses balanced on the front of his cyclo.

Shaking her head, she turned from the window and spied the bed. Her head, thick with jet lag, begged for a pillow. She realized that there was nothing else to do until Dalton and Sky showed up, so she sat on the edge of the bed and removed her shoes.

A cockroach skittered by, which she immediately smacked with the heel of her shoe. She shivered at the thought of the filthy creatures running rampant, but she was just too tired to care.

Checking the bed for any unwelcome bedfellows, she lay down and felt her muscles relax without coaxing. She was dead tired.

A loud knock came at her door just as she was drifting off.

"Mrs. Dalton," a voice came. "Telephone for you."

Paige flew out of bed and yanked open the door.

"Downstairs, telephone," the man said.

"Thank you," she exclaimed, running back to the bed for her shoes.

She hurried down behind him and anxiously took the phone he offered.

"Hello?"

"Paige! You're there."

"Dalton, where are you? I waited at the airport for two hours. I was so scared."

"I'm sorry, honey. Our bus came late, then it broke down on the way to the airport. We had to walk."

"That was you? I saw a broken-down bus on the highway and people were walking."

"That was us. We walked all the way to the airport. That's where we are right now."

"How's Sky?"

"Not happy. I think the fun's already worn off. She's hot, she's sick of the food already, and she says it smells."

"I haven't tried the food yet. But I'll be honest, I'm hot and sweaty, and it is kind of smelly."

"Guess that makes three of us. We just need a cool shower and a good meal and we'll be fine. We're not going to be in Ho Chi Minh

City much longer. I hope to find someone who can help us find Soon Lee's family."

"How do we do that?"

"We can talk about it when we get to the hotel."

"Tell Sky hi for me," Paige said. "I'll be in the room waiting for you."

"We'll get there as soon as we can."

Paige hung up the phone with relief. Finally, they'd connected.

After going back to the room, she decided to try to rest for a few minutes before they got there so she wouldn't be too tired to do something with them later that evening.

It took several minutes for the excitement inside of her to die down. She couldn't wait to see Sky and Dalton again. She knew how happy Skyler would be when she saw all the treats Paige had brought with her from the States.

Feeling exhaustion take over, Paige drifted into a much-needed sleep, wondering what other surprises and strange experiences lay in store for them.

CHAPTER SEVEN

The next morning, after a happy reunion and a wonderful meal at a restaurant that served American and Vietnamese food, Dalton and Paige awoke to a loud scream from Sky.

"Ants," she hollered.

Paige and Dalton raced to the bathroom and there, in the garbage, along with a couple of Snickers wrappers smeared with melted chocolate, were thousands of ants.

Sky ran to Paige and buried her head in her shoulder. Paige took her to the other room while Dalton figured out some way to get rid of them.

"I hope you don't mind me using that bottle of rubbing alcohol," he said when he finally joined them on the bed. "It was the only thing I could think of to kill all of them."

"I don't care what you used as long as you got rid of them," Paige said.

"Dad, this place is giving me the creeps. When are we getting out of here?" Sky begged. "I thought we were going to see where you were a prisoner and stuff and go find Mom's family."

"We are, honey, but I need someone who can take us to the jungle. Someone who knows their way around. We'll find someone today. I promise."

"What else are we doing today?" Paige asked, already feeling the pressing heat and humidity of the day.

"Let's take Paige to the market," Sky offered. "You won't believe some of the weird stuff they have here."

"Sounds fun," Paige answered, not sure if *fun* was really the right word.

They got ready for the day, and before they left the room, they knelt down together to have a prayer. Sky didn't actually kneel on the floor, but on the bed, too afraid that some strange insect would attack her.

After the prayer, they left their room and stepped out into the bright morning sunshine, ready to begin another adventure. To their surprise, Quat was just outside the door of their hotel.

"Quat," Dalton said. "What a surprise."

"You cross road today? You need help?" The boy eyed Paige.

"Oh, Quat, this is my wife, Paige."

Paige smiled and said hello.

"Hi, lady," Quat replied. "You need new clothes, shoes, jewelry? I show you where you can buy. Good price."

Paige laughed. "I'll bet." She remembered telling Dalton how much she'd paid for the taxi ride from the airport and nearly passed out when Dalton told her she'd given the man nearly thirty dollars for a trip that shouldn't have cost more than ten.

"Come, I show you."

They looked at each other, then followed Quat down the sidewalk to a different part of town.

"Quat," Dalton said as he sidestepped an old man sprawled out on the sidewalk near an alleyway. Paige's heart wrenched inside of her at the sight of the old man. Sky noticed it too and took Paige's hand and walked a little closer to her.

Dalton continued. "Do you know anyone who knows about the Vietnam War?"

"Yes, my brother."

"The one who speaks English? How does he know about the war? How old is he?"

"My father was soldier here, in Saigon. He tell my brother many things."

"Where is your father?"

"Dead. When I was little boy."

"I'm sorry," Dalton said.

The boy shrugged.

"Do you think I could talk to your brother? We are looking for someone to take us to some of the sites of the war."

"He will come to here later today. You talk then, okey-dokey?"

Dalton smiled at the girls. "Okey-dokey."

They arrived at another market, this one even bigger than the first. Paige could only imagine the things they could find there. Even in the open, the air was filled with odors, some sweet and spicy, others nauseating and putrid. Paige thought Sky was going to pass out, given how often she held her breath.

Quat left them to go back to the restaurant to help his mother, but not until Dalton slipped him a dollar for his trouble. They agreed to meet at the restaurant at three o'clock to see Quat's older brother. Until then, they were shopping.

"Paige, c'mere." Sky beckoned from one of the stands. An old woman with a cross expression stared at the two Americans in front of her. Paige tried to give her a smile, but the woman merely spit a stream of beetle nut juice on the ground and wiped her mouth with the back of her hand.

Sky lifted up some tarnished, bent dog tags for Paige to see. "We found some at the market yesterday. Dad bought them."

Paige took the tags, the thin metal clinking in the palm of her hand. Together they read the names on the tags: Johnson, Cuthbert, Watkins, Beerman. Who were they? Where were they now? Each tag represented a life, a family affected by the Vietnam War. Had they made it out alive?

"How much?" Paige asked the woman.

The woman held up two bent fingers. Paige calculated the amount in dong and gave her the bills.

After handing the woman the money, Paige clutched her purchases tightly, suddenly afraid someone would seize them.

"Let's find more," she told Sky.

Together they scoured the market with Dalton browsing nearby. He was interested in leather goods and high-tech deals, but wary of quality and dependability.

Paige found several more tags, and she and Sky decided to take them back to America and, if possible, return them to their owners or their owner's families.

"We can ask Quat about museums," Dalton told her. "They might have war memorabilia there."

"Can we?" she asked anxiously.

Dalton wrapped his arm around his wife and gave her a squeeze. "I think it's wonderful that you want to do this." He also gave Sky a squeeze. "And you too, sweetie."

"Look," Sky exclaimed, pointing to a large opening into a metal storage shed. From inside they heard strange noises that sounded like animals. "What's in there?"

They drew nearer out of curiosity, then paused before entering.

"Black-market animals," Dalton told them. "Most of these animals are endangered, but they're hunted and sold illegally."

"Sold to zoos?" Sky asked, confused.

"No, usually to eat or for medicinal purposes."

"What?" Paige exclaimed, then lowered her voice. "What kind of medicinal purposes?"

Dalton didn't have a chance to answer. A man near the door saw them and beckoned them to come inside. They saw rows and stacks of metal cages where they identified several types of animals, mostly macaques and gibbons. There was also a small Asiatic black bear and a sun bear.

The man who had invited them in spoke fairly good English and was open to their questions.

"So, you eat these animals?" Dalton asked.

"No, not all. Some we trade or sell. We had a clouded leopard here the other day, very beautiful. We sold him to man in Taiwan who wanted the fur for a jacket for wife."

"Really?" Paige asked.

"Oh, yes. To dress his wife in fur shows that man has power and much wealth." He smiled broadly, as if certain they would be impressed.

"What about the bears?" Sky asked, obviously not happy about what she was seeing.

"Some people use them for pets, but most of them are killed. We don't always know what will happen to the animals we sell. That is none of our business."

"They don't eat the bears though, right?" Sky asked.

"The gall bladder of a bear is a great delicacy. It contains power to strengthen. We also sell many bears to people from Thailand for bear-paw soup. Very expensive. Two hundred U.S. dollars."

Sky didn't reply but looked at the animals staring out at them from behind metal screens. *If they couldn't be free, these animals should have been in a zoo or some kind of preserve. But bear-paw soup?*

"Let's go, Dad," Sky said, pulling on her father's sleeve.

Dalton thanked the man for his time and escorted Paige and Skyler out of the building.

As soon as they were a distance away, Sky erupted.

"That is the most horrible thing I've ever seen. How can they do that to those poor animals? Did you hear what he said about the monkeys?"

"No," Paige answered. "I was off looking at the little black bear."

"He said that they boil a monkey for three days until it completely dissolves into a thick stew, then it is sold by the cupful because it is supposedly a powerful medicine that can cure anything."

"You're kidding."

"I wish I were," Sky said. "Dad, how do we just stand by and let this happen?"

"Honey," Dalton tried to calm her, "what they are doing is illegal, but we can't stop them."

"We could buy the animals and take them somewhere safe. Don't they have zoos here? Isn't there someone in this crazy country who cares?"

"You have to understand, they think a little differently here."

"A little!" Sky was inconsolable.

As they walked through the marketplace, one man was selling bottles with snakes inside preserved in rice wine. He claimed that the liquid in the bottle had a powerful medicinal value. This fueled Sky's anger even more. The rest of the time at the market, she managed to point out everything negative, from the smells and dirt to the bizarre foods and live poultry waiting to be purchased for someone's evening meal. Although Paige found several more dog tags, which helped take Skyler's mind off of the animals, the girl just couldn't let it go.

By the time they got back to the restaurant to meet Quat, Sky was ready to hop on the next cyclo and head for the airport. She'd had enough of this country and its strange traditions and beliefs. Paige and Dalton tried to reason with her, to explain that maybe fermented snake and rice wine wasn't a cure-all, but these people believed it was, and most of them had no other option. Modern medicine was expensive and hard to come by. They did the best they could.

Back at the restaurant, they ordered *pho* again. Along with the soup they had elephant ear, fish, pork, chicken, and rice.

"I'm sick," Skyler said, pushing away her food. "Don't they have anything here but rice?"

Dalton laughed. "Honey, you'll be back to the land of hamburgers and french fries before you know it."

"Let's get back to the hotel so I can raid Paige's suitcase. I need real food," she said.

"As soon as we talk to Quat's brother, we'll be on our way," Dalton said.

They waited in the sweltering heat, fanning themselves with paper menus. Their entertainment was the small children, Quat's younger brothers and sisters, who ran around the restaurant. Sometimes they stopped to clean dishes off the tables, but mostly they ran around, laughing and chattering to each other.

After some time, a cyclo pulled up in front of the restaurant. A young man who appeared to be in his late teens climbed off and came inside. Quat brought him a drink, and Quat's mother rushed a tray of food to him.

Dalton assumed this was Quat's brother, and he felt his stomach tense anxiously. Hopefully he would be able to help them with their need for a guide.

Quat spent a moment talking to his brother, who looked at Dalton several times as he ate and listened. Then Quat left his side and came over to Dalton and the others.

"He will speak to you after he eats," Quat said.

"Do you think he will help us?" Dalton asked.

"How much money you got?"

Dalton laughed. "I'm sure we can work out an arrangement."

Quat left to help in the kitchen since the restaurant was filling up with people.

"That woman works nonstop in that hot kitchen," Paige said as she observed Quat's mother. "I don't know how she doesn't pass out from the heat."

"She has to provide for her family. She has no choice," Dalton said.

"Their lives seem so hard," Sky remarked. "Kids back home would be lying around watching TV or playing video games, eating junk food, and whining about having to do their homework."

Dalton and Paige exchanged glances.

"These kids probably don't know what it would be like to have a lazy day, you know? To just do whatever they wanted to do."

"You're probably right," Dalton said.

Quat's brother drained the juice from his soup bowl and wiped his mouth with the back of his hand. He then stood up and walked toward their table.

Dalton jumped to his feet and shook his hand, then invited him to sit down.

"My brother said you wanted to talk to me?" he spoke in nearly flawless English.

"Yes. We are interested in going to some of the sites where I spent time while I was here during the war. I need someone who knows their way around, someone who might know where some of the jungle camps were for the prisoners of war."

"You were a prisoner?"

Dalton nodded. "In the jungle and in Hanoi."

The young man nodded and glanced at Sky.

"Do you know someone who could do this?" Dalton asked, knowing this kid would be much too young to know about the camps and battle sites. "I am willing to pay for the service."

"I can do it." He kept looking at Sky.

"You?" Dalton noticed him looking at his daughter.

"Yes. My father told me many things about the war, and my uncle was a soldier for South Vietnam during the war. He showed me many places of the war. He used to drive a delivery truck and would take me with him. I saw many places, heard many stories. I can help you find wherever you need to go. It is possible that my uncle can help us also."

"What is your name?" Dalton asked.

"I am Quang. Nguyen Quang."

Dalton noticed Quang looking at Sky with a strange expression. "Is something wrong, Quang?"

"She should not cross her arms like that."

Sky's face registered surprise, and she uncrossed her arms. "I'm sorry. I didn't know."

"You must be careful not to cross arms or stand with your hands on your hips. This is a symbol of aggression."

"I'm glad you told us," Paige said, putting her arms down by her side.

"Never point at someone. This shows that you feel you are superior. Many Americans do this. You must be very careful in my country so that you can avoid trouble."

"Thank you, Quang," Dalton said. "We appreciate your help."

Quang bowed his head, then asked, "When do you want to leave?"

"As soon as possible. What about tomorrow?"

Quang thought for a moment, then said, "Yes. I think that would work. I will talk to my uncle." He told them that he rented the cyclo from a man and that he had to talk to him and make arrangements to be gone for a few days. He would meet them at their hotel first thing in the morning.

"One more thing, Quang. Do you know where there are any shops that would have dog tags from American soldiers?" Dalton asked.

Quang gave them a few suggestions, then bid them good-bye.

"I think he's excited to do this," Paige said.

"I just hope he can help us," Dalton said. "It's been so long, and I was never completely sure where I was in the jungle."

"All we can do is try," Paige said. "Quang will do his best. He seems like a very nice young man. Nice-looking, too."

"I noticed that too," Sky said.

Paige chuckled and turned to Dalton. "Honey, did you notice? Honey?"

But Dalton wasn't listening. His mind had drifted back three decades to images and scenery that he'd kept buried deep inside. And tomorrow he would return to the places which had been a doorway to death for so many. The only thing that had kept him from going through that doorway himself was a constant prayer that he could make it through one more day, one step at a time, one breath at a time.

And he wondered if he was really ready to face it again.

* * *

Ho Loa Prison, Hanoi, Vietnam, 1971

Dalton woke with a start, the haunting echo of a soldier's screams turning his stomach.

He knew what prompted those cries of agony. Luckily he'd been in the prison long enough now that the Vietnamese guards focused their "persuasive" efforts on the newer prisoners, trying to extract more recent information.

Dalton dragged himself to the wall and propped himself up against it, feeling a slight breeze coming through the small twelve-by-twelve-inch window at the top of his cell.

The jungle camp had been brutal, but at least he'd been able to interact with the other prisoners. Here at the Hilton, there was no contact except for the tap code the prisoners had invented to communicate in secret among themselves. Still, it wasn't the same as having a full-out conversation with someone, and Dalton craved having someone to talk to.

Every day he read the words he'd etched into the wall, reminding himself that he couldn't give up faith or hope. He could never give up. Hope and faith were all he had. The men who gave up died, either mentally or physically. He was determined to survive. He knew there was more in store for him in life than this. In his heart, he didn't feel this was where his journey on earth would end. If it did, it wouldn't be because he gave up.

But discouragement pressed down upon him and the other prisoners like a thick fog.

He thought of his home, of his family, of the friends he'd left behind. Would he ever see them again? And when he got home, would the war have changed him so much he wouldn't fit in?

He worried about this because he had changed. Any soldier who'd seen the things he'd seen, been through the misery he'd been through, couldn't help but change.

Dalton's changes weren't just emotional, however. He was scarred inside . . . and outside.

Glancing down at his right leg that ended just below his knee caused him to close his eyes and wonder what kind of future he had.

Would he only receive pity and scorn for his involvement in the war, or would he be a functional, contributing member of society?

Living life as an invalid just wasn't what he had in mind for himself. He resolved that being an amputee wouldn't be a hindrance to pursuing his goals and dreams, as faded and distant as they seemed. So faded, so distant, that many days they were impossible to imagine.

A movement caught his eye, and he looked up toward the window. There, fluttering as light as air, was a lovely, graceful butterfly with wings of white, wings of an angel.

Dalton held his breath, not wanting to scare away the delicate creature that hovered just inside his room, merely inches from freedom. So close. Freedom was so close, yet for Dalton, so far away.

But the presence of that butterfly gave wings to his broken dreams and sagging hopes. Maybe, in some small but significant way, this was a signal from God that He hadn't forgotten one of His children tucked away and hidden behind moldy, crumbling walls in a country that was filled with war and hatred.

Dalton got onto his good knee, propping himself up with his arm against the wall so he could pray. He needed to thank his Father in Heaven for the reminder that he hadn't been forgotten. God was still aware of him and of all of these men.

Tears leaked down his sweat- and dirt-stained face as he ended his prayer, then watched the fluttering wisp of hope escape through the iron bars back into freedom, into sunshine and light.

He would make it out of here. He had to believe it.

Dalton collapsed onto the floor, the throbbing from his bad leg too much to bear. Keeping it elevated was the only way he could stand the pain. His gaze traveled to the wall, and again he read the words he'd carved there. *Wait on the Lord.* The butterfly had reminded him that the Lord hadn't forgotten him. His life, his fate, was in the Lord's hands. He recalled the words Wilson had told him once. *Courage is not the absence of fear, but the ability to press on in spite of it.*

He would press on.

CHAPTER EIGHT

Once again, Sky's screams awoke Paige and Dalton.

Racing to the bathroom, Paige and Dalton threw open the door and saw Sky on top of the toilet, against the wall.

"What is it?" Dalton asked breathlessly.

"There," Sky whispered, pointing to the adjacent wall.

Paige and Dalton looked and there, attached to the wall, was a scaly, green gecko with bulging eyes.

"Eww!" Paige said, echoing Sky's sentiments as a shiver ripped up her spine.

"What do I do?" Sky whispered, fearing that her voice would cause the creature to attack.

"Climb down off the toilet and come out here," Dalton instructed. "Just move slowly. It won't hurt you."

"I'm scared," Sky said.

"You can do it," Paige told her.

"They're harmless, honey," Dalton assured her.

"You promise?" Sky questioned.

"I promise," Dalton answered.

"Okay." Sky took several deep breaths, then slowly lowered one leg to the ground, keeping her eye on the gecko. After lowering her other leg, she paused, hoping her movements hadn't bothered the lizard. When she was convinced it was safe, she took her first step, then shot out of the bathroom and flew onto the bed.

Paige went to Sky and gave her a hug while Dalton grabbed his camera.

"Hey," Paige said, "just think of all the great stories you're going to have to tell your friends when we get home."

"I'm ready to go home now. I hate this place."

Paige laughed and hugged her again. "We're leaving today. Maybe when we get out of the city, it will be better."

Sky doubted it. Most likely things would get worse. At least in the city they had running water and electricity.

Dalton joined them after the lizard's photo shoot. "Glad you found one of those," he told Sky. "I was hoping to get a picture."

"Dad, it scared me to death."

"I know, but they really are harmless, and they're pretty cool. Some of them can even fly."

Sky's eyes grew wide. "Fly?"

"Well, not really. They just kind of soar through the branches of trees."

"I want to go home," Sky said. "I need fast food and television. And phones. I need to talk on the phone."

"Don't bail out just yet, Sky," Dalton told his daughter. "The adventure's just getting started."

"Oh boy," Sky said with little enthusiasm.

"We'd better get packed," Paige said, noticing her watch. "Aren't we supposed to meet Quang downstairs at eight?"

"I'm not going into that bathroom as long as that thing is in there," Sky complained.

"Well, some of us don't have a choice," Paige said. "My back teeth are going to start floating any minute if I don't get to the bathroom."

Sky and Dalton began packing their things and talking about their next stop. Dalton's goal was to find the location where he got captured. He hoped that Quang could help him, but many landmarks of the war had changed. Rice paddies had replaced battlefields. New growth had covered war zones. Cities had spread and people had built their shabby homes where other homes had been bombed and destroyed.

Before they left their room, the family had their morning prayer. This was as much of a spiritual journey as anything, and this time, Dalton prayed that Quang would be guided and that they would be able to find the places they were seeking. He also prayed for strength, guidance, and protection for all of them.

"Everyone ready?" he asked after he closed the prayer.

"Do you think we'll find more dog tags in some of the other cities?" Paige asked.

"Probably. And I'm sure when we get to Hanoi, there will be plenty of places to look for them," Dalton replied.

"Even if the soldiers have died, their parents deserve to have these tags," Paige said.

"Gathering them will be a big job," Dalton said.

"I'll help you, Paige," Sky offered.

Paige smiled at her stepdaughter. "Thanks, Sky. I'll need it. Besides, I don't care how hard it is, I really want to do this."

Dalton nodded. "We'll both help you. It may be difficult for some of the families to be reminded of such a painful loss, but it also might help them get some closure."

"Thanks, honey," Paige told her husband, then gave him a kiss. "I don't know what I'd do without you."

He returned her kiss. "I don't know what I'd do without you, either. I'm so glad you're here."

"Me too," Sky said as she pulled her backpack over her shoulders.

Paige stretched her arm toward Sky and pulled her into their hug.

"This could be quite an interesting day," Dalton said. "Are we ready?"

"I'm ready," Paige said.

"So am I," Sky answered. "Bring it on!"

* * *

Just as he promised, Quang was there in the lobby of the hotel waiting for them. Another man was with him. He was Hai, Quang's uncle.

Quang explained that his uncle's health was poor but that he wanted to accompany his nephew and the Americans on their journey. Not only had he been a soldier for the South Vietnamese army, he'd also worked as a guide and a translator for the Americans.

Hai's face was worn and tired looking, but his eyes reflected kindness, and warmth filled his smile. He was now an illegal citizen in his own city. His only source of income was odd jobs and working for others, getting paid on the side. His fate had been similar to the fates of most of the South Vietnamese soldiers. Most had abandoned their uniforms when the war ended for fear of their lives and futures under the control of the North Vietnamese. Hai was happy to help Dalton find the places he wanted to go, and he needed the money Dalton was willing to pay.

They went to the family restaurant for breakfast so they could talk about the route to take and the area they needed to cover to locate Dalton's point of capture and his prisoner camps in the jungle.

While they ate the standard breakfast of rice, noodle soup, fish, and some type of fruit none of them had seen before, Dalton, Quang, and Hai discussed the trip ahead.

"I'd kill for a bowl of cereal," Skyler said, stabbing her chopsticks into her bowl of noodles. "Or toast. Can't I just have a piece of toast?"

Paige didn't have a problem with the food, since she loved all types of Asian food—Thai especially—and was used to some of the strange tastes, like fish sauce, chilies, and lime used in a lot of their flavorings. "When we're done here, we can buy some baguettes," she promised. "I wouldn't mind a chunk of bread either."

The Vietnamese had become masters at baking baguettes, a practice that had been introduced to their country during the late '40s and early '50s when the French occupied it. Thousands of loaves of French bread were baked daily in the city.

"So, I guess we're ready," Dalton exclaimed as he got to his feet and shook Hai's hand.

"This will be difficult journey," Hai told them. "Vietnam has rebuilt many of its cities, but country still recovers from war. Napalm destroy villages, and Agent Orange destroy jungles and fields. Roads are not good. We will walk many miles."

Dalton saw Skyler's expression change to one of displeasure. While he was proud of her for not voicing her complaint out loud, he was sure they'd hear about it later.

"We'd better put on our good walking shoes and wear hats," Dalton said.

"What about our luggage? We can't drag that around the country-side with us, can we?" Paige asked.

"We can store your things at the train station," Hai told her. "We ride train to Nha Trang and try and find someone to take us into central highlands. Then we are on foot."

There was nothing more to say. The plan had been made. This was one of the things that had brought them to Vietnam in the first place.

It was time to see where Dalton was captured.

* * *

Shifting her position a dozen times still didn't help Sky find a comfortable place to sleep on the hard train seat. It was hot, and the ride was slow and bumpy.

At first, she had found it interesting to watch out the window and see Ho Chi Minh City fade away into rice fields, muddy rivers, and bamboo shacks—*hooches,* as her father called them. But after a while, all the rice paddies looked the same, and the flat land held no interest for her.

"Paige," she said toward the seat in front of her.

Paige peeked over the seat. "How ya doin', Sky?"

"I think my rear end's gone numb from all this bouncing and sitting. When do you think we'll be there?"

"Another few hours," Paige said.

"Have you got any more Snickers?" An American treat might make things more bearable.

"I sure do," Paige said. "It's probably melted, though."

"That's okay. I'll suck it out of the wrapper if I have to."

Paige handed her the candy bar, which was soft and mushy. Sky didn't care. It would still taste the same.

Licking every last morsel of peanuts and chocolate from the wrapper, Sky sighed with contentment. Then a horrible thought occurred to her. What would they do when they ran out?

"Paige!" Sky banged on the seat in front of her.

Paige peeked over the seat again.

"How many more candy bars do you have?"

"A few. Why?"

"What if we run out? I'll die. I'll die, for sure."

Paige shrugged. "I don't know. I'd think we could find some American candy here."

"Yes," Quang piped up from across the aisle. "Outside of the train station there are shops. You can find candy."

"Oh, thank you," Sky said with relief.

"See," Paige said. "You won't die of Snickers deprivation after all."

Paige turned around and sat down, leaving Sky to herself. She looked out the window and saw more of the same scenery: palm trees, green fields, and bamboo hooches.

"You like M&Ms?" Quang asked her.

Sky turned and looked at the young man across from her. "Yes. Peanut M&Ms are my favorite. How about you? Have you tried American candy?"

"Oh, yes. Peanut M&Ms are very good."

"Have you tried Snickers?"

"No." He shook his head. "Maybe I will try it though."

"You'd love them," she told him.

"Do you miss America?" Quang asked her.

"I miss air conditioning, hot showers, hamburgers, and freeways," she answered, knowing she could go on. "Yeah, I miss it, but I wanted to come."

He raised his eyebrows as if to ask, "Why?"

"We want to see the places where my father was held as a prisoner. And we're going to try and find my mom's family."

He cocked his head.

"My mother was Vietnamese," she told him. "They met before he was captured."

"I see."

Sky wasn't sure why she had told him that. She didn't talk much about her mother to anyone.

"My father," Quang said, "he was an American soldier."

"Did your mother meet him in the war?"

"No, she was just a tiny girl during the war. Her parents were both killed. Only her brother, my uncle, Hai, survived with her. He was a soldier for South Vietnam. Everyone else died. As soon as the war ended, they had to hide. My mother found jobs to earn money to buy them food, but my uncle could not work."

"Why?"

"North Vietnamese soldiers came to Saigon—Ho Chi Minh City—in 1975, and the South Vietnamese government collapsed. They captured many of the South Vietnamese soldiers and took them away. Uncle Hai did not want to leave his sister again, so he found a place in the country to hide. He is still illegal and cannot have a real job."

"That is so sad. What about your father? When did your mother meet him?"

"Over twenty years ago. He came back after the war. He was not happy in America, so he came back. He said the people there were cruel to him and treated him like a criminal. After he met my mother, he helped my uncle set up a cyclo business and my mother a restaurant. They got married. My father told me many stories of the war. He was my hero."

"How did he die?"

"Cancer. He said it was from Agent Orange, even though your government never admitted Agent Orange could cause cancer. He died when Quat was very young, ten years ago."

"But you have younger brothers and sisters."

"They have a different father, but he walked out on my mother."

Sky thought about Quang's life, and how different they were from each other. Then again, the war had changed both of their lives even though it had happened before they were born. And they both came from parents of different races.

"Do people ever bother you about having an American father?" she asked.

"When I was little, I always had a black eye. Kids would tease me and say mean things to me. Not as much now. I look more Vietnamese than American. But inside, I have a great desire to go to America and learn about my father and his family. I feel like I need to do that to understand myself." Quang looked at her and said, "That probably sounds crazy."

Sky shook her head.

"No?" he asked.

"Part of the reason we are here is for my father to visit some places from the war, but the other reason is to find my mother's family. She's dead now. My father met her when he was here in the war. She came to America. I've never met her family."

"That is good for you to meet them," Quang said with a confident nod.

"You think?"

"I do. Their blood runs in your blood. It is your duty to learn about them. You will never be whole until you do. You honor her with your desire to meet her family . . . your family."

Sky nodded. It was true, they were her family. "I don't know what to expect when we meet. I worry how they will treat me and my family."

"But it does not matter. Once you have closed the circle, you will be able to accept what happens either way."

"How do you think they'll feel about seeing us?" she asked him.

"They might be happy to see you because their daughter was able to escape all the horrible things that happened in our country during and since the war. For this they will thank you."

Sky nodded, hoping that would be the scenario.

"But they might be angry because your father took their daughter. And now that she is dead, they can never see her again."

"I hope that's not the case."

He shrugged. "You would rather I lie to you?"

"No, of course not." She fingered her locket, as she'd developed a habit of doing. "Would you like to see a picture of my mother?"

He nodded.

Opening the locket, she showed him the small picture of her mother, smiling and happy.

"This could be you," he said.

"You think?" Sky looked closely at the picture, studying her mother's features. "My nose is much bigger than hers, and she was very petite. I'm almost three inches taller than she was."

"Still, you look very much like her."

"Thanks." Sky closed the locket and let it rest against her skin. Maybe on the outside they looked like each other, but inside they were nothing alike. Her mother had kept her feelings bottled up so tight that they finally ate her alive, robbing her of her will to live. If anything, Sky was usually too liberal with sharing her feelings and emotions.

"So, this woman with your father?"

"That's my stepmother."

"Do you like her?" Quang asked.

"Paige is the best," Sky exclaimed. "She's been like a best friend, a big sister, and a mother all rolled into one. But sometimes . . ." Sky knew that to be honest she had to make a confession. "Sometimes I don't treat her very well, and I don't know why."

"Because," Quang told her, "you must find peace in your soul. Then you can have peace in your life. This will happen when you meet your mother's family."

"How old are you, Quang?"

"I just turned twenty."

"You look twenty, but you talk as though you are much older."

"We do not get to be children very long here in Vietnam. Most children are working by the time they are ten. Our lives can be very difficult."

The train gave a lurch and began to slow down.

"Are we here?" Sky asked, looking out of the window for some sign of a town or village, but all she saw were fields.

"No, there must be a problem."

The train continued to slow until it came to a stop.

"I will find out what is going on," Hai said before crowding into the aisle with the other curious passengers.

Skyler felt as though all her energy had seeped out through her sweat glands. Waiting in the sweltering heat with no breeze coming through the window made the sitting train feel like an oven.

Paige broke out a pack of gum, a piece of which Quang heartily accepted before settling back into his seat, patiently waiting for the train to start again.

Skyler marveled at the amount of patience these people possessed. Were they so used to being inconvenienced and having things out of their control that they'd just learned to accept it and not make themselves crazy worrying about things they couldn't change?

Hai came back inside. "Oncoming train," he said.

"Excuse me?" Dalton replied. "Did you say there was an oncoming train?"

"Yes," Hai answered. "We must wait for it to pass on other track before we go farther."

Dalton exchanged worried glances with Paige and Sky.

Hai waved his hand. "Do not worry. We rarely have collisions here."

Sure enough, moments later the ground rumbled and a loud whoosh followed as the oncoming train barreled past them. Passengers clamored back on board and took their seats, their excited conversations drowned out by the movement of the train chugging forward once again.

Dalton leaned around the seat and said to Sky, "How ya doin', sweetie?"

"Just peachy, Dad," she answered.

"Glad to hear it. What do you think of the countryside? Have you noticed all the water buffalo?"

"I thought those were bulls."

"No, they're water buffalo. They came from China."

"Fascinating," she answered, wondering if the feeling would ever come back into her legs after being bounced and jarred for so long. Then she put her own feelings aside and thought of her father. "How are you doin', Dad? Is this starting to get a little freaky?"

"A little, but it's going to be okay," he told her with an assuring wink. "I'm glad you and Paige are here with me."

"Me too, Dad," Skyler said, knowing that all the discomfort was worth it. "Me too."

"We are close," Hai told them. "It is not much farther. It is too late to continue today. We must find place to sleep, then we start early in morning. We do not want to hike through jungle in dark. There are still land mines in area, and trail is not easy."

With the plan made, they anxiously awaited their arrival in Nha Trang. As they got closer to the city, the landscape changed from banana and palm trees to clusters of rustic dwellings. Green rice paddies gave way to dirt streets filled with bicycles and pedestrians, all busily going about their day, doing whatever they needed to do to secure their next meal.

Sky was the first one in their group to step off the train. She had never been so grateful to stand on solid ground as she was at that moment. Her legs felt weak and wobbly from sitting so long.

The passengers crowding onto the platform forced her away from her family like an undercurrent she couldn't fight. She tried to turn to see where Paige and her father were, but they hadn't gotten off the train yet. Holding tightly to her backpack, which she hadn't had a chance to put on, she resisted the sea of bodies pushing her ahead. Hai had told them to be careful in crowds. He said some thieves had been known to slit the bottoms of backpacks and empty the contents before the person wearing the backpack even knew what had happened.

Panic caused her heartbeat to race. She felt someone grab her arm and pull at her. While yanking herself free, she fought for the safety of some stairs to her left, hoping she could look out over the crowd and maybe locate her group.

Again someone grabbed at her, and this time she heard him call her name.

She turned to see Quang behind her. Relief filled her, and she allowed him to steer her out of the way toward the stairs she'd spotted.

"Thank you," she said breathlessly as they climbed the stairs. "I didn't know how far I was going to have to go to get free."

"People have been trampled before. You must be careful. Better to wait until the train is empty. You got off so quickly, I did not have a chance to warn you."

"I'm glad you caught up with me."

They watched the steady stream of people until Quang spotted Dalton, standing head and shoulders above the Vietnamese passengers.

They caught Dalton's attention and soon joined him and Paige and began their walk from the station to a hotel Hai recommended that was located just across the street. Nha Trang was significantly smaller than Ho Chi Minh City, but just as crowded. As Quang had promised, Sky saw several stands selling newspapers, magazines, Coca-Cola, and candy, some of which was American.

Just outside the hotel stood a young girl Sky guessed to be around seven years old wearing a pale blue dress with a Peter Pan collar.

"Please, sir," she said to them, holding up a handful of flowers. Her big, almond eyes were pleading and sad.

Hai paid no attention to the girl, but Dalton stopped and looked down at the beautiful child.

He held out a few coins for her, which she eagerly took, then handed him the bouquet of flowers that looked like forget-me-nots.

Sky was glad her father had helped the little girl. A few dong meant nothing to them, but they meant everything to a starving child who probably had hungry brothers and sisters at home.

"Here, sweetie." He handed the flowers to Sky.

She noticed his eyes were moist. "Dad?"

Dalton shoved the flowers into her hand and stepped quickly through the hotel doors.

Paige looked at Sky and shook her head. This was something they could talk about later.

CHAPTER NINE

"Wow, Dad, look at that sunset." Sky gazed out the hotel window at the glowing red of the setting sun. It was a spectacular sight.

Dalton joined her at the window and rested an arm around his daughter's shoulders. "I remember these sunsets," he said with a wistful tone in his voice. "You'd think after thirty years I would have forgotten it. I thought I had forgotten it, but here, now, I remember taking a break from my duties to stop and watch a sunset just like this the night before I was captured. I never thought I'd enjoy another sunset again."

Sky sensed the pain in his voice and gave her father a hug.

"Reminders are all around me," Dalton told his daughter. "Like that child earlier today."

"The one selling flowers outside the hotel?" Sky asked.

"Yes, the one with the sad eyes. She reminded me of your mother when I first saw her."

Sky rested her head on her father's shoulder as he described how beautiful Soon Lee was but how sad she often looked.

Just then, Paige came out of the bathroom, where she'd taken a shower to rinse off the dust, sweat, and grime of the day of traveling.

Sky wished she and her father could have had a few more minutes of privacy. She loved hearing her father talk about her mother. Each conversation helped her feel closer to her.

* * *

"What in the world is that noise?" Paige asked as she rolled over in bed and pulled the pillow over her head.

"The villagers have finished their morning Tai Chi exercises, and now the government is playing the morning broadcast."

"Why didn't I bring earplugs?" Paige complained. It had been so hot and muggy the night before that she had had a hard time falling asleep. Then it seemed as though Dalton had tossed and turned the entire night. Now the morning wake-up call in Vietnamese was too much. She was going to be a zombie all day.

"We need to get up anyway," Dalton said. "Hai wants to get an early start. Sky, are you awake?"

Paige lifted her head and saw Sky still asleep with a pillow over her head too. The girl was one of the deepest sleepers Paige knew. Back at home, it had taken nothing short of a nuclear blast to wake her up. Obviously the morning broadcast hadn't even bothered her.

"Sky?" Dalton said louder.

Sky groaned and threw her arm across the pillow to shut out her father's voice.

"Let her sleep a little longer," Paige said. "We can both get showered and dressed, then she can get up."

"All right," Dalton said. He gave his wife a kiss on the forehead, then yawned.

"Did you have some trouble sleeping?" Paige asked him.

"Did I wake you up?"

"I couldn't sleep. It was too hot."

"It wasn't the heat bothering me as much as the dreams," Dalton said. "Being here has stirred up all the memories."

"Do you regret coming?"

"I don't know. I don't think it's going to do as much for me as I had hoped. But I still feel like this is important for Sky."

Paige stroked her husband's cheek, her heart aching. "Maybe it will help you. Especially today after you've seen the places that have haunted you all this time. You'll be able to replace the old memories with new ones."

Dalton kissed her again. "How'd I get someone so smart?" he asked her.

"I am pretty smart, aren't I?" she teased. "I was smart enough to marry you, wasn't I?"

"And I was lucky enough that you'd have me, even though I've got all this emotional baggage in my life."

"Hopefully we'll get rid of some of that baggage," she said. "And I'll do anything I can to help you."

"I know you will. I'm so glad you joined us."

"Me too," she said. Then in a quiet voice she added, "I just hope Sky doesn't regret asking me to come. She still doesn't seem quite herself with me."

"Try and be patient," Dalton responded softly. "She's nervous about meeting Soon Lee's family. She'll be fine once we get that over with."

"I hope so," Paige answered.

* * *

The bumpy, dusty road took them from the green rice paddies to flat lands of deep red soil, barren and dry with few trees and sparse vegetation. They drove past oxen, wooden carts, and small, run-down villages. The farther they got from the Mekong river and its tributaries, the fewer people they saw, until they felt as though they were the only people within a hundred miles.

Hai knew right where to go and seemed convinced he knew the spot Dalton was seeking. Even though Dalton had resigned himself to the fact that they would never find the exact spot where he and his men had been attacked, to know he was in the area was enough for him.

Quang, the driver, kept the rusty van speeding along the bumpy road until Hai called out for him to stop.

Sky, who'd managed to fall asleep, sat up with a jolt.

"Are we there?"

"No," Hai told her. "From here we must walk."

Sky looked around them and saw nothing to walk to. There was a wide river and some green, rolling hills in the distance, but that was it.

She exchanged glances with Paige, who shrugged. Just how far was this walk anyway?

They pulled the van off to the side of the road until it was well concealed, then took their necessary supplies of food, water, and other sundry items and lined up outside the van.

The sky was overcast, which helped with the heat, but the humidity was unbearable. Paige had braided Sky's hair and then clipped it up, so it was off her neck. Even in the lightest of clothing, they were drenched with sweat.

"We cross river up there," Hai said. No one said anything, but all fell in line as Hai led them toward the river. For an elderly man, Hai kept a steady pace. He had peddled cyclos for many years and was strong and sturdy.

After following the bend in the river, they finally came to a narrow neck and stopped. Dalton, Paige, and Sky stared at the thick rope spanning the river.

"What's that?" Sky asked.

"Rope bridge," Hai said.

"That's it? That's how we cross?" Sky immediately pictured herself falling into the churning water and being washed away, ending up somewhere in the Mekong delta.

Paige looked at Dalton with alarm. "Honey, do you think it's safe?"

"Probably not, but it's our only way to cross. I've done it before. It's not too hard."

Sky's eyes opened wide. "You're serious? We're going across on that rope?"

"It's going to be fine," Dalton assured her.

"I will go first, to show it is safe," Quang volunteered. "No big deal."

He stood on the bank, where the rope was easily accessible, then grasped it with both hands and swung his feet up, hooking them over the rope. Slowly, like a worm hanging upside down, he inched his way across, stretching out his legs first, then sliding his hands, stretching and sliding. It didn't look hard, but the roaring water below made it seem terrifying. Within minutes, he was on the other side, waving his hands and flashing the OK sign to them.

"Dalton, you go first," Hai told him. "Then Mrs. Dalton." He pointed at Paige. "Then daughter. I will go last."

"Honey," Paige asked her husband, "are you going to be able to do it?"

"Sure." He nodded. "I think I can manage fine." His prosthetic leg was attached below the knee, so he could hang from the rope without too much trouble.

Sky wasn't sure she wanted to do it, but she didn't have a choice. She certainly wasn't going to wait on this side of the river by herself. Plus, she'd come all this way to see these places, and she wasn't about to miss out. With conviction and determination, she took her place in line and pushed her fears aside.

"Just take it slow and easy," Dalton said as he grabbed hold of the rope. "It's not that far." He swung up to the rope and wrapped his legs around it, then began his wormlike crawl across the river.

Sky's stomach knotted, but she didn't give in to her fears. She could do this.

"Now you, Mrs. Dalton," Hai said as Dalton got about a third of the way across.

"Are you sure the rope is strong enough for two of us?" Paige questioned.

"Oh, yes," Hai answered. "I have seen four people cross at same time. Is good."

Paige hesitated a moment before latching onto the rope. She gave Sky a worried look.

"You can do it," Sky told her.

"Let's see if all those Pilates classes have helped," Paige joked. After she grabbed the rope, Paige announced that they were in for some serious rope burns and began to cross. Her foot slipped, and she dangled for just a moment with one leg hanging close to the surface of the water, but she got her leg back up and continued.

"You okay?" Sky hollered.

"I'm fine," Paige said. "Come on."

Dalton reached the other side and hollered at them so they'd know he'd made it.

"You're doing great, Paige! Hang in there," he yelled jokingly.

"Very funny," Paige hollered back over the rush of the water.

Progress was slower for the two women, but they both finally arrived on the other side.

"Ow!" Sky said, checking her wrists and ankles. "I think I've rubbed off all the skin. That's going to kill going back across."

They turned to watch Hai expertly maneuver across the rope, crawling more like an agile monkey than a frightened worm. He made it across it no time at all and was ready to continue on.

"Good job," Quang said to Sky as they began their walk to find the spot where Dalton had been captured.

"Thanks," she replied. "I'm a dancer, not an athlete."

"I can tell."

"Gee, thanks."

"No," he said, obviously surprised she'd misunderstood him. "I mean, I can tell you are a dancer."

"Oh, okay. Thanks."

"You do ballet?"

"I've taken a lot of ballet training," she said. "I do a lot of different types of dance, though. What about you? What kinds of things do you like to do?"

"Football. I wish I had time to play football. But in America, I guess you would call it soccer. And music. I love American music."

"Who do you like to listen to?"

"The Rolling Stones," he exclaimed.

Sky laughed. "I like the Stones too."

"I know all the words to their songs," he told her. "We have a radio station here that plays American rock 'n' roll music."

Dalton heard them talking. "Did you say you know all the words to all of their songs?"

"Yes," Quang answered.

"All right," Dalton said "Why don't we play a game? I'll give you a title, and you have to tell me the first line of the song."

"Sure, okay," Quang agreed.

They were all grateful for something to do to make their trip on foot more bearable. One thing Sky was grateful for was that there was finally some green on the ground instead of just red rocks and soil—and dust everywhere.

The game helped. Before they knew it, they had traversed the flat land and crossed into low, rolling foothills. The soil was still deep red, but the vegetation grew thicker as they headed deeper into the hills. The thick-growing grass made their steps more difficult, and Sky felt sweat from the effort and the humidity trickle down her back. Occasionally she took a drink from one of the several bottles of water she had in her backpack. Both Quang and Hai wore a *non la,* one of the conical-shaped hats worn by most of the Vietnamese. And as the sun broke through the clouds, Sky found her visor did little to shield her from the pounding heat.

"I need one of those hats like you have," she told Quang.

"Yes, they are very practical. Keep you cool."

"But they look so weird."

"You would rather not look weird and be hot?"

He was right. This was not the time for vanity. Being practical made more sense than anything.

"I would rather be cool," she said.

"Then I will let you use my hat," he said, taking the *non la* from his head and handing it to her.

"No, that's fine, you don't have to do that."

"I will trade you for a while. I will wear what you are wearing. It is called?"

"A visor."

"Visor."

"Yes." She slid the visor from her head and handed it to him.

"Ah, Nike," he said. "Very cool. Michael Jordan."

Sky laughed and put on Quang's hat. It was so lightweight, she could barely feel it on her head. The wide circle of the hat cut the sun's rays immediately.

"Wow, this thing really does work."

"Vietnamese work outside most of their days. They have for hundreds of years. They know what is best to protect from the sun."

"I guess they do. How do I look?" she asked.

"You look like a rice farmer."

Sky laughed again. "And you look like a soccer player," she said.

Quang smiled. "Nike!"

"When I get back to America, I'll send you a Nike soccer ball. Okay?"

Quang tilted his head, his expression confused. "You would do that for me?"

"Sure," she said. "Wouldn't you want one?"

"Oh yes, very much. But that would cost a lot of money."

"I have a job. I'll save my money."

"What kind of job do you have?"

"I work at a water park."

"What is a water park?"

"It's a place where they have these big, long slides that you go down, and then you land in a pool of water. Some of the slides are dark inside and have flashing lights, then you shoot out into the sunlight. Or some are really high and drop almost straight down."

His eyes grew wide. "These slides sound very fun."

"They're a blast. If you ever come to America, I'll take you there. And to Disneyland."

"Ah, yes. Disneyland."

"Do you think you'll ever come to America?"

"I would miss my family very much, but yes, I will come to America. I will come and get a job and make money and bring my family to live with me. I will buy my mother a car, and we will have a garden where she can spend her time growing flowers instead of working so hard at the restaurant. And I will take her to the beach."

Sky smiled at him. It was thoughtful of him to be so concerned about the welfare and happiness of his mother. "That sounds wonderful. I hope it happens for you."

Suddenly Dalton stopped. Sky nearly ran into him. Dalton slowly backed up, and Sky got scared.

"Move back slowly," he said. "Very slowly."

She peeked around her father and saw a coiled snake straight ahead.

Everyone froze, watching to see what it would do. After what seemed like an eternity of waiting, the snake slowly uncoiled and slithered away into the tall elephant grass.

"That was close," Dalton said. "Everyone okay?"

Sky nodded. "Was it dangerous?"

Hai answered her question. "That was two-step snake."

"Two-step?"

"Yes, because it bites you, two steps later, you die."

"I'm not sure we should continue," Dalton said. "I don't want to put any of us in danger."

"No need to continue," Hai said. "Because we are here."

Dalton's eyebrows lifted. He looked around himself in a wide circle, then looked back at Hai.

"X-ray Landing Zone, right?" Hai verified.

Dalton nodded.

"Over there, where it is flat. That was landing zone."

A flash of recognition crossed Dalton's mind. Somewhere within a several-mile radius was where he and his men had landed and found cover. Then, most of his men had been killed—everyone but him and the youngest member of his group, Beckett, who'd been severely wounded, losing one arm and the use of his legs after taking a bullet to his spine.

Following the low slope of the hill to the flatland below, they walked in reverent silence, somehow sensing they were on hallowed ground. Occasionally they stopped so Dalton could describe some of the battles that had taken place in the area. Men had died upon the very ground where they stood.

"No wonder the dirt is red," Sky said.

Dalton nodded.

"It looks much different now," Dalton said. "But I think this would be a good place to stop." From his pack he removed sticks of incense. Then, gathering a few rocks, they made a small mound of stones. Sky picked wild flowers and placed the bouquet in the center of the stones. Each of them took one of the smoldering sticks of incense, and following Hai, they bowed three times, then placed the sticks around the rocks and flowers.

"This represents those who have died before us," Hai explained. "This is now neighborhood for dead. By placing incense here, we pay tribute to those who died here."

Smoke rose from the incense sticks, filling the air with their pungent odor. They all bowed one more time, then Dalton said a few words. "Heroes earn their status by the way they live and the way they die. These men are my heroes. I was proud to serve with them, and I wouldn't be here today if it weren't for them. Someday I will see them again and thank them for their courage and sacrifice."

Tears trickled down Dalton's face.

"A good friend told me once that 'courage isn't the absence of fear, but the ability to press on in spite of it.' I believe this is true. We will all be faced with difficult situations in life, but we have to believe. We cannot give up hope." The whisper of a breeze wafted the incense smoke, sending it dancing through the air.

Sky felt her heartbeat quicken and fill her chest with its powerful pounding, an outpouring of the Spirit moving her to tears also.

Wiping at her eyes, Sky felt Paige's arm slip around her and pull her close. She laid her head on Paige's shoulder, and for a brief moment, she felt that she finally understood to a small degree what her father had experienced. It allowed her to share a bond with him that she knew would last for eternity, and she hoped that someday, she too could thank these men for giving their lives for their country.

After a moment of silence, Hai cleared his throat. "We must go if we are to find trail where you were in jungle. I fear it might rain before we go too far." Sure enough, the dove-gray clouds had turned a deeper shade of gray, the breeze coming with more purpose.

"Just a minute," Sky said. Removing her backpack, she pulled out a pint-sized container and knelt down on the ground. Using the lid of the container, she began digging at the hardened clay-like soil. "I want to take some of this dirt back with us," she told them without looking up. "So I never forget."

Dalton knelt down beside her and helped fill the container. Then, when it was full, they embraced, and their tears flowed again.

"Thanks, honey," he told his daughter.

"I'm glad we came," Sky told her father. "I understand better now."

When they stood, Dalton received a hug from Paige. They held each other until Hai cleared his throat again. They'd come too far to turn back now, but none of them wanted to get caught in a rainstorm. Without further delay, they began their trek into the hills. This time their goal was to find any remnants of the jungle camps.

CHAPTER TEN

Just as Hai had predicted, it began to rain. It was not wise to turn back, since the rain had likely turned the river into a dangerous torrent. Additionally, they were a five-hour walk from the van. They were going to have to sleep in the jungle.

Drenched and cold, Paige and Sky huddled together beneath a rain poncho on a rock while the men tried to construct some sort of shelter out of bamboo and palm leaves. Hai and Quang worked as though they'd devoted their lives to building shelters, but then they probably had built such structures many times before.

Dalton felt anguish at the thought of making his wife and daughter sleep in the jungle. He had hoped that they wouldn't have to travel too far from the point of capture so they could see some of the jungle spots where Hai suspected the prison camps were located. Then they could get back to the van before dark. But the hike had taken longer, and the rain had closed in, and now they had no choice. Trying to get back to the van was one thing, but crossing the river on the rope bridge was an entirely different thing. Dalton knew he'd rather have them sleep in the jungle than attempt a crossing in the middle of what could be the beginning of a monsoon.

The shelter was quickly ready, and once a few dry twigs and branches were found, Dalton had a fire going. At first the smoke from the fire had them all choking, but soon the flame began to burn steadily. The light and heat from the fire was a welcome blessing from the pouring rain.

Paige brought out granola bars, a bag of trail mix, and, of course, Snickers bars.

Hai looked at the trail mix in his hand and said, "I am to eat this?"

Sky was quick to reply. "It's better than some of that cra—"

"Skyler!" Dalton cut her off before she could finish.

"It's good," Sky restated.

"Yes," Quang echoed, reaching in the bag for more of the raisins, peanuts, and M&Ms.

Taking a raisin between his fingers, Hai examined it closely. "Looks like bug."

"It's a dried grape. Go ahead," Paige urged.

Hai nibbled the edge and tested the flavor. The skeptical expression on his face turned to one of pleasure. "Yes, very good." Before long, he was munching his way through several handfuls of trail mix.

The sky grew dark and the rain continued. Keeping a fire burning was essential, so everyone decided to take shifts to supply it with wood. They'd gathered enough dry pieces of wood to keep the fire going all night.

Dalton took the first shift, and his family and their Vietnamese friends drifted to sleep. Grateful for the food Paige had brought and for the warmth of the fire, Dalton thought of the last time he'd been in this jungle, how he would've given anything for real food instead of the meager meals of rice and animal fat and occasional bananas found in the jungle.

He stretched his legs out toward the fire, basking in its warmth. How many nights had he shivered through rainstorms like this one when he was a prisoner of war? He didn't want it to, but his mind drifted to thoughts he'd kept buried, memories about those months he'd spent in the jungle . . .

"It's dead," the marine named Ron Sherman told Dalton. "The camp commander's gonna flip when he sees his favorite pig dead."

Even the animals kept by the camp cadre were hungry there in the jungle. Could they help it if the sow's favorite meal was found in the latrine, the latrine where the pig had died with its nose buried deep beneath the contents?

Sherman had been right. The camp commander was livid at losing his precious animal. But what Sherman didn't expect was for the commander to point at him, then at the pig.

"What?" Sherman asked the interpreter.

"You fix," the interpreter said.

Sherman was stunned. With his medical training, he could have helped many of his men through their agonies from injuries and illness, yet he'd never been allowed to practice his medicine. And now the commander wanted him to revive a dead pig?

Shaking his head, Sherman said to the interpreter, "You tell the commander to give the pig mouth-to-mouth resuscitation. That'll do it."

The meaning got lost in the translation, and the commander nodded, then walked away.

The pig was later butchered and the meat eaten by the camp staff. The prisoners also received a portion of the pig—the head. And they ate every morsel of meat they could scrape from the skull, not even caring if it was safe.

It had been like Thanksgiving to have actual meat in their stomachs. But the few moments of satisfaction didn't last long and left them longing for more . . .

"What's that?" Paige awoke with a start.

Dalton sat up with a jerk and strained to listen.

The sound of a sputtering motor was headed their way.

"I think we have trouble," Hai said.

"Why?" Dalton asked.

"Restricted area. Patrolled by guards. They do not like visitors, especially American."

"What do we do?"

"Let me speak to them," Hai said. "Do you have dong?"

"Yes," Dalton said.

Hai told him to quickly take some of his money and put it in his pocket. He told him how much to offer, but to be willing to give it all if necessary.

Moments later, a soldier on a rickety motorcycle fishtailed through the mud on his way toward them.

Hai immediately stood and bowed.

The soldier glared at him and barked out a string of harsh words.

Quang leaned in closely to Dalton. "He wants to see our papers."

Dalton's stomach tensed.

The soldier continued his diatribe while Hai, with his head hanging down, took the verbal beating. Then, a moment later, the soldier was off his bike, sloshing toward their shelter. Peering inside, he let loose with another heated verbal assault, and Hai immediately turned to them and told them to step outside the shelter and line up.

Dalton stood between his wife and daughter, holding onto their hands. He vowed he would do anything he had to, to protect them against the young soldier who carried a rifle on his back.

The soldier looked them over several times, then his gaze lingered on Sky. She looked away, avoiding his eyes. Dalton felt anger ignite inside him.

Taking a step closer to Sky, the soldier stared at her with lust in his eyes, and Dalton vowed that if the kid took one more step or reached his hand even a fraction of an inch toward his daughter, he wouldn't know what hit him.

Suddenly Hai spoke up, distracting the soldier.

The soldier replied, and Hai then said, "Mr. Dalton, he want to see our papers. I tell him we have more important papers to show him."

Sliding his hand into his pants pocket, Dalton separated a handful of bills from the wad of dong and presented it to the guard.

The guard laughed and reached for his gun.

Hai spoke again. "More, Mr. Dalton."

Knowing that he had to act as though he were giving up every cent he had, Dalton eased a few more bills out of his pocket while keeping a keen eye on the soldier the whole time. Any quick movement and Dalton was ready to pounce.

Dalton stretched his hand toward the soldier and presented more cash.

The soldier took the cash but kept his hand on his rifle. He turned again toward Sky.

Dalton reached into his pocket and pulled out the last of the cash. He also slid his cheap, imitation Rolex off his wrist, a watch he'd bought for twenty bucks the last time he was in New York. He was glad he had the watch for a moment like this.

Handing the soldier the money and the watch, Dalton stared the kid in the eye, stood tall, and expanded his chest, trying to look intimidating.

Obviously the soldier had decided he'd gotten enough out of them, and with one last glance toward Sky, he said something to Hai and walked to his motorcycle.

Hai didn't answer but bowed his head. "You must bow," he hissed to the others, who quickly dropped their heads as the soldier fired up his bike again. After backfiring several times and sputtering nearly to the point of stalling, the engine finally roared to life. Giving Hai one last command, the soldier jammed the bike into gear and roared through the mud, slipping and nearly tipping over but catching himself before he fell.

As soon as he was out of sight, they all released a collective breath of relief.

"What was all that?" Dalton insisted.

"We are in restricted area and must leave at once. I'm sorry, Mr. Dalton. You will not be able to continue your journey without permission from government. Very difficult to get."

"Oh, Dalton, I'm so sorry," Paige said.

"You know what? That's okay," Dalton said. "I think spending the night in the rain in the jungle is as close as I need to get to my old camps. They probably don't exist anymore anyway."

"Government destroys all evidence of camps," Hai told Dalton. "There is nothing to see except jungle and snakes."

"I don't need to see any more of those," Sky said.

Dalton gave his daughter a nod of agreement. "Then what are we waiting for?"

"We must hurry," Hai said. "You gave him more money than he make in year. He may have comrades who also want to get in on good fortune."

"Then let's get out of here."

The rain had stopped, but a heavy mist kept everything wet and slick. No one minded the mist or the mud—all they cared about was getting back to the van.

"Mr. Dalton," Quang said as they trudged ahead of the others. "I want you to know that I would not have let that soldier touch your daughter."

Dalton reached over and gave Quang a pat on the shoulder. "Thank you, son. That means a lot to me."

With the terrain slanting down toward the flatlands, the group was able to move quickly in spite of their progress being hampered by the mud.

"Nice touch with the watch, honey," Paige said. "I never would have thought of it."

"I saw him glance at my wrist and knew it had caught his eye. I figured it would sweeten the deal. Besides, we brought along some watches to give out when we get to Soon Lee's village, didn't we?"

"I brought five of those watches I found at that clearance sale."

"He scared me," Sky said. "I didn't like the way he looked at me."

"All he would have gotten to do is look," Dalton assured her. "None of us would have let anything happen to you."

"I'll be glad when we get back to the van and get out of here."

"Me too, sweetie. I've seen everything I need to see."

"How did you do it, Dad? How did you survive it? I could barely handle it for one night, and we had food and a fire and I knew I was leaving. But you didn't know if you would ever get out."

Dalton didn't answer for a minute, then he said, "I didn't want them to think they'd won, that they'd finally broken me down. By surviving, I won. They could take away everything except my faith in God and my will to survive."

"I swear, I will never complain of anything ever again," Sky told her father.

"Oh, ho, ho!" Dalton laughed. "I'd better get some witnesses to this," he teased. "Paige, did you hear that?"

"I did, and I feel the same way. We're very spoiled in America. We have food and clothes and homes and . . ." she added soberly, "freedom. We have freedom."

"And that's the most important thing of all," Sky remarked. "Isn't it, Dad?"

"Yes, Sky. It is. Freedom is the greatest gift we have."

* * *

They'd arrived back at the hotel mud-caked and rain-soaked. After their night in the jungle, their hotel seemed like the Taj Mahal. Even with geckos on the walls and creepy crawlers and mosquitos in the room, Sky felt like a queen.

The next morning, the group made plans to continue their journey. Rain fell but didn't deter them from their plans or the people in the village from going about their morning duties.

"Doesn't anything faze them?" Sky commented as she looked out the window at the busy street. Vendors had opened shops all along the road, which was filled to capacity with bikes and a few cyclos. "I've never seen anything like it."

Paige zipped her backpack and placed it on the bed next to the bag of wet clothes from their trek the day before. "I wonder if our clothes will ever dry."

"Maybe we can find a Laundromat somewhere along the way," Sky replied.

"I think those are called rivers," Paige joked.

Sky laughed.

"Our clothes are going to be stained with that red soil. They'll never come clean."

"That's okay," Sky said. "I'll be so sick of wearing the same things by the end of this trip, I'll probably drop my backpack into the garbage at the Los Angeles airport on our way to the car. I'll never want to see them again."

This time Paige laughed.

"What's so funny?" Dalton asked as he stepped out of the bathroom, carrying his toothbrush and toothpaste.

Paige was about to explain what they were talking about when Sky got a strange look on her face, an expression of being puzzled and in pain at the same time.

"Sky, what is it?" Paige asked, rushing toward her.

Sky pushed her out of the way and headed for the bathroom.

Paige and Dalton waited anxiously outside the door.

"Sky." Dalton tapped on the door. "Are you okay?"

"No."

"Are you throwing up?" Dalton asked.

"No, wrong end."

"Uh-oh," Dalton said.

"I have just the thing for her," Paige said, racing to her backpack. She rummaged through her emergency first-aid kit and found what she was looking for.

Sky emerged from the bathroom holding her stomach and looking miserable.

Dalton helped her to the bed.

"I knew this weird food was going to kill me," Sky said.

"I have something that will help you feel better." Paige sat down next to her on the bed and offered her two pills—one to coat her stomach to help settle it and one to stop the diarrhea.

"Are you sure this will help?"

Paige promised her it would and helped her sit up so she could drink some water to wash down the medicine.

"I've been feeling a little queasy myself," Dalton said. Just as a precaution, they all decided to take the medication. The last thing they needed was to get sick, especially with the types of medical remedies the Vietnamese recommended.

"Uh-oh," Sky said as she raced for the bathroom again.

Dalton looked at Paige. "This isn't good. We're supposed to be on a train in half an hour."

"What about giving her a blessing?" Paige suggested.

Dalton didn't have time to answer. A knock came at the door.

Quang and Hai were ready to go for breakfast.

"We have a small challenge," Dalton told them. "Sky isn't feeling well."

Just then, Sky emerged from the bathroom, holding her stomach and groaning.

Paige helped her to the bed, where Sky curled up in a ball. Stroking her forehead, Paige tried to soothe her and convince her that everything would be okay.

"We get medicine," Hai offered. "At market."

"No," Sky cried. "I won't drink boiled monkey, or snake juice, or . . ."

"Honey," Dalton said, "it's going to be okay. Paige suggested a priesthood blessing. Okay?"

"Thanks, Dad. That's sounds much better."

Hai and Quang took a seat in the corner and watched as Dalton took a small vial of oil from his key chain and placed a drop on Sky's head. He then laid his hands on her head to seal the anointing and to give her a healing blessing. Not only did he bless Sky to recover quickly from her stomach trouble, but he also told her that the Lord would be with them and guide them throughout their time in Vietnam and that they were in His care. It was a beautiful blessing and brought tears to not only Sky's eyes, but Paige's too.

When it was over, Dalton hugged his daughter and wife. Now all they needed to do was exercise faith that the words he had spoken had been prompted by the Spirit.

Just then, Sky let out a groan and raced for the bathroom. Paige and Dalton exchanged worried looks.

Their bags were packed, and a break in the weather signaled that it was the perfect time to get on the road and head for their next destination, the Tunnels of Cu Chi, on their way to Soon Lee's village.

But not if Sky was sick.

A few minutes later she came out of the bathroom again. She still looked weak, but there was some color in her cheeks.

"Honey?" Dalton said. "How are you feeling?"

"I think I'm going to be okay," she said. "I don't know if it's the medicine or the blessing, but I think the worst is over. I am a little hungry."

"You are?"

"Yes, and a bowl of rice sounds perfect right now. But without fish sauce," she said. "No, wait, a baguette. Can we find one of those?"

"I'm sure we can," Paige said, giving her a hug. "I'm glad you're feeling a little better."

Dalton clapped his hands together. "I guess we're back in business then. Let's have a prayer before we go."

Paige and Sky knelt down with Dalton, holding hands as they got ready for the prayer. Then, before starting, Dalton looked over at Quang and Hai, who'd been completely quiet during the entire ordeal. "Would you like to join us?" he asked them. "We want to have a family prayer before we go."

Quang jumped right to his feet, but Hai wasn't as quick to follow. Still, a moment later, he followed his nephew to the side of the bed, where they both knelt down.

Dalton asked Paige to say the prayer, which she gladly did. She expressed gratitude for all of their blessings, especially for helping Sky to feel better. She also expressed gratitude that Quang and Hai could be with them. Then she requested that they be protected and kept healthy so they could continue their journey to find Soon Lee's family. She then closed the prayer.

Hai and Quang were the last to get on their feet. They looked as though they had questions about the prayer, but they didn't voice them.

"Sky, honey?" Dalton asked. "Are you sure you feel well enough to keep going? We have a long train ride ahead of us today."

Sky nodded. "I think so, Dad."

After checking the room for any stray items, they grabbed their bags and headed out for the next new adventure.

CHAPTER ELEVEN

"I have a question," Quang asked as the train rumbled along the track.

Sky nodded and swallowed the last bite of her baguette, then took a drink from her water bottle.

"That prayer your father gave you. What was that?"

With so many of her friends being nonmembers, Sky was used to answering questions about her beliefs. "The men in my church—the Mormon Church—hold the priesthood, which is the power to act in God's name on the earth. My father used that priesthood to bless me to help me get better. He gives me special blessings like that all the time."

"But didn't Mrs. Paige give you medicine? Maybe that's why you feel better."

Sky nodded and smiled. "Sure, I think the medicine did help. Heavenly Father expects us to do what we can with the resources we have available, but He helps to make up the difference. Yeah, the medicine helped, but I know my father's blessing helped my body respond to that medicine so I could feel better even faster. We don't have time on this trip to sit around while someone is sick. I believe very strongly that Heavenly Father helped me today. I've had a lot of experiences like this in my life. I know these blessings have helped me."

Quang thought about what she said for a moment. "I have seen a picture of your temple in America. In Utah. Salt Lake City."

"You have? Where did you see that?"

"My father had a picture of his parents in front of the temple. This is where they got married."

"Wow, really? So was your father LDS?"

"LDS?"

"Mormon."

"When he was a little boy. He did not go to church when he grew up. He had your Mormon Bible too, but he did not read it."

"Have you ever read it?"

"No. It is gone. My mother said it was too painful to have reminders of him in our home, so she got rid of everything. She does not allow us to talk about him."

"Wow, I'm sorry. That must be hard for you. You probably want to know about your father. Do you ever talk to your grandparents in America?"

"They are both dead," he told her.

"I'm sorry," she replied. "At least they are all together now."

Quang's brow knitted. "What do you mean?"

"Up in heaven. They are together in heaven. That's where my mother is too. Someday I'll see her again, and you will see your father and meet his parents."

His forehead furrowed. "You believe this?"

Sky replied, "I know this for sure." She looked him straight in the eye. "Quang, don't you believe in heaven?"

"We do not go to any church. I do not believe in anything."

"Do you believe I'm telling you the truth?"

"I believe that you believe you are telling me the truth."

"Here," Sky said, taking a pad of paper and a pen from her backpack. "Let me show you something." She continued to explain to him the plan of salvation, drawing it out for him on paper, like she'd learned in seminary.

"So, I will see my father again, even if I am not Mormon?" Quang asked.

"Yes, of course you will. Quang, this life is just a small moment in time."

Looking out the window, Quang silently watched the landscape pass by.

Sky wondered what was going through his mind.

A few minutes later, he turned and said, "Do you think we can get a Mormon book for me? I could use the money your father pays me."

"Yes, of course," Sky said as a warmth inside her chest grew to fill her whole body.

"Thank you. I would very much like to read this book."

Sky glanced out the window. "We're coming to a city. Is this the place where the tunnels are?"

Quang read the signs as they went by. "Yes, we are almost there."

Sky was anxious to visit the Cu Chi Tunnels. She'd learned about them in school and was fascinated by the fact that the Vietcong had dug 125 miles of tunnels beneath the ground in trilevel networks of mess halls, meeting rooms, hospitals, sleeping chambers, and even a tiny cinema. The Vietcong hid in these tunnels sometimes for weeks, entering and exiting through concealed trapdoors.

"Sky?" Quang said as the train began to slow. "Do you think we could talk about your church some more, another time?"

With a smile, Sky said, "We can talk about my church anytime you want, Quang."

Quang returned her smile and looked out the window at the train station coming into view.

Sky thought about their conversation. Quang apparently had questions about the meaning of life. He missed his father, and he needed answers. And she was grateful for any part she had in helping him find answers to his questions.

* * *

They were greeted at the tourist site by young Vietnamese women in black pajamas. A man in green fatigues led the group of tourists down a narrow trail, where they soon arrived at an open-sided hut. The young women in black showed the tourists to their seats. Moments later, on a big-screen television set, scenes from the Vietnam War began: B-52s dropped strings of bombs, villagers ran for cover, and communist guerrillas launched their attacks.

The narrator began: "Cu Chi, the land of many gardens, peaceful all year round under shady trees. Then merciless American bombers ruthlessly decided to kill this gentle piece of countryside. Like a crazy bunch of devils, they fired into women and children. The Americans wanted to turn Cu Chi into a dead land, but Cu Chi will never die."

The sound of gunfire from a nearby firing range, where visitors could pay a dollar a bullet to shoot an AK-47 rifle, strangely knit the past and present together.

Paige leaned over, put her arm around Dalton, and kissed his cheek. "You okay?" she asked.

Dalton had easily dismissed the propaganda presented in the film. He'd learned to do that while in the Ho Loa prison. "I'm fine," he said, returning her kiss. They looked into each other's eyes. "Have I told you how glad I am to have you here?" he said.

She nodded. "Only a hundred times a day," she replied. "And I'm glad to be here."

When the movie finally ended, it was time to enter the tunnels.

"Dad," Sky said quietly to her father as they moved toward the entrance behind the group of tourists, made up mostly of natives, "that was all a bunch of garbage, right?"

"Yes, honey," Dalton told her.

"Why do they do that? Why do they make Americans out to be such monsters? Does it bother you?"

"No, honey. The war was hard for both countries. Don't forget, they had over three million casualties from the war. The country and the people suffered a great loss."

Sky hugged her father, and Dalton felt grateful that his daughter was gaining an understanding of this event in his life that had changed him forever. She'd always asked questions about the war and his involvement in it, but being here, seeing things firsthand, was answering her questions in a much better way than he could.

Much of the scenery and sights had changed since the war, but Dalton felt the wounds inside himself slowly closing. He'd kept his grip so tight on the memories that had burdened him for such a long time that it felt wonderful to finally let go, and he experienced a sense of freedom and release, a feeling he'd hoped would come from this trip but one he hadn't dared dream he'd receive.

A sign near the entrance said, "Please try to be a Cu Chi guerrilla. Wear these uniforms before entering tunnel." Black pajamas, pith helmets, rubber sandals, and old rifles were available for those who wanted to get the full tourist experience. Neither Paige nor Sky opted to put on the soldier's garb, and when Dalton saw the size of the tunnel entrance, he wasn't sure he even wanted to attempt going inside.

Hai wanted nothing to do with the tunnels. He opted to wait outside for the others. Quang's curiosity got the best of him, and he volunteered to be first in their group to enter.

Once inside, they had to crawl on their hands and knees to the first stop, a large open room called a conference chamber. They were amazed at how clean it was, and the guide told them that workers dusted inside the tunnel every day.

Their next stop was the kitchen, where they would be allowed to eat some of the food that the soldiers ate during the war. When Dalton found out it was about thirty yards to the kitchen, he decided it was time to leave. He'd seen enough, and even though he never struggled with claustrophobia, the dark, confined, underground space was just too tight for him. "I'll meet you guys outside," he told Paige and Sky. "I don't want to take a chance of getting stuck in one of those tunnels."

Before another group of tourists clogged his escape, he found a sign indicating an exit through an escape tunnel. As he emerged aboveground, he immediately pulled in a long breath of air.

Glad to be free from the musty, underground maze, Dalton couldn't help but be impressed with the ingenuity and industry of the Vietcong. Until the discovery of the Cu Chi tunnels, no one could understand how the Vietcong seemed to materialize out of thin air. Hidden exits and entrances to the tunnels were everywhere, which allowed the enemy to pop up anywhere, like prairie dogs, armed and ready to defend their territory.

Finding a shady spot under a tree, Dalton sat on a boulder and watched the workers at the site, busy keeping groups of curious tourists moving through the different areas of the tunnels.

The rustling palms, the moist, humid air, and the pungent smell of the earth brought a startling sense of déjà vu. For a moment, Dalton's memories flashed to the past, to memories filled with loneliness, pain, and hunger. He'd never forgotten how it felt to starve and to be so overcome with dysentery that death was a preferred alternative.

Involuntarily, his stomach reacted to the memory with a hungry growl. Earlier he'd shoved a granola bar into his shirt pocket, and he decided now was the right time to eat it.

Munching on the snack, Dalton found himself amazed that he was really here with his wife and daughter. It was something he'd thought about for years, and now it was happening. He also thought about seeing Soon Lee's family. They'd never met, and he prayed that their first meeting would go well, especially for Sky's sake. He wanted her to have a positive impression of them and their country. Whether or not she liked it, it was part of who she was. Their blood ran in her veins. She'd inherited characteristics and physical traits from them, and she had a bond with them. Hopefully, that bond would become emotional as well. Either way, whether Soon Lee's family rejected or accepted them, Sky would have the chance to meet them and draw her own conclusions. Then she could choose to accept or reject them. Giving her that choice was the most important part of this journey.

A high-pitched voice startled Dalton, jarring him from his thoughts. He looked up to see a young man coming his way, and by the tone of his voice, he wasn't happy with Dalton about something. An unexpected wave of panic came over him. What had he done? What was going on?

"No litter," the man said, wagging his finger at Dalton, the overexcited tone still in his voice.

Dalton didn't know what the guy was talking about until he looked around the rock where he sat. Then he saw the wrapper to his granola bar on the ground. He thought he'd put it into his pants pocket, but obviously he hadn't crammed it in far enough.

"Oh," he exclaimed, reaching for the wrapper, "I'm sorry. I didn't know that fell out of my pocket."

The man glared at him with narrowed eyes.

Dalton shoved the paper clear down to the bottom of his pants pocket. "There," he said, "all taken care of." Not allowing the man to intimidate him, Dalton stared back at him.

"Good," came the reply, and the man turned on his heel and headed down one of the jungle paths to another area of the site.

Dalton remembered what it was like to look into eyes full of hatred and anger. He remembered the pain he'd suffered at the hands of those men. These weren't memories he welcomed, but he made himself confront them nevertheless. Once those memories surfaced, they seemed to disappear. They would never go away completely, and in many ways he didn't want them to, but the pain and agony associated with the memories was being lifted from his shoulders.

"Dad," he heard Sky's voice call. "There you are."

Dalton looked up and saw his daughter, smiling brightly, running toward him. He stood and greeted her with a hug.

"That place was amazing," she said, talking excitedly. "We saw where the soldiers slept and where the hospital was. It's unbelievable. I don't know how they found their way around down there. I felt like an ant."

Dalton chuckled and hugged his daughter.

Quang came right behind her, walking with Paige.

"What did you think, Quang?" Dalton asked.

Pulling a face, Quang answered, "I could not live down there like an animal."

"Me either," Paige said. "I should have left when you did, honey. Once we got past the conference room, there wasn't another exit until we were almost done. By then I had no choice but to finish the tour. I think I'd go nuts underground like that. The guide said some soldiers stayed down there for two and three weeks at a time."

"Maybe they felt differently when they knew their alternative was going above and getting shot at." Dalton looked at Paige's wristwatch. "I guess we'd better get back to the train if we want to get to Hue by tonight. Has everyone seen enough?"

The response was unanimous—everyone was ready to find a place to eat, then go to Hue where Quang and Hai would help them find Soon Lee's family. Once they accomplished this, Quang and Hai would be paid and return to Ho Chi Minh City.

One more train ride, and they would be there.

CHAPTER TWELVE

"Are you nervous?" Quang asked Sky. They'd talked nonstop on the ride to Hue, making the long, uncomfortable train ride bearable.

Quang had many questions about America. He wanted to know what the schools were like, what Sky did for fun with her friends, what Disneyland was like. He never knew a day of sleeping in or going to the beach to play volleyball and lie in the sun. The fact that Sky had her own car, went through drive-up windows for fast food, and was heading for college in the fall seemed like impossible dreams to him. Anything he received he worked for. Nothing came at an easy price. Every meal was a result of hard work and physical labor. And Sky gained a whole new appreciation for all she had back home in America: an abundance of food, clothes, comforts, and, most of all, freedom.

"I'm excited and nervous," Sky replied. "I've dreamed about meeting them for so long, I can't believe it's finally going to happen. I don't know what to expect, but I know I need to do this. I have to have some sort of connection with my mother's family. I think I would regret it my entire life if I didn't."

Quang nodded. "I would like to meet my father's family. I have wanted to go to America ever since he died. I would like to learn more about my father. I feel like part of me is over there and that I need to find it to be complete."

"That's exactly how I feel, Quang," Sky said, marveling at how uncanny it was that they would have so much in common, even though they came from separate worlds. "If you ever come to America, I hope you will come and visit us," she offered. "We'll help you find your father's family, just as you have helped us."

"You would do that?" Quang asked in amazement.

"Of course we would."

The train gave a sudden lurch as it began to slow. "Oh my gosh," Sky exclaimed, grabbing Quang's arm. "I think we're there."

Quang looked down at her hand on his arm.

"Oh, I'm sorry," she said and quickly pulled her hand away.

"No," he said, smiling at her. "It is okay."

Sky felt a flush of embarrassment color her cheeks. Her action had been completely unconscious. There was such a sense of comfort and companionship with Quang, she hadn't even hesitated to touch him.

As he looked out the window at the upcoming train station, Sky looked at him. She liked the smooth, creamy brown of his skin. A hint of his father's features defined his face. Instead of being round and full, his face was narrow, his jaw square and solid, his cheeks chiseled and angular. His black, glossy hair was short and neatly trimmed. He really was handsome.

His smile brightened his face, and it was apparent that his difficult life and circumstances hadn't snuffed out the anxious, optimistic twinkle in his eye.

He turned and caught her looking at him, causing him to smile. "Are you ready?"

She returned his smile. "Yes, I think I am."

* * *

The next day, the van rattled along the bumpy dirt road, winding its way through villages. They were on their way to a smaller city, somewhere west of Hue.

Most of the homes were ramshackle dwellings, poor and run-down. Sometimes children would run alongside the van, waving and laughing. Many only wore a T-shirt and were thin and dirty, but their beautiful smiles and chocolate-colored eyes made them irresistible.

Paige, Dalton, and Sky found a van driver willing to take them the distance to Soon Lee's village. Without Quang and Hai there, Dalton doubted they would have been able to talk the man into the trip, even though he obviously needed the money badly. They learned that the area through which they had to travel was surrounded by poppy fields, which meant opium and rebel movements with private armies. Strangers and foreigners—especially Americans—weren't welcome there.

Hai explained to them that opium was important to the area's economy and that this area and an area referred to as the Golden Triangle, where the borders of Laos, Myanmar, and Thailand met, supplied two-thirds of the world's demand for opium.

"If we are stopped," Hai told them, "you must keep your faces down. You will also need to pay them."

Dalton took Paige's hand in his and gave it a squeeze. They exchanged worried glances. He felt great concern for the safety of his family. His goal was not to put them in danger, and he seriously reconsidered whether or not to proceed.

He glanced at Sky, sitting in the seat behind him. Her expression also reflected concern.

The driver spoke to Hai for several minutes, then Hai turned and explained to them what he'd said. "City where your wife's family lives destroyed in war. They try to rebuild, but they are very poor."

"Hai," Dalton said, "do you feel it is a mistake for us to come here? Is it too dangerous?"

"Perhaps. We can explain why you are here, and they may not see you as threat. Still, have money ready. It is not much farther."

Luckily, the train station had an ATM where Dalton had been able to get cash. He never knew when they would be near an ATM, so he made it a point to get as much as he felt safe carrying. Hai had instructed him to split up his cash and carry most of it hidden away in his backpack. He kept some in his wallet and some in the pouch he wore around his neck containing his passport and travel papers.

"What do you think?" Dalton asked Paige. "Should we continue?"

"We're almost there," Paige said.

"Dad, we can't turn around now," Sky added. "Not when we're this close."

The decision was made. They kept going, praying that they would be protected. With each mile they traveled in uneasy silence, watching for signs of trouble, praying for safety. The road had long since turned into a dusty dirt road filled with potholes and rocks.

"How much farther?" Sky asked.

Not a second later, the driver brought the van to an abrupt halt.

Panic struck Dalton's heart, and he scanned their surroundings to see what the trouble was. Expecting to see soldiers or guerillas wielding weapons, he instead saw nothing.

"What is it, Hai?" he asked their elderly guide.

"The bridge is out. We must walk the rest of the way. It is not far."

Paige looked at her husband with concern.

"We'll be okay," Dalton assured her, knowing he had no right to promise anything of the sort. He was as worried as she looked, but they'd committed to seeing this all the way through, and there was no backing out now. He hoped he didn't live to regret their next move.

After climbing out of the van, everyone waited while Dalton paid the man the agreed price for the trip. The money had barely touched the man's hand before he was back in his van, making a hasty retreat out of the area.

"Well," Dalton said, wanting to break the uncomfortable silence that settled upon them after their driver left. "What are we waiting for? Which way, Hai?"

"We follow river this way." He pointed. "Village is not far."

Dalton knew that *far* for an American on foot and *far* for a Vietnamese on foot were two different things. The Vietnamese were used to walking nearly everywhere they needed to go. But the distance wasn't Dalton's biggest concern—it was the possibility of a surprise attack.

Soon, several homes appeared in the distance. Several young children, out playing on the banks of the river, ran toward them while their mother slapped clothes against a rock and scrubbed them.

"Hello, hello," the children shouted, barely able to form the American word in their mouths.

Sky laughed at their enthusiasm. "I have suckers," Sky said to Hai. "Can I give them one?"

"Yes, of course," Hai said.

To the children's delight, Sky found suckers and balloons in her backpack.

The children giggled with glee as Dalton blew up the balloons for them. They batted the balloons back and forth, playing with as much excitement as a kid on Christmas morning. The smallest child, a little girl, held her pink balloon and looked at it wide-eyed, as if seeing the most beautiful and magical thing in the world.

Grabbing her camera, Paige stopped and snapped a picture of her.

Dalton smiled as he watched his daughter interacting with the lovely children, who even in destitution, were able to be happy. He was glad if their brief visit gave these children joy.

Sky laughed at the eager children grabbing at the suckers she held in her hand. Dalton found his own camera and took several pictures of his daughter and the village children. These pictures would be treasures beyond any price.

A rumble in the sky urged them ahead, and the smell of rain filled the air.

"I have rain ponchos," Paige said. "Do you think we need them?"

Dalton glanced up at the distant clouds and said, "I think we'll make it to the village before those clouds reach us. We need to keep moving, though."

With the children waving good-bye, the travelers went on their way, following the narrow dirt road that ran parallel to the river.

Sky caught up to her father and they walked side by side.

"I can't quit thinking about Mom," she said. "She probably traveled this very road."

"Yes, honey. We're probably walking through the fields where her family planted rice. This was where she grew up."

"Do you think this is where it happened? You know?"

Dalton looked around. "It could have been. She wouldn't talk about it much."

"You've never told me the whole story, Dad. You've always said I was too young to understand. Don't you think I'm old enough now?"

"Yes." Dalton nodded. "I think she would want you to know."

The breeze kicked up and the pungent odor of dust and rain filled the air as Dalton began.

"Their village was raided by the Vietcong. Someone tipped them off that the people living in the village had been helping the Americans and were spying on the North Vietnamese. It was all untrue, but the Vietcong didn't care. Instead of trying to learn the truth, they decided to just get rid of the problem altogether. When they invaded the village, the men tried to protect the women and children who had gone into hiding. You knew your mother was married before and that she had a baby who died."

Sky nodded. "A baby boy."

"Right. When the NVA came, your mother and the other women took the children and hid under some camouflage they'd made out of bamboo and straw and palm leaves. Your mother's baby was only a few weeks old, and he was asleep, but when the soldiers started shooting their guns, it woke up the baby, and he started to cry. She knew that if he didn't stop, every one of those women and children would be killed. So she did what she had to do."

Sky swallowed and could barely speak. "What did she do, Dad?"

"She suffocated her child."

Tears filled Sky's eyes and fell onto her cheeks.

"The worst part is, they were still discovered and were then forced to watch as all the men and boys were gunned down in front of them. She lost every man in her life that day—her father, her two brothers, her husband, and her son."

Sky swallowed hard, trying to keep her emotions at bay.

"Maybe this helps you understand why she was always filled with such torment inside. She never forgave herself for what happened. They were then taken captive and brought to camps, where many of them, your mother included, were raped and some even sold as slaves. During an air raid one night, your mother managed to escape, and she made it to Saigon. She never heard if her mother or sisters survived."

Dalton put an arm around his daughter's shoulders. "That's when I found her on the streets of Saigon. That's why I rescued her. I had to take her away from the horror she'd lived through and the horror her life had become."

"I love her so much, Dad," Sky said through her tears. "Even though she's gone, I still love her, and I don't want to forget her. I'm glad you told me about what happened."

Dalton gave her a squeeze.

"And I'm really glad we came here," she assured him.

"We're going to meet your mother's family soon," Dalton said. "How do you feel about that?"

"I wish I weren't so nervous. But I'm also—" Sky stopped dead in her tracks.

Dalton followed her frightened gaze. There, in front of them, with gun barrels trained on them, were four men who looked more like teenage boys. The group of visitors stopped and huddled close together.

"Give me your backpack," Quang whispered to Sky. She slipped it quickly from her shoulders, and he slid it onto his own.

Hai came forward, standing next to Dalton.

One of the boys rattled off something in Vietnamese, his tone menacing, his eyes flecked with displeasure at the sight of the unwelcome visitors.

Hai said a few short words, but the boy shouted something back immediately.

Hai then spoke to Dalton. "He wants to know how much our lives are worth."

"How much should I offer?" Dalton asked.

"Give them one hundred American dollars."

"I will start with fifty," Dalton said.

He reached into his pocket and took out the money.

A different boy limped forward and reached for the bills. One of his legs was crippled and shorter than the other one. He handed the money to the boy who'd spoken with Hai, who then laughed at the handful of bills. He then said something to his friends, who all laughed with him. The boy addressed them again with sharpness in his voice. "He is insulted. That would not keep his own grandmother alive."

Dalton took another fifty out of his pocket, wondering if he had enough cash to appease them. He only had fifty more and a few thousand dong. That was it until they got to the next town and found an ATM.

The same boy limped forward and took the money, handing it to the leader of the group. The boy made another remark, causing his buddies to laugh again.

He spoke to Hai again, then Hai told Dalton what the kid said. "He says he knows that Americans' pockets are lined with money. It is not enough."

Dalton felt anger grow inside but knew it wouldn't help him, his family, or their guides if he got upset. Pulling out the rest of his American dollars, all the dong he had, and a pack of gum, Dalton reached forward, presenting all the contents of his pockets.

Taking the rest of his money, the boys laughed as they divvied out the sticks of gum and fought over the few dong. The American money went to their leader. He put the money into his shirt pocket and addressed Hai again, speaking at length. Hai bowed his head and stepped back.

Dalton expelled a relieved breath. It seemed as though the worst was over.

But Dalton's relief was premature. The leader of the guards suddenly shouted out, causing Dalton's stomach muscles to tighten. This time the leader himself approached the group. He bypassed Quang and Hai, but stood directly in front of Dalton and took a long look at him, then pointed at Dalton's camera and wedding band.

Dalton knew what the guy wanted but didn't hand it over immediately. His blood boiled, pulsing through his veins, but he maintained his composure.

The leader barked out another command.

"He will shoot you if you do not give him what he wants," Hai said.

Dalton had over a hundred pictures from their trip on his digital camera. He could never get those back. And even though he could replace his wedding band, it had great sentimental value for him.

But he had no choice.

After Dalton surrendered the items, the leader took them and handed them to one of the other guards who had stood back, almost as if watching the scene as a bystander. The young man held the items and waited for further commands. As he waited, he made eye contact with Dalton for just a moment, then he quickly looked away.

Dalton tensed as the leader stepped in front of Paige. She'd been warned about wearing jewelry or carrying valuables. She too had a cheap watch, but no ring. She pulled a wad of dong from her pocket, which pleased the leader, but that was all she had. The leader demanded her backpack, which she gave reluctantly. Except for clothes and personal items, there was nothing of value in the backpack. Not even her passport and important papers were inside. She wore them around her neck in a pouch like the rest of them.

Balling his fists as the leader stood in front of Sky, Dalton grew increasingly agitated. He couldn't stand by and watch anything happen to his daughter. He didn't like the look in the leader's eye or the disgusting smile that played on his lips.

The leader lifted his arm and reached his hand toward Sky, who whimpered and shut her eyes.

Dalton's muscles twitched, knowing what he had to do.

The leader reached for her throat, and at the same time Dalton swung his arm to stop him.

A shot rang out.

Dalton staggered back, clutching his shoulder as blood oozed through his fingers. Paige and Sky both screamed.

The leader turned and yelled at the soldier who had fired his rifle, then without another thought, he reached for Sky, yanked the necklace from around her neck, then retreated. He yelled something at Hai, then gathered his men together and took off through the trees where they'd come from.

As soon as they were gone, Paige and Sky rushed to Dalton's side.

"It's not bad," Dalton said. "I think the bullet just grazed my shoulder."

"Let me see," Paige said, peeling away the bloody fabric from his injury.

Sky turned her head as a wave of nausea washed over her.

Relief filled Paige's eyes. "You're right, it just nicked the surface, but it's bleeding like crazy."

"Guess I'm lucky that guy has bad aim," Dalton joked.

"It wasn't luck," Paige told him. "You were being watched over."

"She's right, Dad," Sky said, forcing herself to look at her father. "I know Mom's been with us while we've been here. She's our guardian angel."

Dalton smiled at his daughter and nodded. "I believe that too." He glanced around. "I think we'd better get out of here before we have any more trouble."

"We need to put something on your wound though, so it doesn't get infected. I've got some bandages in my—" Paige stopped.

"They took your backpack," Sky lamented. "And the necklace you gave me, Paige."

"It's okay, honey. You couldn't stop them." Paige looked back at the wound. "But I do need something to stop the bleeding."

"I might have something we can use in my backpack." Sky turned to Quang. "That's why you took my backpack, isn't it?"

"I thought it would be safer with me," Quang answered, handing it to her.

She dug through the contents and found a clean pair of cotton socks she hadn't worn yet. "What about these?"

"Those will do," Paige said taking the socks and laying one out flat on Dalton's wound. Putting her hand over the sock, she applied some pressure to help stop the bleeding.

"That's good," Dalton said. "Now, let's get going. I don't want them to come back. I'm surprised they didn't go after the suitcase."

"Thank goodness Quang was pulling it," Sky said.

Attached to the suitcase was a metal stand with large wheels that managed on the uneven ground without too much trouble. They had all taken turns pulling and were lucky that Quang happened to be the one taking his turn at the time they were ambushed.

"I agree with Mr. Dalton," Hai said. "We should leave."

Helping Dalton to his feet, Paige offered a supporting arm. "Here," she said, "can you hold the sock in place?" she asked her husband.

"I think so," Dalton said. "Let's get going. We can deal with it later."

They began to walk until finally they were far enough away they no longer felt threatened. They were within the outskirts of the village.

Dogs barked at them, and people stopped what they were doing and stared at them, but they continued walking.

"We must find the marketplace and I will ask around about your family," Hai said. "I think it would be best not to tell anyone about the shooting." Hai left, promising to be back in fifteen minutes to report.

"They took my Neosporin," Paige said, looking at his wound. "I'm afraid of infection."

"Quang," Dalton said, feeling a bit wobbly. "Could you help us? We need to find an ATM and get some medical supplies."

Quang held up his hand. "I would be happy to find both," he answered.

Paige helped Dalton find a place to sit in the shade while Quang and Sky went to locate medical supplies.

After they left, Paige checked the wound again. The bleeding had finally stopped. "If we were home, I'd take you to the doctor for a couple of stitches. As it is, I'm afraid you're going to have a scar."

"We'll just have to make do with what we can find," he told her. "It'll heal fine without stitches. Won't be the first scar I've gotten over here," he joked.

Paige smiled, still wishing there was something more she could do for him. Then her smile faded.

"What is it?" he asked.

"I was so scared when I heard that gun go off, and you fell backward. I thought they'd killed you."

"Oh, honey," Dalton said, wrapping his good arm around her. He winced from the pain the movement caused him. "I'm sorry."

"I hope this is the worst thing that happens on this trip," she tried to add with a laugh.

"I'm sure it will be. We're here now. We'll be safe in the village for a few days, then we'll go on to Hanoi, and after that we're on our way back home. The worst is over."

"I hope you're right, sweetie. I hope you're right."

CHAPTER THIRTEEN

"So how weird is this for you, being here?" Paige asked Dalton as they watched the busy, open market, swarming with activity.

"I don't think it's really hit me yet. I know I'm here where Soon Lee grew up, but it doesn't seem real."

"It's hard to believe all that happened here over thirty years ago," Paige observed. "I look at these people, and they are obviously hard-working and strong, but they seem so gentle." Dalton nodded. "Are you doing okay, honey? How's your shoulder?"

"It still hurts, but it's going to be fine," he assured her. He didn't tell her how much pain he was in because he didn't want to worry her.

They both sat up when they saw Hai hurrying toward them. "I found them. I found out where your wife's family lives."

Dalton felt relief at the news. Part of him hadn't dared hope they would still be here.

Suddenly, it all became real.

* * *

"I don't know how to thank you," Dalton said to Quang and Hai as they approached the bamboo-walled home that housed Soon Lee's family. The roof was made of tightly bound grass, and the door was no more than a piece of canvas material pulled aside to allow access to the dwelling. "We never could have made it without you."

"It has been our pleasure," Hai said.

Quang nodded.

Sky squeezed her father's hand. She held it tightly as she looked at the dingy home with litter strewn about and clothes hanging on a droopy clothesline. At one corner of the yard was a garden plot with healthy green plants, in neat rows, thriving in the moist, tropical climate.

A pen of chickens in the other corner filled the air with lively squawking.

Around the corner of the house came a squealing pig, and behind the pig came three children at full speed, screaming wildly. They all skidded to a stop at the sight of strangers. The pig continued running and squealing around the other side of the house.

The youngest, a little girl, quickly darted behind an older boy, taking a shy peek at them. Sky gave the little girl a warm smile, causing the little girl to pull her head back in hiding, then slowly again, she dared to take another peek.

Hai came forward and stood next to Dalton. He addressed the young children, and the oldest boy gave him a quick answer. Hai asked him another question, and the boy bowed, then, followed by the younger boy and little girl, they dashed inside the house. Once they were inside, their voices erupted excitedly.

"I ask them if elder of home is here and that we request to visit with him."

Dalton nodded and gave Sky a wink. She took in a steadying breath.

Paige stepped closer to Sky and slipped her arm around the girl's waist. Sky was glad to have her stepmother there with them and planned to find a moment to tell her so.

A shuffling at the doorway caught all of their attention. They watched as an elderly, bent figure shuffled outside. A twisted piece of wood, used as a cane, aided the man as he walked.

Following Hai's lead, they all bowed to the man. He himself bowed his head briefly, then with a weathered face and worn expression, he looked at them, his tired eyes imploring the reason for this visit.

Hai began to speak. He gestured toward Dalton, then toward Sky.

The old man looked at them as Hai continued explaining who they were and why they were here.

After a moment, the old man interrupted Hai. He turned toward the front door, where the three children lingered in the shadows, trying to find out what was going on. The grandfather voiced a command, and the oldest went running inside.

It wasn't long until the boy emerged with a woman, who was talking rapidly to him as she dried her hands on a cloth. She continued chattering until she looked up and immediately stopped, her mouth remaining open. Her eyes darted to the old man, then to the group standing before her.

Before the old man had a chance to say anything, the woman looked at Sky, her expression turning to disbelief. She dropped her cloth, stepping on it as she walked toward Sky, her eyes filling with tears. Then, without a word, she threw herself at Sky, who gathered the tiny woman in her arms and held her as the woman sobbed uncontrollably. Sky looked at her father, unsure of what to do and what was going on.

The old man wiped at his own eyes as he watched the emotional display. The children at the doorway ventured farther out and came to stand by the old man.

Another woman tentatively came through the doorway. The old man spoke to her and soon she, too, had her arms around Sky, sobbing.

Sky couldn't help but cry at the overwhelming display, not sure who was hugging her, but knowing, at least, that their presence was welcome. For that she was grateful.

The oldest woman, the first one to hug her, finally stepped back, taking both of Sky's hands in hers and looking at Sky for several minutes. Then, lifting one wrinkled hand to Sky's cheek, she stroked Sky's face, speaking through her continuous stream of tears.

The old man came forward and looked at Sky, then spoke to Hai.

Hai responded and then told them what he'd said. "They are honored by your presence. They want you to come inside."

The woman didn't let go of Sky's hand as they crowded into the house.

The room was devoid of furniture except for several homemade stools and some woven bamboo mats where they all sat down except for Sky. The older woman took her to an area of the room where a beautifully decorated altar was located. There were carvings and ornate statues on a silk-covered stand and above it, on an intricately carved shelf, were pictures. And there, directly in the middle of the shelf, was a picture of Sky's mother as a young girl.

If Sky hadn't known better, she would have sworn that it was a picture of herself.

Sky pointed to the picture, and the older woman nodded and wept. Sky understood. The older woman was also amazed at the likeness between Sky and her mother.

The elder spoke to all of them, and Hai translated.

"This man is Soon Lee's uncle, her mother's brother. He is only surviving male in her family from war. Woman holding Sky's hand is Soon Lee's mother. She feels her daughter has returned home. This is great day for them."

Sky looked at her father as tears trickled down her own cheeks. She then looked at her grandmother, barely five feet tall, and smiled through her tears. Then she wrapped her arms around her grandmother and hugged her, holding her, feeling the connection and the closing of the circle. These people were her family. As Quang had said, their blood ran in her veins.

Her grandmother's frame shook as she sobbed in Sky's arms.

It took several minutes for their tears to stop. Everyone in the room wiped at their eyes, even Hai and Quang.

The other woman, the grandmother's sister, returned to the room with a tray. On the tray was a teapot and small ceramic cups.

Dalton asked Hai what kind of tea they were serving, and Hai inquired for them. Hai then told Dalton that it was herbal. The family was too poor to buy black tea and had to gather herbs to make their own.

Through the help of Quang and Hai, Dalton explained to the family about their daughter and her constant yearning to see her family again and to find out if they had survived the war.

The uncle explained that after their release from the camps where they were held, Soon Lee's mother, Tao, had gone to live with her sister, Tung, and her husband for many years. After the death of Tung's husband, they returned to Tao's village to live with the aging uncle. Tao had never wanted to return again to this village. It had only filled her life with horror and pain. But her duty was to her uncle, and she had no other choice.

Tung's daughter, Anh; her son, Nu; and his three children also lived in the home. During the day Anh worked at a noodle shop, alongside Tao and Tung. Nu worked in the fields and spoke some English. His wife had died from complications following the birth of their last child. All of them lived in this small home, the way it was with most Vietnamese families. And they were more than happy to make room for their visitors.

When Dalton told them that they only planned on staying a few days, Grandmother Tao was pleased but indicated that she wanted them to stay longer. Dalton explained that Hai and Quang needed to return to Ho Chi Minh City the next day and that he, Paige, and Sky were on their way to Hanoi to catch a plane home at the end of the week.

Sky felt a pang of sadness in her heart at the thought of telling Quang good-bye. She looked over at him and found him looking at her with an expression on his face that matched the ache in her own heart. Quang had become an important friend to her, one whom she knew completely understood the complexities of who she was, inside and outside. She wasn't ready for their friendship to end.

"Hai, I am concerned about what we will do after both of you leave," Dalton said. "Ask them if their nephew will be able to translate for us when you are gone."

Hai asked the question and was told that the nephew's English would be sufficient, although he wasn't home very often, sometimes arriving home late at night only to be gone early the next morning before most of the family was even awake.

Grandmother Tao and Aunt Tung offered them food along with their tea and bustled around the kitchen area preparing it for them.

Hai translated as Uncle Kiem explained to them that most of the people in the area were rice farmers. He also said there were other crops in the area too but didn't elaborate. Sky knew he referred to the illegal opium crops.

Uncle Kiem spoke continuously, and Hai translated. "There is curfew," Hai told them. "From dusk to dawn, no one is to be out. This is forbidden. You are not allowed to take photographs, either.

There are patrols everywhere. It is against the law to take pictures of any police or military. This is for your safety, especially because you are Americans. You must be very careful."

The three Americans nodded. The last thing they wanted was trouble. They'd found enough of it while trying to get to the village.

"While we are waiting for food," Paige said to Dalton, "let me check your wound. We need to put something on it to prevent infection."

Sky helped Paige remove the stained sock, and, taking one of Dalton's T-shirts, they cut it in strips and made another bandage that they could wrap more securely.

"I wish we had my antibacterial ointment," Paige said. "I'm really concerned about infection."

"It'll be fine," Dalton assured her. "I've had worse."

Sky knew her father referred to his time in the POW camps, and even though she'd never know just how bad it was to be in such an awful place, Sky's understanding of her father's experience had grown immensely during their time in Vietnam.

"We should tell Uncle Kiem that we have gifts for them and for the schools."

"Hai, could you tell him that for us?" Dalton asked.

Uncle Kiem nodded as Hai told him about the gifts the Americans had brought for them.

"He is pleased," Hai said. "He will have one of children go to school and arrange meeting for you to give gift tomorrow."

"Can you go with us to the school?" Sky asked Quang. "You're the one who dragged that suitcase most of the way. You should at least be able to see the children receive the gifts."

"Uncle?" Quang asked.

Hai nodded. "Yes, we go with you. Then we make our departure so you can be with your family."

The meal was placed on a low-lying table. They sat around the table on the floor and filled bowls with noodles, then added bits of chicken and vegetables. The noodles were delicious, lacking the fish flavor of the others they had eaten. Even Quang remarked at how delicious they were, explaining that his mother ran a noodle shop in Ho Chi Minh City.

Aunt Tung explained to them that her daughter, Anh, worked at a noodle shop in the market. It was grueling work, and Anh got home late in the evening and left early in the morning to get the shop ready each day. Aunt Tung and Grandmother Tao helped out at the shop most days during lunchtime, when the shop was the busiest, and in the evenings they helped clean the shop, make the noodles, and cut up vegetables and meat for the next day.

Sky was amazed that at such an old age, these women still worked so hard. But there was no retirement for them, no 401(k)s. If they wanted to eat, they had to work. And then, when it was no longer possible to work, it was the obligation of the children to take care of the elderly.

After the meal, Grandmother Tao brought out another dish. It was made of sticky rice, grated coconut, sugar, and grilled sesame seeds. Sky had not tasted anything that delicious since she'd arrived in Vietnam. Her grandmother was overjoyed to tears when Sky asked for more because, her grandmother explained, this was Soon Lee's favorite treat as a girl.

Once the adults were finished, the children were allowed to eat. They sat still and ate in silence as the adults continued to talk.

By this time Sky felt comfortable enough with her relatives to begin asking questions about her mother. Grandmother Tao glowed as she told Sky about her mother, especially as a young girl.

"She had beautiful voice," Hai translated for her. "When she sang, it was as if bird from heaven sang. Everyone loved to hear her sing, and she performed often.

"She also loved to work in fields. When she was very young, she would ride water buffalo as her father plowed fields to plant rice. Your mother was hard worker. Many times she worked more than her brothers. This made them mad, but they could not deny that she was strong and determined."

Dalton nodded. These were words he also would use to describe Soon Lee. Without her determination, she never would have escaped the prison camp or survived on the streets of Saigon.

Uncle Kiem had been quiet for most of the conversation, but suddenly cleared his throat to speak. Everyone turned to listen.

"The war in Vietnam made enemies out of brothers. It destroyed our country and took away our fathers and sons. The American soldiers helped us. You," he said, looking straight at Dalton, "helped our Soon Lee when she was alone and desperate. When she knew of no family to turn to for help, you were there for her." He bowed his head. "We give you our gratitude."

Dalton had to clear his throat before he could speak. It took him a moment to respond. Finally he said, "She always remembered her family and her country. She wrote many letters and made many calls to find you."

Grandmother Tao wiped at her eyes.

"She passed away before your letter arrived," he said.

Tears filled Sky's eyes also. She'd often wondered if her mother would still be alive today if that letter had arrived sooner.

"We weren't sure whether to come find you," Dalton said, "but we felt it was important for Sky to know who her mother was and know her mother's family."

Sky nodded to her grandmother, uncle, and aunt.

"We are honored that you are here, but it is dangerous for you to be here," Uncle Kiem said. "It is good that you brought your Vietnamese friends with you. They will be able to return home safely, but while you are here, you must always have one of us with you."

The children had finished eating and had gone outside, but they soon returned in a whirlwind of chatter. They quickly grew silent and stood still, bowing at their great-grandfather.

Everyone listened as the oldest child spoke. Hai told them that the children had been to the school and had told of the Americans who wanted to give gifts to the school.

"Village elders will be there to receive gift," Hai said, translating for the boy.

Paige smiled and said, "This is wonderful. And thank you, Quang, for helping to drag that suitcase all of this way. I knew it would be worth it once we got here."

Quang also smiled. "It is a great thing that you do for the children here. They will become better educated and be able to help their own people." He then told the uncle and two women what he'd said. They all nodded in agreement.

"Tell them, Quang, that we brought things for them also," Paige said.

Opening the suitcase, Paige motioned for Sky to help her. Sky was grateful that Paige had insisted on bringing the gifts for the schools and for Soon Lee's family, and she realized that Paige didn't want to take credit for the gifts. She wanted them to come from Sky.

The first thing she gave them was a scrapbook that Paige and Sky had worked on that contained pictures of Soon Lee, Dalton, and Sky, from Soon Lee's arrival into the United States, her wedding, and Sky's birth, until her unfortunate passing. There were tearful reactions and even some delighted laughter at pictures of Sky as a chubby infant and precocious toddler.

Sky then presented her grandmother with a beautiful, red silk jacket with black trim and buttons and a mandarin collar. She also gave her a strand of pearls, small and delicate, just right for Grandmother Tao's tiny neck. Speechless, Grandmother Tao was overcome with her expensive gifts. Aunt Tung's eyes shone brightly as she gazed upon the lovely items, much more elegant than anything they could afford.

Paige and Sky hadn't known what to bring, since they weren't sure whom they would meet, but there were plenty of items to bestow upon each member of the family. For Aunt Tung they had a lovely comb, brush, and mirror set, along with a small gold band containing a sparkling ruby. For Uncle Kiem there was a book of pictures from around the world—a nice, hardbound volume of breathtaking places they had never seen or even known about. They also gave Uncle Kiem one of the watches Paige had in the suitcase. Even though he probably didn't have a great need for it, Uncle Kiem was grateful for the gift, and after putting the watch on his wrist, smiled proudly as he showed it to them.

The two boys were each given a Lakers T-shirt, and Sky also gave each of them a soccer ball. Quang took out the pump and inflated the balls for them while they danced around with excitement. Sky gave the young girl a lovely porcelain doll that was dressed in traditional Vietnamese clothing. The girl ran straight to the two older women to show them her treasure, all the while speaking excitedly.

Even though Anh and her son, Nu, weren't home, they presented gifts to be given to them also. Seeing the looks upon their faces gave Sky a wonderful feeling inside, a feeling of being connected, of being . . . family.

Gathering around Uncle Kiem, the children looked at the pictures in the book, oohing and aahing at the amazing beauty of the Grand Canyon, Mt. Everest, and the Hawaiian Islands.

"Quang, will you please ask Uncle Kiem if it would be okay to take some pictures of the family?" Sky asked. "I would like some to take home with me."

Uncle Kiem agreed, and Sky was delighted to see how happy they all were to pose for pictures. She promised to give them all copies of the pictures when she got home to add to the scrapbook.

Sky felt a closeness with these people, and more than ever before, she felt close to her mother, a closeness she'd missed and yearned to have for many years. She knew coming here had been the right thing to do. She would leave a part of herself here, but she also would take a part of them home with her.

CHAPTER FOURTEEN

"This is exciting, isn't it?" Paige said to Dalton as they followed Grandmother Tao, Aunt Tung, and Uncle Kiem into the village. The youngest girl walked with them, but the two oldest children were at the school.

"If the teachers and elders of the city are half as excited as Soon Lee's family was to get the gifts, it will be worth dragging that crazy suitcase halfway across the country with us," Dalton answered, steadying the luggage as it rolled over the bumpy dirt road.

"I was thinking of keeping the suitcase to take home souvenirs with us, but I don't know if I want to carry an empty suitcase with us all the way to Hanoi. We can buy most of our souvenirs in Hanoi and buy a cheap bag to take them home in."

"I'd rather do that," Dalton said. "Maybe Quang would like this suitcase. I'm sure he's grown attached to it after all the miles he's logged with it."

Paige laughed.

"Besides, it sounds like he may be coming to the States to visit. He might need it."

"Fine with me if you want to offer it to him," Paige replied.

"Honey, I need to ask you something." Dalton wasn't sure if he'd been dreaming or not. "Did you hear something in the middle of the night last night?"

"Like what?"

"Like the sound of gunshots?"

Paige's forehead wrinkled as she thought for a moment, then she opened her eyes wide. "Yes, now that you ask me, I remember waking up, but I was too tired to even think it might be gunshots. But you're right, that's exactly what it sounded like."

"As much as I'd like to stay an extra day or so, I think the sooner we move on, the better," Dalton told her.

Paige nodded. "I think you're right."

"While we're in town this morning, I'll make arrangements for us to leave tomorrow."

"Sky's going to have a hard time leaving," Paige said. "Look at her."

Sky walked next to her grandmother and, with Quang's help, was engaged in a conversation with her. Dalton watched his daughter as gratitude filled his heart. Seeing his daughter bonding with her grandmother and other members of Soon Lee's family left no doubt in his mind that coming here was the right thing to do.

The marketplace was a bustling center of commerce. Kiem pointed to the noodle shop where they would go for lunch following the presentation. Even though it was midmorning, all the outdoor seats at the noodle shop were filled.

Dalton noticed an abundance of policemen at the market and other military men patrolling the streets. It was hard to say what they were patrolling for. Perhaps it was the prevalence of the illegal opium fields that kept the place so tightly guarded. He wondered if the guards were keeping watch to protect the opium growers or the townspeople. Either way, having so many guards around made him uncomfortable, and as much as he enjoyed being with Soon Lee's family, he would be happy to be away from this area.

"We are near," Hai told them. "We wait outside until they come for us."

The school was nothing more than gray cement blocks and a clay-tiled roof, yet it looked fairly new in comparison to the dingy, crumbling buildings of the town.

"Well, this is it. We made it," Dalton said to the group. Presenting these gifts had been another one of their goals for the trip. They'd accomplished many of the things they'd already set out to do. The only thing left once they finished their business with Soon Lee's family was to go to Hanoi and visit the place where Dalton had finished his time as a prisoner of war.

Paige's eyes glistened with excitement. "I hope they like what we brought. I can't wait to see the faces of the children."

"I know," Sky said. "We worked so hard finding all those chalkboards and making the kits." Paige and Sky had spent a lot of time putting together learning kits for the children. They contained everything a child would need for school: chalk and a small chalkboard, scissors, paper, pencils, erasers, glue, crayons, a ruler, and more.

After a few moments, Anh's oldest grandchild came to the door to bid them to come inside.

With the suitcase rolling behind them, they entered the concrete-floored building and followed the boy down a narrow hallway past several small offices. Then, opening a door, he led them inside a large room where four rows of desks were filled with young children, all watching with anxious anticipation.

The teacher, a young man probably no older than Quang, greeted them with smiles and bows.

Hai translated for him. "He is honored by our presence and these gifts. Their school is very poor, and many children have to share and take turns with books. Learning is very slow and difficult for them and frustrating for him. These generous gifts help children to learn faster and learn more."

Dalton, Sky, and Paige bowed.

At the front of the room near the teacher stood four men, all of them looking as old as some of the surrounding mountains and as bent over as some of the twisted tree trunks.

The teacher requested that the three Americans come forward and stand in front of the class. With Hai translating, the teacher told the children why the Americans came to their village and why they wanted to bring such generous gifts. He told them about Soon Lee and about Dalton being a soldier in the war against the North Vietnamese and how he'd been a prisoner for many months.

With complete attention, the children listened as Hai continued to explain what the Americans had brought for them. Not only were the children receiving educational gifts, but there were enough T-shirts for each of them, as well as toothbrushes and toothpaste, candy bars, balloons, and a bottle of bubbles for each of them. It was more than any of them had seen in their lives at once, and many sat in stunned silence while others could barely contain their excitement.

The teacher rapped his knuckles on his desk to bring them to order, which took less than a few seconds. The students looked straight ahead in stone silence. Then one of the elderly gentlemen stepped forward. Through Hai, he communicated his gratitude for the gifts. He confirmed that the future of their village was in the hands of these children, and that the more education they had, the brighter their future would be.

After he spoke, he bowed to each of the American visitors, then motioned for them to greet the other elders. Dalton led the way, and in front of each of the other men, he bowed and received their words of thanks.

Dalton bowed to the last man, but instead of looking up at him and saying "thank you" like the other men had, the man kept his head down, his gaze directed toward his bare feet. He did the same thing as Paige and Sky went by.

With Quang's help, a learning kit was then distributed to each child, with plenty of extras for the teacher to store for new students and future use. The teacher kept the candy and toys for a time when the children were allowed to play outside and have treats. All the time they were handing out the gifts, Dalton noticed that the one elderly man kept his gaze shifted away from the activity in the classroom.

The children stood as the Americans prepared to leave. They all bowed politely on their teacher's cue. Paige blinked to clear the tears in her eyes. She hugged Sky, who wiped at her own tears. Dalton smiled at his wife and daughter and knew what they felt. His heart was also full of gratitude for being able to help, in some small way, this tiny community struggling to break the bonds of the past and hopefully build a better future for themselves.

With one last bow to the elders, and still no eye contact with the last man, the Americans departed with their Vietnamese friends and family and filed outside into the hot, muggy morning.

"Wow," Sky said, giving her father a hug. "That was awesome."

"It sure was, sweetie. Definitely worth all the work, wasn't it?"

"For sure," she replied. "I wish we could do more for them." Then Sky turned to Paige. "Thanks for all you did for them."

Paige smiled as she received a hug from her stepdaughter. "I hoped it would feel this good when we finally gave them our gifts. Actually, it's better than I thought it would be."

"For me too."

Hai checked his watch. "Now we go to market and wait for our ride." They'd arranged a ride for Hai and Quang with a driver who made deliveries to Hue.

"You still have a few minutes for some lunch, don't you?" Dalton said, wanting to feed them before they left.

Hai bowed. "Yes, of course."

They walked back to the market to eat at the family's noodle shop.

"How do you think it went, Uncle Kiem?" Dalton asked.

Hai translated and received Uncle Kiem's reply. "They have not seen such generosity before. Government provides only barest of necessities. It is wonderful thing you have done."

Dalton was grateful for their approval and was glad they'd gone to the trouble of bringing so much with them.

"Honey," Paige said to her husband, "I need to buy a few things. I appreciate you letting me borrow your toothbrush, but I could really use my own."

"Of course," Dalton said. "As soon as we finish lunch and say good-bye, we will do some shopping."

"Maybe I can find some more dog tags," Paige said.

Dalton held Paige's hand as they walked and, slowing his pace, allowed the others to walk ahead.

"I need to ask you something," he said to Paige.

She looked at him with concern.

"Did you notice that one elder on the end, the one—"

"Who wouldn't look at us?" she finished for him.

"Yes! What was that all about?"

"Maybe he's shy, or maybe he hates Americans. I don't know. I couldn't figure it out either. He didn't seem like that when we first walked in. In fact, I thought he was kind of a cute little man," she said. "But he seemed to get very uncomfortable the longer we were there."

"That's what I thought," Dalton replied. "I don't get it. I guess it doesn't matter. Yet . . ."

Paige waited for him to go on. "Honey, what is it?"

"It's just that there was something about him." Dalton thought about it for a moment longer then shook his head. "Oh well, I guess it doesn't really matter."

"I think Sky's going to have a hard time telling Quang good-bye," Paige observed.

"Yeah, I think so too," Dalton answered. "He's a great kid, isn't he?"

"I hope he does come to see us sometime. We could take him so many fun places."

"He seemed excited about us giving him the suitcase," Dalton told her. "He didn't seem to mind dragging it home. Especially since it is empty now, and he can actually lift it."

Paige laughed. "We had every inch of that thing stuffed full. I'm surprised we didn't wear the wheels out."

They arrived at the noodle shop and were greeted by Anh, who looked tired but happy to see them. She was glad to hear that the gifts were so well received. She offered to feed her American relatives for free, but Dalton refused, wanting to help the family out as much as he could.

While the food was being prepared, Dalton went to make arrangements to have money wired for the rest of the trip, and Paige wandered around the noodle shop to a small area stocked with candies and gift items. She admired many of the lovely handcrafted items, but was especially interested in the beautiful pottery and lacquerware vases and jewelry boxes. The fine detail and craftsmanship were captivating. She brought back several of the pieces to the table.

"Dalton, look at these beautiful things." She handed him one of the pottery vases. "Sky, wouldn't you love one of these lacquerware boxes for your jewelry?"

Sky ran her fingers over the smooth surface of the box, then lifted the lid, exposing the silk lining inside. "It's beautiful. Dad, can we get one?"

"They have smaller ones you could take home to your friends for a souvenir," Paige suggested.

"That's a great idea," Sky answered with enthusiasm.

Uncle Kiem said something to Hai, who then told them, "Your grandmother and aunts make boxes and pottery."

Sky's mouth dropped open.

"They make these?" Paige asked with disbelief.

"Yes, family makes pottery and lacquerware for many generations. Grandmother Tao teaches them how."

"I know about this lacquerware," Paige said. "It takes a very long time to make because once they paint the artwork onto the wood, they have to apply seven coats of lacquer. Each layer takes seven days to dry."

"Whoa," Sky exclaimed. "Why so long?"

"That's what gives it such a hard surface. It's very durable."

Uncle Kiem pointed to Sky and said something.

Hai translated. "Sky's mother was wonderful artist. Her steady hand allowed her to create most intricate of paintings."

"I didn't know Mom was an artist," Sky said.

"She used to draw a lot when you were little," Dalton told her, "but after a while she quit. She always said she'd get back to it. I've kept her artwork in storage. We can get it out when we get home."

Sky smiled. "I'd like that."

"Honey," Paige said to Dalton, "I wonder if the family would be interested in shipping some of these things to the United States. I know we could sell them at the design store. Some of these bigger pieces would be fabulous to use in decorating, and the smaller ones would be great for gift items."

"Hai," Dalton said, "would you mind asking Uncle Kiem?"

Hai spoke to Uncle Kiem about the possibility of selling the artwork in the United States. Kiem's face lit up, and he called out to the women in the kitchen.

Immediately Grandmother Tao, Aunt Tung, and Aunt Anh appeared, each of them carrying bowls of rice, noodles, vegetables, and different meats.

Uncle Kiem spoke to them with great enthusiasm, which transferred immediately to the women's faces. Grandmother Tao clasped her hands together and bowed toward Paige. Then she spoke to Uncle Kiem, who then spoke to Hai.

"They say that you bless their lives, and they will be forever in your debt." Hai continued to explain, "With Uncle Kiem,

Grandmother Tao, and Aunt Tung all growing old, it is harder to find ways to provide for all of them. Aunt Anh needs help in the noodle shop, but Tao and Tung are too old to continue much longer. One thing they do is pottery and wood pieces because they do this at home. They worry great deal over this matter. What you offer allows them to provide for themselves and their family."

"Paige, you really think these will sell?" Dalton asked.

"Yes, of course. Plus Asian art is huge in the San Francisco shop. I've seen similar artwork, but nothing this detailed. I know it would sell."

The discussion around the table grew lively and excited. There were so many details to work out, and Hai was a great help in translating between the two groups.

They decided that it was important to get Anh's son, Nu, involved since he was the one family member who could speak English. He would have to handle most of the business for them. He hadn't been home yet since they arrived, but he would return later that evening, and they could then work out the arrangements.

After the meal, the older women hurried back to the kitchen to handle the noon rush.

"Dad," Sky said, "can Quang and I go to the market and look around before he leaves?"

"Sure," Dalton said, feeling confident that she would be safe with Quang. "Stay together, though." He watched them leave. "They've become close through this trip, haven't they?"

Paige nodded. "They have a lot in common. I think she's finally found someone who understands who she is. None of her friends back home know what it's like to have half of you belong to a whole other culture and people."

Dalton leaned forward and gave his wife a kiss. "I'm glad this trip has turned out so well. I have to be honest, I worried that something might happen while we were here."

"So did I," Paige confessed. "But it's been wonderful."

Dalton turned to Hai. "I don't know how to ever thank you for all you have done for us. We never would have made it this far without you and Quang."

"It is pleasure," Hai said, bowing his head.

"Hai, could you ask Kiem something for me?" Dalton knew that after Hai and Quang left, the chance for questions and answers would be gone. "Could you ask him about the elders who were at the school, particularly the man on the end?"

Hai nodded and turned to Kiem. After hearing the question, Kiem answered with short, abrupt answers. He shook his head several times and continued talking a moment longer, then threw his hands in the air and heaved a heavy sigh.

"What did he say?" Dalton asked.

"He says this man is great mystery. No one knows much about him. He was gone during war for many years, but he never speak about it to anyone. Some say he was with North Vietnamese, but no one know. His wife dies many years ago, leaving him to take care of his oldest son, who was born deformed, believed to be that way because of Agent Orange during war. Son was great burden to him, but he recently died. He had another son who left home and has not returned. It is believed that he lives in America now and plans never to return. His father refuses to leave Vietnam, so it is possible they will never see each other again. This is also very difficult for him to bear."

Dalton nodded, wondering if this explained the man's reaction to them at the school. Perhaps the man hated Americans because of the war or because that was where his son now lived.

Sky and Quang came racing into the noodle shop. "Paige, we found dog tags—dozens of them. You have to come and see."

Paige jumped up. "Do you mind, honey?"

"I'll take care of the bill and find out about transportation for tomorrow. I can check and see if the money I had wired from our account arrived. Then we'll find you at the market," Dalton said. He invited Kiem to join them at the market, but Kiem was too tired and chose to stay at the shop where they could meet before Hai and Quang caught their ride home.

After paying a generous sum for their meal, Dalton was ready to make their travel arrangements. For some reason, he felt anxious for them to be on their way.

Kiem and Hai bowed to each other as they said good-bye. Then Hai and Dalton walked to the market, where they located a small travel office that helped them secure a spot in a delivery van the following day.

With that taken care of, Dalton and Hai found Paige, Sky, and Quang at one of the shops, each of them holding half a dozen dog tags in their hands.

"This place is a gold mine," Paige said excitedly. "I don't think these people understand how valuable these are to us or they would have charged us much, much more for them."

Dalton chuckled at the enthusiasm his wife and daughter showed at locating these wonderful pieces of history and personal items that hopefully they could somehow return to families of soldiers in the war.

* * *

"I have something for you," Sky said, reaching into her backpack for the book. She handed it to Quang.

He looked at the cover and ran his finger across the words *Book of Mormon*. He looked at her, his eyes filled with gratitude. "Thank you."

"When I get home, I'll send you the Vietnamese version, okay?" She looked up at him and felt tears sting her eyes. She'd grown to treasure his friendship and enjoy his company. He had a subtle sense of humor that made her laugh. They talked with the ease of old friends. But most of all, he understood her. He completely understood her.

"I am going to save the money your father gave me so I can earn enough to come to America," Quang told her.

Sky smiled. "That's good."

"And I will read this book. I want to read it before I meet my father's family."

Sky nodded. Someday he would experience exactly what she had just been through—meeting strangers who were family and bridging the gap between their two worlds.

"If you want me to, I will be with you when you meet his family, just like you were with me," she promised.

"I would like that very much."

Hai said something to Quang in Vietnamese, and Quang answered. Then he turned to Sky. "I must go now. But I will see you again."

Sky couldn't stop the tears, even though she did her best to do so. They trickled onto her cheeks, but she quickly wiped them away. "Thank you," she said to him.

They hugged, and Sky held on tightly to Quang, feeling his strong arms around her. There was an amazing bond between them—they both felt it. Even her father and Paige had noticed it, and Sky knew that she would indeed see him again.

To her surprise, he brushed a quick kiss on her forehead before he let her go. Sky's heart fluttered in her chest. She had to force herself to let go of his hand, feeling an ache grow inside of her.

Hai bowed to them one last time and then, with Paige's big suitcase stowed in the seat behind them, he and Quang climbed inside the van that would take them to Hue where they would catch the train back to Ho Chi Minh City.

Dalton slipped an arm around Sky, as did Paige, and the three of them waved as their two friends drove away. Sky felt a piece of her go with Quang and knew she would never be content until she saw him again.

"A little harder than you thought it would be?" Dalton asked her.

She shook her head and sniffed. "I knew it would be hard."

"We'll see him again," Dalton assured her.

"I know. But who knows how long it will take before he can earn enough money to come to America."

"I gave him a little extra to help him," Dalton said.

"You did?" Sky felt her love for her father increase even more at that moment.

"He's a good kid. He deserves a little help."

"I'd be sad if I thought we'd never see him again. Do you think Hai would come over with him?" Paige asked.

"I hope so," Dalton answered. "I feel like they were brought into our lives for a reason."

They all agreed there was something very special about their friendship with Hai and Quang. With the hope that someday they would see each other again, they walked back to the noodle shop.

CHAPTER FIFTEEN

"I don't want to go tomorrow," Sky told her father as they sat outside the bamboo house after dinner that evening, watching the sun set over the rice paddies and banana trees. Grandmother Tao was making noodles for the next day at the shop, Aunt Tung was getting the children their supper, and Uncle Kiem was resting inside.

The evening shadows grew long, and the night air felt cool and fresh.

"I've already made arrangements for us to go on the van. I've already paid our money." Dalton didn't tell his daughter that he felt uncomfortable about them staying longer.

"Isn't there some way we can stay even for another day?" Sky begged. "I don't know when—or if—I'll ever come back. I may never see my grandmother and the rest of Mom's family alive."

Dalton didn't know what to say. The last thing he wanted to do was pull his daughter away from Soon Lee's family. But he couldn't deny that something didn't feel right about staying. Still, what would one more day matter?

"We still need to meet with Nu and talk about the artwork," Paige said.

"Well," Dalton weighed the matter in his mind, telling himself that he was probably just being overly cautious, "all right. I guess if you really want to. But I thought you two were ready to get back to the land of fast food and indoor plumbing."

"Just one more day, Dad," Sky said. "That's all I ask."

"I guess we're staying one more day," Dalton replied, happy to see his daughter's yearning to spend more time with her mother's family.

"Thank you," Sky said, giving her father a hug. "Grandmother Tao was going to show me how to paint on a wooden jewelry box. I know I can never finish it here, but still, it will be fun to have her teach me."

"I'll go to the market tomorrow and work things out so we can stay one more day."

Suddenly the three children burst outside and, with squeals of delight, ran down the dirt road. Moments later, their chattering announced their return, but they were not alone. A young man was with them.

"This must be Nu," Dalton said.

Paige and Sky turned to watch the arrival of the only family member they hadn't yet met.   But as he got closer, Dalton, Paige, and Sky had a startling realization, one that sent a collective chill through all of them.

Nu was one of the soldiers who'd held them up and taken their valuables.

"Dalton," Paige whispered, "what do we do?"

"Nothing," Dalton said. "Just act natural."

"His friend shot you," Paige said. "He could've killed you. How do I act natural?"

"If you don't, we might all get killed."

"Dad, I'm scared," Sky said.

"It will be fine. Don't forget, he is family. I'm sure the others won't let anything happen to us."

The children and their father approached. Nu was completely engrossed in his children's excitement and didn't see the three Americans until he was just a few feet away. When he did see them, he stopped. He'd been holding his daughter, but he quickly put her down and said something sharp to the children. They ran inside the house without another word.

Sky's heart thumped wildly in her chest as she saw the man recognize who was sitting before him. His eyes glanced to Dalton's shoulder, to the wound concealed by his shirt.

"Hello," Dalton said, getting to his feet.

Nu had no chance to reply, for his mother, Anh, came through the door, obviously anxious to see the safe arrival of her son.

Greeting his mother, Nu said a few words to her, and she bustled back into the house.

Nu approached them, his disapproving expression causing Sky to feel very frightened.

"We have come to visit you and your family," Dalton said. "I'm Dalton McNamara. I was married to your aunt, Soon Lee. And this is our daughter, Skyler," he said, putting his uninjured arm around her.

"And I'm Paige," Paige said. "It's nice to meet you, Nu."

He studied Sky for a moment, then looked at Dalton. "You were soldier in war?"

"Yes," Dalton replied. "I met your aunt in Saigon during the war."

Nu thought for a moment, then nodded his head slowly. "We are honored by your presence."

Dalton thanked him, but no one knew what to say. Nu's family thought he worked for the police, but the reality was he worked for an illegal opium farmer.

Anh came to the door and called him inside.

Nu replied to her, then turned to them. "We can talk more inside. Please," he said, motioning toward the door.

They followed Nu inside, none of them speaking.

Grandmother Tao immediately began making Nu and the Americans comfortable. Within minutes, steaming bowls of rice, vegetables, and meat were brought to the table for Nu to eat. His children sat nearby, obviously thrilled to have their father at home.

Sky doubted any of them understood how dangerous Nu's job was. But she also understood that he probably earned much more money working for the opium dealer than for the regular police in the village. She thought it was sad that some people felt it necessary to risk their lives doing something illegal just to provide for their families.

Uncle Kiem had skipped the earlier meal but after resting was ready to eat, so he joined Nu at the table. Kiem spoke to Nu, nodding occasionally toward Sky, Paige, and Dalton. Sky figured Uncle Kiem was telling Nu about the proposition to send art to America.

After hearing his uncle's explanation, Nu turned to Dalton. "Is this true? You want us to send these things to you in America?"

"Yes," Dalton said. "My wife works at a store that sells decorations for homes. These pieces would do very well there."

Paige nodded.

Nu said a few things to his uncle, then turned back to them. "This is very generous of you. It would not be difficult to arrange. I know many people who could help me send shipments to you. How soon do you want them?"

"Right away," Dalton said. "We will take a few pieces with us and have you send the rest. I will also leave money with you to pay for the cost of shipping."

Nu nodded to Dalton, then to Uncle Kiem. The deal was made.

When their father finished eating, the children gathered around him, since they had to go to bed soon. It had grown dark, and everyone was tired.

As Dalton, Sky, and Paige later settled down on mats in the front room, they heard a rustling in the hallway that led to the only other room in the house, a back room where the family slept.

Sitting up, Dalton squinted through the darkness and saw Nu standing near the kitchen area.

"I am sorry to disturb you," Nu said. "But I must apologize to you for what happened. How is your shoulder?"

Dalton's wound was tender and he feared infection. "I think it will be fine. My wife had some ointment in her bag that would have helped, but I will be okay."

Nu was silent. "The men I work with do not always act wisely. But we can take no chances. Still, shooting you was not necessary."

"I understand, Nu," Dalton said. "You had no control over it."

Again, quiet filled the room until Nu finally said, "I will let you sleep."

"Good night, Nu," Dalton said.

* * *

Sky couldn't believe her eyes when she woke up the next morning.

"Paige," she whispered, nudging her stepmother with her elbow. "Paige, wake up."

"What's the matter?" Paige mumbled, rolling away from Sky.

"Your backpack. Look, it's here."

"My what?" Paige said.

"Your backpack." Sky got up and lifted the pack, carrying it back to Paige.

Pushing herself onto her elbows, Paige lifted her head. "Where'd that come from?"

"I bet Nu got it. He probably felt guilty and went and got it last night."

"Dalton, honey, look," Paige said. "Nu brought my backpack to me."

Dalton covered a yawn as he sat up. His hair stuck up all over his head, and his eyes were mere slits. "Well, I'll be."

"I'm so happy to see my toothbrush," Paige said, rummaging through her pack. "And look, honey, my first-aid kit. Now I can take care of that wound better."

"I'll bet that's why he went and got your pack. I told Nu last night that you had something in your pack to fix my wound."

"Pretty cool," Sky said. "I mean, it's still freaky that you even got shot, but I bet it was a major hassle for Nu to go get your pack in the middle of the night."

"I'll make sure to thank him."

"Here," Paige said, sitting down next to Dalton. "Let me take care of this right now." She exposed the bandaged area of his shoulder and removed the soiled dressing. Yellow pus oozed from the wounded flesh. "We got this back just in time. I'm afraid you have an infection."

"Well, hopefully that ointment will take care of it."

"I don't know. It looks pretty bad. I think you could use an antibiotic."

"We'll have to wait until we get to Hanoi," Dalton said. "I doubt we'll find anything like that here. Besides, by tomorrow it may be doing better. That reminds me, I'd better go to town and make arrangements so we can leave tomorrow."

"You have to leave so soon?" a voice said.

They looked up and saw Nu standing just inside the room.

"Good morning, Nu," Dalton said. "Thank you for getting this pack."

"Yes," Paige echoed. "Thank you."

Nu bowed his head to them.

"We've been here much longer than we planned to be," Dalton explained.

"I see," Nu said.

Grandmother Tao came into the room at that moment. She bowed to her guests and, with Nu's help, told them good morning. She then spoke to Nu with urgency.

"My mother needs supplies for the noodle shop," Nu said. "There is a place not far from here where I go for these things." He directed his next comment to Dalton. "Perhaps while you go to the market to make arrangements, I can take the others with me. There are many things to buy there."

"Shopping!" Sky announced. "Please, Dad, can we?"

Dalton's first impulse was to say no, but Nu was obviously very eager to make up for the damage that had been done to them. Dalton felt that Nu wouldn't allow any danger to come to them.

"Are you certain it's safe?" Dalton asked Nu.

"I give you my word," Nu told him.

"What do you think, Paige?" he asked his wife.

"I think it sounds fun. Who knows what we'll find?" she answered.

"All right then. I guess you can go."

"Uncle Kiem will go to the market with you," Nu said.

With the arrangements made, Grandmother Tao began preparing their breakfast, then they were off for their day of adventure.

* * *

A rumble in the distance caused Dalton to turn and look at the sky. Gray clouds hung heavy in the distance, slowly covering the sky like a giant blanket.

He and Uncle Kiem picked up their pace as they made their way across the market square to the noodle shop where they would have lunch. It had taken longer than he'd expected to get everything arranged for their ride back to Hue so they could catch a train to Hanoi. First they had to track down the man who knew a person who made delivery trips to Hue, and then, once they located him, they had to find the driver of the delivery van. They ended up waiting for him to return from a delivery, and Dalton only could imagine what kind of cargo he hauled back and forth in the back of his van.

Still, he was their only way back to Hue.

Dalton paid more for their travel than he wanted to, but the arrangements were finally made and their transportation was secured. As much as Dalton had enjoyed the time with Soon Lee's family, he was ready to move on, to finish their exhausting tour of Vietnam.

With a sudden gust of wind kicking up, many people scurried to finish their shopping and get indoors. The scent of rain on the air was unmistakable—they were in for a big storm.

The sun disappeared behind the clouds, casting a dark shadow across the village. Dalton hoped Paige and Sky were safely back at the hut, waiting for him.

Sweeping inside with the wind, Uncle Kiem and Dalton entered the noodle shop just as the first drops of rain fell. The drops started out as a smattering but soon turned into a heavy downpour. Dalton remembered rain like this—as a soldier and then a prisoner. Day after day he'd endured the steady deluge of rain while tromping through mud and jungle trails or sitting in his hooch, shivering from the dampness in his old, rotting prisoner-of-war garb.

Shaking his head to clear it, Dalton looked up to see Anh approach them. "You want noodles?" she asked in broken English.

Dalton nodded.

Uncle Kiem said a few words, then Anh rushed away. The shop had a few other customers, but once the rain began, the market square emptied.

Moments later Anh brought out steaming bowls of noodles and vegetables, with chunks of white fish on the top.

Dalton was enjoying the meal when the door opened and a hunched, rain-soaked figure entered the shop. When the man turned, Dalton was surprised to see the old man from the school, the one who had reacted so strangely to him.

The man looked up and saw Dalton and paused, then slowly found a seat at a table on the far side of the room.

Anh attended to him immediately, and several minutes later, he too enjoyed a bowl of her wonderful noodles.

Dalton didn't mean to stare, but it was driving him insane. What was it about that man that had him so intrigued?

* * *

"Because our village is not near a main highway or located near a tourist attraction, we do not sell many of the things my family makes," Nu explained as they drove back from their visit to the market north of his village. "We try and send things to the market in Hue, but it is very difficult because I am the only one who can go, and I must work on the patrol."

"I think we will do well with these items in the United States," Paige told him. "Maybe you won't have to keep working on the patrol."

"It is not that easy, once you are in it," he said. "I know too much. There are secrets. They would think of me as a threat."

Sky felt bad for Nu. He didn't seem like a bad person; he was just doing what he felt he had to do to provide for his family. The burden of support lay upon his shoulders, and it was a heavy load.

"Why can't you just move somewhere else and start over?" Sky asked.

"I have thought of this, but it is not so easy. The elderly do not wish to leave, and if they do not come with me, they are in danger because of my job with the patrol. My family would suffer, and I cannot allow this."

"I'm sorry," Sky said. "I wish it could be different." She thought about Quang, wanting to better his life, which would allow him in turn to better the lives of his family.

"Sending the art pieces to the United States will help us a great deal."

"I'm very glad this is going to work out, Nu," Paige said. "We are happy that it will help your family."

They bounced along in the strange little vehicle that seemed like a truck version of a golf cart. It had a miniature truck bed in the back, and there was barely enough room for all three of them in the cab, but they were almost home. And it was just in time, because a heavy rain had begun to fall.

Sky had loved the market with its fascinating foods and items for sale. It was the closest thing she'd seen to a supermarket since they'd arrived in Vietnam. Even though the store was small, it was filled to the brim with goods. But she was also glad they were almost back to her grandmother's house. Her stomach was troubling her again.

Sky noticed Nu slowing down. Nu's eyes darted to each side of the road and out to the field of poppies to their right.

"Nu?" Sky asked. She and Paige looked at each other, then back at Nu. His face was as white as a sheet.

"Is something wrong?" Paige asked.

Just then, Nu slammed on the brakes. "Get down," he screamed, throwing his hand across their shoulders and forcing their heads to their knees.

A second later, there was a loud explosion and the truck rocked on impact.

"Stay down!" Nu yelled.

Another blast sounded and hit the truck, then another, and another.

"What's going on?" Sky screamed.

"It's a military raid."

"Why are they shooting as us?" Paige cried.

"They are shooting at me," he yelled.

"Paige!" Panic consumed Sky. "What do we do?"

"I don't know," Paige answered, grabbing Sky's hand. "Pray!"

The blasts continued, and they heard voices coming their way.

"Nu," Paige said, "what should we do?"

Sky looked over, waiting for his reply. But his face was blank, his body lifeless and still.

"He's been shot!" Sky cried.

"Hold on, and don't let go of my hand," Paige said. "We have to stay together."

CHAPTER SIXTEEN

Where was everyone?

Dalton looked around and found no one at home. He'd trudged through the muddy road to get home in case Sky and Paige were waiting for him. But obviously he'd beaten them home. He wondered how much longer they'd be, then remembered they'd gone shopping. He figured they must have found some wonderful things to buy.

But still, something didn't feel right, and Dalton didn't like it.

He looked out at the steady downpour and realized he was ready to move on to their final stop. He'd saved the worst for last, knowing that many of the ghosts he'd dreaded meeting while on the trip were in that old prison. It was possible that the nightmares would never go away completely, but he was now convinced this trip had helped him let go of some of those horrible memories. They'd achieved everything they needed to here with Soon Lee's family, and it was time to say good-bye.

Uncle Kiem was going to stay back at the market until the children were finished with school, then he would walk home with them. But Dalton had wanted to come back to meet Paige and Sky.

So where were they?

* * *

"I'm scared," Sky said to Paige as the guard opened the door to the van they'd been riding in and motioned them outside.

They stood in the pouring rain as the guard slammed the door shut and the van pulled away. He said something in Vietnamese, then, realizing they didn't know what he was saying, he pointed to the front door of a building and nodded toward it.

"I think we're supposed to go—" Sky received a sharp stab in the back with his gun. Suppressing the urge to cry out in pain, Sky stopped talking and walked toward the door.

Paige gave her a look filled with sympathy, but she didn't speak. Obviously, as Sky had painfully discovered, that was not allowed.

They made their way through the door, then stood inside and looked at the men behind a long counter. The guard received some orders, saluted, turned, and walked away.

Clasping each other's hands, Paige and Sky tried not to panic. Paige knew that as soon as Dalton found out about what happened, he would come and get them. Right now she was grateful to still be alive—any one of those bullets could have easily hit either her or Sky.

She swallowed as the man in front of them scowled, still saying nothing to them.

What was going on?

A moment later, the sound of footsteps echoed toward them. Paige and Sky turned to see their guard and another man approach.

The men stopped in front of them. The new man spoke to them. "You are American?" He eyed Sky suspiciously.

Paige answered, "Yes."

"Come with me," he said. He turned and walked away. Sky and Paige followed, their guard bringing up the rear.

Following the maze of hallways, they soon arrived at another counter where a Vietnamese woman stood. Her hair was pulled back severely in a tight bun at the back of her head. The two guards exchanged words, and the woman behind the counter glared at Sky and Paige with contempt. The woman then came around the counter and took her place next to the man.

"You will go with her," he said. "Later you will meet with the judge to decide your sentence."

"Our sentence?" Paige asked.

"Yes, drug charges are very serious."

"What?" Paige exclaimed. "We weren't—"

"Silence!" the man said. Then he quickly addressed the woman. She answered abruptly, then grabbed Paige's arm and shoved her toward a doorway. She did the same to Sky. They went through the doorway and walked down a long hallway to another room where a different woman, busy at her desk, spoke to them without even looking up. When Sky and Paige didn't respond, the woman behind them grabbed each of them by the arm and pushed them forward.

The two women exchanged words, then the woman behind the counter went to a cupboard and pulled out some items. She plopped the things onto the counter. Sky realized what was going on, and tears stung her eyes. Fighting with all her strength to not cry, she steadied her trembling lip and took in several deep breaths, but wondered how this could be happening to them.

The woman with the bun said something and jabbed them both in the back. Sky and Paige somehow understood that they were to pick up the piles on the counter. After doing so, they turned and followed the woman to another room. Here there was a tiled floor, several showerheads, and a hole in the floor.

The woman said something with a perfunctory nod.

Sky and Paige looked at each other.

The woman spoke again, this time her loud voice echoing against the tile. She made a motion of unbuttoning her shirt, then pointed at the showers.

Inside, Sky felt sick with fear.

Meeting Paige's own panicked gaze, Sky removed her clothing, but it was obviously not quickly enough for the guard, who startled them with a loud command.

Once they were undressed, they stepped underneath the showers and pushed a button, allowing cold water to wash over them. Closing her eyes to wash her face, Sky offered a prayer for help, then finished her shower and stood next to Paige to get dressed in the prison garb that looked like the same pajamas most of the population of Vietnam wore, only theirs were a drab tan color. Slipping their feet into some type of woven flip-flops, they left their civilian clothes behind and followed the woman.

Paige managed to reach out and give Sky's hand a squeeze before they walked through a locked gate exiting into a large, outdoor common area where several dozen women, all dressed in the same clothes, stopped what they were doing and watched as Paige and Sky followed the guard to a large building that looked like an outdoor animal cage, with iron bars for walls and a thatched roof. The guard inside opened the door and let them in.

The two guards spoke a few words. One of them must have said something amusing, because they both laughed and looked at the American prisoners.

Their escort finally left, and the other guard led them to a far corner, where two rolled-up straw mats stood in the corner. She pointed at the mats and at the small area in the corner, then walked away.

A handful of Vietnamese women were also inside the building, and while most of them ignored the newcomers, others stared at them.

Again, tears threatened, but Sky forced herself to be strong, at least until she could cry without an audience. She wondered how long it would take before her father got them out of there.

* * *

Dalton had to sit down before he passed out. All around him were sobs of sorrow.

Nu had been shot and left for dead. Paige and Sky had been taken to prison for being with a known drug trafficker.

The blow was too much for the family to bear.

Gathered around Nu's still form lying on the floor in the middle of the room, the family released its pain. Grandmother Tao wailed at the top of her lungs. The three children sat on the floor surrounding her and cried until the youngest one finally cried herself to sleep. Auntie Anh had run out of the door screaming. And Uncle Kiem rocked back and forth, muttering as tears streamed down his face.

Nu was near death. He'd lost so much blood, that there was no way he could survive. It would only be a matter of time before he passed away.

The family's cries of sorrow crowded Dalton's thoughts. He couldn't concentrate, couldn't think. Not only was he shocked with the news of Nu getting shot, but also with the fact that his wife and daughter were in prison. From what he had gathered, having a family member in prison brought great shame to the family. Death was better than prison. The townspeople would mourn with them if someone died, but having family in prison would cause the townspeople to shun them.

Wondering whom to talk to and where to turn for help, Dalton knew that he had to act fast. He had to get Sky and Paige out of prison. He knew he could prove they weren't drug traffickers, but the problem was they were American, and that was the worst thing they could be at that moment. He'd heard about the prisons in Vietnam, the horrible conditions as well as the treatment of prisoners, especially American prisoners. His heart ached at the thought of Sky or Paige getting injured or being treated poorly.

There had to be an attorney he could talk to—someone who would be willing to help him. But who?

Dalton finally stood and walked outside. Then he started down the dirt road toward town, wondering how the family was going to survive this blow if Nu died. If by some miracle he didn't die, he would go to prison. Either way, the family was doomed.

Dalton knew he had to contact the American consulate. Hopefully they would tell him what to do.

* * *

Sky stared down at the slop on her plate and looked at Paige. The brown broth with globs of white pig fat and a few chunks of vegetables turned her stomach.

Luckily they each got a hunk of dry bread to eat with their meal. They hoped that would sustain them.

Keeping to themselves, Paige and Sky found a place at the table to sit. The roomful of women, mostly Vietnamese, ate their food hungrily. Sky wondered if they were that hungry or if they really enjoyed the food. Sky doubted the latter and broke off a piece of her bread to fill the hollowness inside her stomach. Surely her father had contacted the authorities by now, and she and Paige would soon be released. Maybe by tomorrow they would be able to leave. That hope kept her sane, because it was the only thought she could bear to entertain. All the other ones struck fear in her heart.

Keeping their heads bent to avoid the glares of the other women, Paige and Sky nibbled at their bread, not tasting the slop. Hopefully they wouldn't be there long enough to get hungry enough to eat it.

A sudden outburst of yelling startled them. Two women jumped up from opposite sides of another table and attacked each other, slamming into the floor as they both fell in a tangle of hair-pulling and biting.

Sky watched in horror as the women went after each other, but was even more horrified when two female guards, wielding thick wooden sticks, approached and began beating the women. The women let go of each other and curled up in balls to protect themselves from the vicious guards.

Finally the beating stopped. One of the women whimpered as blood poured from a gash on her forehead. The other woman remained silent and still. One guard yelled at both of them, and the bleeding prisoner somehow managed to roll onto her side and attempt to get up. The other woman didn't respond. The guard kicked her in the ribs, her body jackknifing with the blow, but still she didn't move.

The first woman, her clothes stained with blood and a patch of her head bald from having her hair ripped out, finally stood and limped in agony behind one of the guards.

There was still no response from the other woman, and when the guard gave her one last nudge with her foot, it was obvious she'd been beaten to death. Another guard was summoned, and together the two guards picked up the dead woman by the armpits and dragged her across the floor, leaving a trail of blood. They exited through some doors, leaving behind the rest of the prisoners, who sat in stunned silence.

Sky closed her eyes and pulled in some long, deep breaths as a wave of nausea threatened. She pled for strength and for help that her father would get them out of there—fast!

* * *

"But I can't wait three days," Dalton yelled into the phone. "Who knows what kind of treatment my wife and daughter are receiving in that prison!"

"I'm sorry, sir," the woman's voice on the other end of the line said. "We cannot have a representative there before then. Have you tried the local authorities? Perhaps they could help you."

Dalton shut his eyes as anger coursed through his veins. "No. They are the ones who put my wife and daughter there in the first place."

"Then I suggest you contact an English-speaking attorney in the meantime. He can start the process of getting them before the judge and getting them released."

"This is unbelievable," Dalton muttered.

"Excuse me, sir?" the woman said.

"Nothing," Dalton answered. "Please, if there's any way you can send this person sooner, I would appreciate it."

"Yes, of course," she said. "We'll do our best."

Dalton shook his head and slammed the phone onto the receiver.

He was on his own for the next three days.

He had used the phone at the noodle shop and left some money for the use of it. Anh robotically went through the motions of preparing food for patrons, but Dalton knew that inside she was crying and filled with worry for Nu and his fate. Still, the woman had no choice but to keep working.

"You need help, sir?" a man at one of the tables said to him in English. Dalton looked at him. "I'm sorry. I couldn't help but hear your conversation."

Dalton approached his table.

"Actually, I could use some help," Dalton said. "My wife and daughter were in an accident with one of our relatives. They were taken to jail, but they are innocent of the charges that put them there."

The man nodded. "They are also American?"

"Yes," Dalton answered.

The man shook his head. "It will be difficult, but I think I know a way."

Dalton pulled out a chair and sat down, willing to listen to anyone who would help him.

"My name is Kito," the man said.

"Nice to meet you," Dalton said. "You speak very good English."

"Thank you. I learned in the war. I helped the Americans as an interpreter."

"What would you suggest I do?" Dalton asked.

"There is one thing our people understand, and that is . . . you are from America. They know you have money."

Dalton opened his mouth to speak, to explain that he wasn't a wealthy man and that this trip had already cost him much more than he'd even dreamed, but he knew that compared to the Vietnamese, he lived like a king.

"Go on," Dalton said.

"In our country, money is power. You offer money to the right person, and your family is free."

"How do I know who the right person is?"

The man got a sly look on his face. "I can tell you."

Doubt filled him. Dalton wasn't sure about this man, nor was he sure that he wouldn't make the situation worse if he tried to bribe someone to release Paige and Sky. The risk was too great until he had more information.

"I need to think about it," Dalton told him. "Could we meet again, later?"

"Certainly. I will be here at five o'clock. We can talk then."

"Thank you," Dalton said, standing as Kito left the table.

"It is my pleasure," the man said.

Dalton watched Kito exit the noodle shop and wondered if the man really was the answer to getting his wife and daughter released. There was no amount of money too great to pay for their freedom, but he didn't want to land himself in jail, either.

He needed help from someone, but who?

* * *

"Why are you here in Vietnam?" the man in the wrinkled suit asked Paige and Sky. He stood next to the desk where the judge sat. Armed guards hovered off to the side.

"We are tourists," Paige said. "We came to this village to visit family. We didn't know our relative was involved in drug trafficking."

"You were with him as he made a delivery," the man told them. "We had people watching."

"No," Sky burst out. "We rode with him to the market to get supplies for my grandmother."

The judge sitting before them scowled at her outburst.

The man in the wrinkled suit continued, "We know you have made arrangements for shipments to the United States."

"Not for drugs," Paige said. "For art pieces—pottery and lacquerware—to sell at the interior design shop where I work."

Sky felt her hopes crashing down around her. From their perspective, their activities did look suspicious. These men were twisting the facts and making it sound exactly the way they believed it was.

"Merely a cover for the illegal trafficking of drugs," the man said.

"No, we just wanted the art pieces the family made," Paige said quickly, her voice beginning to tremble.

The judge slammed his hand on his desk. He spoke at length to the man in the wrinkled suit, who then turned and said, "You must engage the services of an attorney. The judge has seen similar situations and will not be fooled again."

"But how long will this take?" Paige cried.

"As long as we need," the man replied. He nodded to the guards, and before they knew it, Sky and Paige were on their feet and heading back to the dirt compound.

Sky had barely made it through the door to the compound when she burst into tears.

Paige wrapped an arm around her and said, "It's going to be okay. Your dad is doing everything he can right now to get us out of here."

"How did all of this happen?" Sky cried. "How did we even get here?"

"I know, I know," Paige soothed, stroking the girl's hair. Then, her hand froze and Sky felt Paige stiffen.

"What's wrong?" Sky sniffed, lifting her head. She looked into Paige's face and saw a look of alarm.

Slowly, Sky turned her head. Ten Vietnamese women had surrounded them.

A woman with eyes of steel stepped forward.

"You American," she stated, pointing at Paige.

Paige nodded, holding Sky close.

"What are you?" the woman asked, pointing at Sky.

"She's also American," Paige said. "Her mother was Vietnamese. From this village."

The woman smiled. Half of her teeth were missing, and the other half were stained brown from beetle nut juice. She walked toward Paige and Sky, holding her hand out to Sky.

Sky swallowed, not knowing what to do and afraid of what would happen.

"Come," the woman said. But the woman's smile made Sky uncomfortable, and she clung to Paige.

The woman's gaze narrowed, and Sky became even more afraid of what would happen if she didn't go with her.

"Come!"

Sky reached out, and the woman took hold of her hand, leading her to the others who stood in a semicircle around them.

The woman spoke rapidly to them, causing them to laugh and jeer at Sky. Immediately Sky pulled away, turning toward Paige for help. The woman yanked at her arm, and the circle began to close around them.

"Stop," Paige yelled from outside the circle. She tried to break through, but one of the women backhanded her and sent her flying to the ground.

As the circle tightened around her, Sky felt her knees weaken. What were they going to do to her?

The woman peered at her with a leering expression and cackled. Sky's skin crawled.

Hands reached out and grabbed at her, pulling at her arms and hair. "Ow," Sky screamed as they yanked on her long braid. "Stop!" she demanded as they clawed at her arms.

They forced her to her knees, and their punching became more painful. Blows to her back and head caused her to cry out in pain. Sky heard Paige in the background yelling for her, but the crowd was like an angry barrier that couldn't be broken.

They yelled names at her in English. Horrible, despicable names.

"No, please," Sky yelled as they pushed her onto the ground, where she received blow after blow from their feet and hands. She thought of the women in the lunchroom and cried even harder. They were going to kill her!

Then, suddenly, a shot rang out, and the beating stopped.

Sky lay still, waiting and wondering what was going on.

The woman, obviously the leader of the group, said something quickly and all of them stepped back and turned around, their backs to Sky.

Paige rushed over and gathered her in her arms.

Sky's lip was swollen and split open, bleeding freely. A huge bump had formed on her forehead, and her back, arms, and legs felt as though they were one giant bruise. Every breath she took was accompanied by piercing pain in her rib cage.

"Help me up," Sky said through gritted teeth.

Paige helped her stand just as one of the guards arrived and began yelling at the women.

The group of attackers dispersed to various spots in the compound. The guard stopped for a moment, staring at Sky and Paige, her face lacking compassion or concern.

"Who started this?" the guard asked.

Sky knew that telling the guard wouldn't change what happened and would probably only make matters worse for them with the other prisoners.

Paige opened her mouth to answer for Sky, but Sky shook her head. Obviously satisfied, the woman turned and walked back to her post.

Standing together, Paige and Sky looked around at the compound of prisoners, all staring at them, waiting to see what they were going to do.

"Let me help you back to the cell," Paige offered.

"No, I need to walk by myself," Sky insisted. "I can't let them think I am weak."

"Are you sure you can make it?" Paige asked.

"I have to."

Her left leg collapsed beneath her on her first step, and she nearly fell, but she caught herself and managed to limp, putting as little weight as possible on her left leg. It was a slow, painful trip across the compound to the cell block that housed half of the inmates, but they made it to their mats, where Sky finally allowed Paige to help her lie down on the hard surface.

Using her own shirt, Paige wiped the blood from Sky's mouth and chin and checked her other wounds.

"Why, Paige? Why did they do this to me?"

Paige smoothed Sky's hair back and swallowed hard so she could speak. Shaking her head slowly, she admitted, "I don't know. I don't understand. You would think they hated me more because I'm American."

"Quang told me how many of the Vietnamese feel toward children of mixed blood. They resent the Vietnamese women who married American soldiers. Is that why they did this? Because they hate me for being American and Vietnamese?"

"I wish I knew," Paige said. "I was so scared. I thought they were going to kill you." Tears streaked down her cheeks. "I tried to get to you."

Sky looked up and saw that Paige's right eye was swollen shut and her cheek was already discolored and swollen where she'd taken a blow from one of the women.

"I thought I was dead too," Sky said.

"How much do you hurt?" Paige asked.

"On a scale from one to ten, about one hundred," Sky said. There wasn't a spot on her body that hadn't been kicked or scratched.

"I think you have bite marks on your hand," Paige said.

"It didn't break the skin, did it?"

"No, thank goodness. A rabies vaccine was one shot we didn't get before we came."

Sky chuckled, causing her ribs to seize with pain. Her laughter quickly turned to tears, and Paige encircled her with a hug and held her. If this was an indication of what they were going to endure while they were here, Sky was frightened. She wouldn't survive another beating like this.

* * *

"How much should I give the guard?"

"One thousand dollars," Kito said. "That is the price."

"Tell me how this works again."

"The guard will leave the door from the compound open for five minutes at ten o'clock, right before they have their final lockdown for the evening. Your wife and daughter will slip through the door and go around to the back of the building where there is a restroom. There they will find an unlocked window that they will crawl through. They will follow the building and wait for your signal."

"How long will all of this take?"

"We have less than ten minutes before the final head count."

"Is that enough time?"

"If everything goes right, yes. If you get out of town before they catch you, you will be safe. Do not be fooled. Many of the police in this town are also involved with the trafficking of drugs. They do not want to risk bringing attention to themselves. They will not pursue."

"Have you helped others escape?"

"Yes, many," Kito said.

"Have all of them been successful?"

Kito didn't answer right away. Finally he said, "I will not lie to you. What we are doing is very risky. I have seen many escape to freedom, but I have also seen others not so fortunate."

"They've gone back to jail?"

"No. They are shot."

Dalton knew then that he couldn't go through with it. Not unless he knew they could escape safely. He shook his head.

"If your wife and daughter are convicted of drug trafficking, they will spend the rest of their lives in prison," Kito told him. "Illegal activity is going on all around this town, but getting caught is worse than death."

"I need some more time to think about it," Dalton said.

"We will meet again, here, in the morning," Kito said.

"Yes, in the morning."

CHAPTER SEVENTEEN

The noise woke Sky from a fitful night's sleep. She ached all over, and sleeping on a hard floor didn't help much.

Turning her head, she realized that the noise, a soft whimpering, was coming from Paige.

Reaching out her arm, she touched Paige on the shoulder, causing the woman to jump.

Paige quickly wiped at her eyes and rolled over.

"Paige, what's wrong?" Sky spoke in barely a whisper. Nothing would be worse than waking one of the other prisoners.

"I feel so bad about what happened to you," Paige said. They positioned themselves so their foreheads were touching and they could speak without disturbing anyone around them.

"I'll be okay."

"We have to get out of here."

"I know."

Sky stroked Paige's hair, trying to comfort her. This whole situation seemed like a horrible, unbelievable nightmare, one they just couldn't seem to wake up from.

"I keep thinking about your dad in the camps. He went through much worse than this."

"I know. I've been thinking about that too. He's a hero for surviving."

"I hope we can get out of here so we can tell him," Paige said.

"Me too."

The woman next to them groaned and rolled over, causing them to cease talking. It was best to be quiet now. They would have plenty of time to discuss things later. In fact, they had all the time in the world.

* * *

"I'll do it." Dalton handed the man an envelope containing one thousand American dollars. "How do we arrange it?"

"It has all been taken care of. Your relative, Nu, has a friend who owns a delivery van."

"Yes, he was going to take us to Hue," Dalton said.

"He is going to help us. He has done this before. You will need to give him one hundred dollars."

Dalton chuckled sardonically. "Why does that not surprise me?"

"I am sorry, but this is risky for all of us. But I promise you, the prison system here is corrupt at best. Money is power. The only way to get your wife and daughter out of prison is to buy their way out."

"How do I tell my wife and daughter about the arrangements?" Dalton asked. He'd still not been able to visit them no matter how hard he'd tried. Until he had representation from either an attorney or the American Embassy, he was not allowed to visit.

"I will take care of it," Kito said.

"How can you do that? Why would you risk so much for my family?"

"One of the guards at the prison is my wife," Kito said. "She does not like what goes on inside, and she is willing to help, if the price is right."

So that was it. Dalton finally understood. Kito and his wife had a regular "prisoner assistance" business going. But Dalton didn't care. The sooner they were out of here and away from this place, the better. He hadn't eaten or slept since Paige and Sky were captured. He couldn't function until they were safe again. Thoughts of his own incarceration haunted him unceasingly. Now, more than ever, he regretted putting his family in harm's way.

If he'd only listened to his heart, if only they'd left when they'd planned to leave, none of this would have happened.

"I will see her this afternoon, when she is on break. She will talk to your daughter and wife today, and tomorrow we will carry out the plan."

Dalton nodded but wished they could take care of it today. Who knew what unspeakable things were going on in that place?

"Meet me in the marketplace in the morning, and we will go through our plan one last time," Kito said.

"Why not here?"

"Someone might get suspicious. It would not be wise to draw attention to our actions."

"I see," Dalton said, his stomach tensing.

"And Nu, how is he doing?" Kito asked.

"Still unconscious, but alive. He lost a lot of blood."

Kito nodded, then said, "I must be going. I will meet you here in the morning."

Dalton agreed and watched him walk out the door. Dalton was the only one left in the noodle shop besides Aunt Anh. Dalton had seen her watching him with Kito. She approached him. Her small, overworked body seemed near collapse. Dalton's heart went out to her. They shared a common bond, that of trial and hardship.

"Is good," she said in English to him.

"Kito?" he asked.

She nodded. "Is good."

Relieved that she approved, Dalton dipped his chin to show his respect for her.

Knowing that tomorrow when they left they would have to leave the family behind made Dalton feel guilty. If Nu died, or survived and was sent to prison, the family would suffer a great deal. Dalton doubted that the plan to import some of their artwork would pan out now. The only way he could feel good about abandoning them was to leave them with enough money to help support them until more of the children grew old enough to take care of the elderly.

Hoping there was enough in his bank account to make another sizable withdrawal, Dalton left the noodle shop to take care of one last piece of business. Then he would go back to the house and wait until it was time to set the escape plan in motion.

* * *

"That woman keeps looking at us," Sky said softly to Paige. She'd noticed the woman watching them ever since they'd arrived at the prison. Even when Sky didn't see her, she felt the woman's eyes on them.

"She's not Vietnamese. I wonder why she's here," Paige said.

Sky tried to roll onto her back to get a look, but it was still just too painful. The bruising and swelling was worse today, and it was all she could do to endure lying on her side.

The prisoners were supposed to be outside in the compound, but Sky and Paige had been allowed to remain inside.

Slowly, one by one, the other prisoners returned to find refuge from the sweltering heat of the afternoon sun.

The woman staring at them had a shaven head, an indication that she was being treated for lice. Her eyes were round and sad, ringed by sunken, dark circles, her shoulders so thin that her clothes looked like they were on a hanger, not a human.

"She looks like she's one breath away from death," Paige said. "The poor thing. I wonder how long she's been here."

"I don't know," Sky said. "You don't think that's where we're headed, if we stay here."

"We aren't going to stay here," Paige assured her. "Your father would storm this place like Rambo before he'd let us stay here."

"I wish he'd hurry. How come he hasn't come to see us yet?"

"I don't know, honey, but I'm sure he's doing everything he can."

"You're right," Sky said, letting her eyes drift shut. She felt sleepy from the heat, and she also knew that resting would help her body heal. With a long yawn, she began to drift into a mindless state, escaping reality if only for a moment.

* * *

Sky awoke with a start, and when she opened her eyes, she found herself staring straight into the sunken eyes of the strange woman who'd been watching them.

"Paige," Sky cried, scooting back from the woman, causing herself unwelcome pain.

"It's okay," the woman said. "Paige asked me to keep an eye on you. She went to the latrine." Her clipped English accent didn't fit her appearance even remotely. "I didn't mean to startle you."

"Who are you?"

"I'm Beatrice Wixom. And you're Skyler McNamara."

"How do you know—"

"Paige told me all about the both of you while you were sleeping. Sorry about the beating. I guess the only thing worse than being white around here is being half white and half Vietnamese."

"So I've learned."

"You've handled it well. They respect you for not telling on them. Not that it would have done any good anyway."

"How long have you been here?" Sky asked Beatrice.

"I've actually lost count of the months, but close to five years, I'm guessing."

"Would you mind if I asked why you were here?"

"Not at all, deary. I'm a photojournalist, and I spent nearly two months following the Ho Chi Minh Trail, making a documentary of sorts. I used to be very fascinated with the Vietnamese people. Not anymore, I'll tell you."

Sky found herself warming to Beatrice. She looked terrible, but her mind was still sharp.

"As for why I'm in prison, I was a victim of circumstances—in the wrong place at the wrong time, you could say. I've got many people on the outside working for me, but the Vietnamese have found ways to bring charges against me that I never even knew about."

"What happened?"

"My camera."

"Your camera?"

"Yes. I got a little lost and found myself in a field. I happened to film some military maneuvers and got caught."

"That's it?"

"Doesn't sound like a problem, does it? Until you add the word *spy* to my charges and suddenly you've got half of the military force in Vietnam surrounding you."

"You're kidding." Sky felt horrible for Beatrice.

"I wish I were. I've had help from every foreign official I could think of, but the Vietnamese government considers me a threat to their security, and I have been sentenced to twenty years here."

"No!"

"It was supposed to be only ten years, but I happened to have a small altercation with the police in Cambodia, and after the Vietnamese government found out about it, they doubled my sentence."

"What did you do in Cambodia?"

"I couldn't bear the sale of wild animals being used for medicinal purposes, so I bought as many as I could and set them free in wildlife preserves. I soon ran out of money and thought I could sneak into one of the shops at the market and open up the cages and let the animals out. My plan didn't work too well."

"You were so brave to try and release them. I hate what they do to animals here."

"Well, I think *stupid* is a better word than *brave*. My efforts put me in a cage just like the animals I was trying to free."

"Why aren't you in jail in Cambodia?"

"I managed to escape and sneak across the border in the back of a poultry truck. I would have been fine if I hadn't gotten into trouble here, but once the Vietnamese authorities heard of what I'd done there, they were certain I was a spy."

"And there's nothing you can do?" Sky couldn't believe Beatrice was stuck here for fifteen more years.

"I would do anything to get out of here," Beatrice told her. "I will not live another fifteen years in this place. Already I've lost so much weight my teeth have begun to fall out. My bones ache constantly. Besides the lice I had, which are now gone, I've had some kind of parasite that won't allow my body to absorb any nutrients. Soon I will die from malnourishment."

"If we get out of here, we'll help you. We'll send you medicine and things you need," Sky told her.

"That's lovely of you," Beatrice said, "but they won't let me have any type of drugs they don't prescribe themselves."

"We have to find a way. We can't leave you here like this."

Beatrice smiled, showing diseased gums and gaps from lost teeth. "Thank you, my dear. That's the nicest thing I've heard in the last five years."

Paige returned from the latrine and sat down beside Beatrice and Sky. "I see you two have met," she said, smiling.

"I gave Sky quite a start when she woke up. I must look worse than I feel. I wouldn't know, since there are no mirrors here. Haven't seen myself in five years. Apparently I'm not aging well. Too bad, too. I used to be quite a good-looking woman."

"You're still beautiful inside," Paige told her.

Beatrice didn't speak, but closed her eyes and nodded.

They didn't see the Vietnamese guard approach until the woman spoke. "You are McNamara?" Her English was horrible but still understandable.

"Yes, I'm McNamara."

"Come with me."

Sky immediately clamped her hand onto Paige's arm, not wanting Paige to leave her.

"You leave now," the woman shouted when Paige didn't move fast enough for her.

Paige jumped to her feet, and when she turned to look at Sky, the woman jabbed Paige in the back with her club.

Watching in terror as the guard led Paige away, Sky felt a sob in her throat that threatened to tear loose, but fear held her mouth tightly shut. The last thing she wanted to do was make Paige's ordeal worse.

"What do they want with Paige?" Sky managed to ask Beatrice.

The English woman shook her head. "Hard to say. Maybe they didn't like the way she ate her last meal, or used the latrine, or looked at one of the guards. It doesn't take much."

Just as they got out of sight, Sky heard the crack of the club, and Paige cried out in pain.

"No," Sky whimpered. "Why are they doing this? She didn't do anything."

"Be still," Beatrice said sharply. "You don't want to make it worse for her or have them turn on you."

The thought of Paige getting beaten with a club sounded worse than getting kicked with someone's foot, as Sky had. Sky put her hands over her ears and curled up like a ball. Tears ran from her eyes as she prayed like she'd never prayed before. The words *Deliver us from evil* ran through her mind over and over and over again.

* * *

Nu's mother, Aunt Tung, kept a constant vigil over her son. She wiped constantly at her eyes as she sat near him, rocking and stroking his arm and hand. Grandmother Tao stayed nearby, leaving her sister's side only long enough to prepare a meal or tend to the children's needs. Uncle Kiem knelt often at the altar before the pictures of deceased family members, appealing to them to help Nu.

Dalton wished there were something he could do. In a hospital in America, Nu would have probably received the treatment he needed and then be on his way to recovery. An illness or injury that would be treatable in the States by an antibiotic or a few stitches, could be fatal here in Vietnam.

With several hours to go until he met the driver at the noodle shop, Dalton used his time to pray and ponder over the situation they were in and the plan that was about to unfold. He was trusting complete strangers with the lives of his wife and daughter. But desperation motivated him to do something he normally wouldn't have.

As he listened to the low, mournful prayer Uncle Kiem offered, Dalton found himself drifting off to sleep, something which had escaped him the last few nights. His nightmares had returned, and shutting his eyes was the surefire way to invite horrible memories of his life as a prisoner here. Haunting him like ghosts were the faces of the men he'd known, men who had suffered and died.

After the dreams, he'd wake up in a cold sweat, shaking uncontrollably. Remembering the memories was like reliving his past, and along with those memories came the pain.

He had to get his family out of that prison. He just had to.

Aunt Tung let out a loud cry, then began to sob and laugh at the same time.

Startled, Dalton looked over and saw what all the commotion was about.

Nu was conscious.

The tears of joy that followed evidenced what a great moment it was for the family. Nu's children were allowed inside to see their father, kiss his cheek, and offer a prayer at the altar.

While the family was busy giving Nu small sips of broth to build his strength, Dalton placed the envelope of money on the altar for them. He couldn't tell them what he was doing or where he was going. Aunt Anh knew, but it was just between them.

Grabbing their three backpacks, Dalton slipped unnoticed through the door and outside into the dimming evening light. They had to be at the prison at dusk, and then, as soon as Paige and Sky were in the van, they had only a few minutes to get out of town and be on their way to Nha Trang.

Kito had told him that his wife gave the head count to the head guard. She would tell them that the prisoners were accounted for at bedtime. This would give them a longer period of time to get away before anyone came looking for them.

Hoping that they'd thought of every possible detail, Dalton prayed that whatever they missed, God would take care of. They couldn't do this without His help.

* * *

"Let's go to the latrine before they lock us in for the night," Paige said to Sky.

"But I already went, and it hurts too much to walk."

"Sky, I need to go, and I need you to come."

Sky didn't argue any further. After the beating she'd taken today, Paige hadn't seemed herself. The funny thing was, Sky hadn't noticed a lot of injury or bruising as a result of the beating.

Sky felt like something odd was going on, but Paige didn't seem to want to talk, so Sky finally gave in and slowly got to her feet.

The guard nodded as the two of them approached her to ask for permission to use the latrine. She unlocked the door, and Sky held her ribs as they walked toward the horrible-smelling room they used for a toilet.

"Paige," Sky said. "I have to tell you about the dream I had this afternoon. My mother was with us, and she kept telling us not—"

"Shh!" Paige interrupted. "Not now, Sky."

Clamping her mouth shut, Sky didn't say another word. Paige was acting weirder by the second.

Inside the latrine were several other prisoners who were just finishing as Sky and Paige entered. Sky waited patiently for Paige, but it seemed as though Paige was moving extremely slowly on purpose.

Soon the latrine was completely empty.

"Can we go back now? I'm tired," Sky said.

"We're not going back," Paige told her.

Sky smiled. "Funny, Paige. Now come on."

"Sky, we're not going back. We're escaping."

Sky glanced down at the holes in the floor. "And how do you propose we do that?"

"Your father arranged it all. One of the guards here took a bribe to help us. We have to go—now."

Sky felt her knees weaken. "Are you sure? Paige, I'm scared."

"Don't be scared, Sky. We have to be brave."

"But what if we get caught? They'll hurt us. Paige, they'll kill us."

"We don't have a choice," Paige said. "Do you remember what your father told us?"

"No," Sky whispered, her stomach tightening.

"He said, 'Courage isn't the absence of fear but the ability to press on in spite of it.' The guard assured me that everything will go fine."

"Which guard?"

"The one who took me today. She didn't really beat me. She just banged her club on the ground, and I yelled. She told me I had to be convincing or people would suspect her. I can explain everything later. We have to go."

Digging deep for her courage, Sky followed Paige, praying with each step they took.

At the end of the latrine was a door, one that was usually locked. But when Paige tested it, the door was open. Sky looked at Paige in amazement. They were really sneaking out. And her father had arranged it.

As she stepped through the door, Sky prayed even harder. They closed the door behind them and looked up and then down the dark hallway. Paige pointed one direction and took Sky's hand.

Trying not to make any sound at all, Sky and Paige took slow, measured steps until they arrived at another hallway, this one dimly lit by a bulb hanging from a wire. Sky followed Paige as they turned a corner and tiptoed noiselessly along the polished floor. The muffled sound of a television carried along the corridor, reminding them that they weren't alone.

At the end of the hallway, they found a door. Sky held her breath as Paige tested the doorknob. Relief flooded her when the knob turned, but it was quickly replaced by fear as Paige slowly pushed the door open, unsure of what they'd find on the other side.

But it was just a restroom with a shower, toilet, and sink.

Closing the door behind them, Paige then went to a window. Sky watched with amazement as Paige carried out the plan.

The lock opened with a snap that seemed to magnify as it echoed in the room. They both froze, holding their breath to see if the noise caught anyone's attention. After a moment of waiting, Paige continued by pushing the window open. It would be tight, but they could fit through the opening.

Paige reached toward Sky to help her through the window when a sound outside the bathroom door stopped them, and they both froze with fear. Then, to their horror, the doorknob rattled, then began to turn.

"In here," Paige whispered, swinging open the shower door. They flew inside and crouched down against the wall as the door to the bathroom opened. Someone stepped inside but didn't turn on the lights. If the lights remained off, they would be safe.

Then, to their complete shock, someone whispered, "Paige. Skyler."

"Oh no," Paige mouthed.

Sky knew immediately who it was. Beatrice.

"It's Beatrice," Sky whispered.

"Are you sure?" Paige asked.

Sky nodded.

"Paige?" Beatrice said again. "Skyler?"

"In here," Paige whispered.

Opening the shower door, Beatrice poked her head inside. "Take me with you. I'll do anything. Please don't leave me here to die."

"But—" Paige started.

"Please!"

"We don't have time to debate this," Paige said. "We have to go now."

They got out of the shower and paused near the window.

Sky looked at the open window, their chance for freedom, and felt her blood turn to ice.

"We can't do it," Sky said. "It's not safe."

"What?" Paige questioned.

"My dream, Paige. I didn't understand it until now. In my dream my mother told us to stay. To wait. It's not safe."

"Sky, your father is out there right now, in a car, waiting for us. We have to go."

Tears stung Sky's eyes. "It's not safe."

"We don't have time to argue," Paige said. "This is our only chance."

"Wait," Beatrice said. "I'll go first, then you two follow. I'll show you it's safe, okay?"

"Sky?" Paige said.

The dream had seemed so real, her mother's warning so powerful. But Paige was right. Her father was fifty feet away, ready to take them to freedom.

"Okay," Sky said.

"Where do I go?" Beatrice asked as she hiked one leg up on the windowsill.

"Straight along the side of the building. Wait there for a signal, then run across the street."

"What kind of signal?" Beatrice had her other leg up and was sitting on the sill.

"A small flash of light."

"Okay, okay, I got it. I'll see you two in the car."

"Good luck," Paige said.

Sky clenched her fists so tightly that she felt her nails dig into the flesh of her palms.

With a soft thud, Beatrice landed just outside the bathroom window. She paused just a moment, then slipped away into the darkness.

Sky and Paige held their breath as they waited and listened. The eerie quiet seemed to intensify their nerves.

"You think she made it?" Paige asked.

"I think so."

"Do you want to go first?"

"Okay. I'll wait for you outside the window," Sky said.

With a little boost from Paige, Sky swung one leg over the windowsill and was just about to swing the other one over when a loud explosion filled the night with a simultaneous flash of light.

Startled, Sky lost her grip and fell back. Paige caught her before she tumbled to the floor.

"Come on," Paige said, dragging Sky from the bathroom. "We have to go back."

"They shot her," Sky cried.

"I know, and we're next if we don't get back now!"

After pulling the window shut, they raced through the hallway as an alarm sounded. They slipped through the door to the latrine, then peeked out into the compound and waited for the right time to cross.

"Stay in the shadows," Paige said. All around the prison, streams of spotlights flashed while sirens screamed through the air.

Sky felt panic constrict her chest, making her breathing difficult. She still couldn't believe that one moment Beatrice was with them, and in the next she'd been shot and killed.

"Wait," Paige said. They stood back against the building and watched as several armed guards ran past.

"Let's go." Paige grabbed Sky's hand and pulled her toward the cell. The guard wasn't at her post.

"How will we get in?" Sky cried, knowing that if they were caught on the outside, they would receive painful punishment.

Just then, one of the prisoners from the inside came to the cell door and pushed a button behind the guard's desk that allowed the door to open.

Paige and Sky rushed inside.

"Thank you!" Sky said to the prisoner, her words followed with a gasp. The prisoner who'd ganged up on Sky and started the beating had let them inside.

The compound swarmed with activity. Paige and Sky hurried to their corner, where they huddled together, looking out through the bars, both of them wondering, hoping, that Dalton was safe.

The reality of what had just taken place began to slowly sink in, and together Paige and Sky mourned the loss of their friend, even though they'd only known her for one day. She'd risked her life for them, and they were alive because of her.

As they realized the fact that they wouldn't have survived the escape, another reality hit them. If that hadn't worked, how in the world were they going to get out of this place?

* * *

Dalton didn't sleep the entire night. He hadn't recognized the woman who'd run into the road from the shadows, but he knew it wasn't Paige or Sky. But who was she, and why had she come in their place? Were they okay? What was going on?

The biggest question that remained was how he was going to get them out of there.

Nu remained in the main room, near Dalton. Grandmother Tao took a shift to watch over him through the night. The family kept a constant vigil over him. It was amazing that he was still alive, though he was understandably weak. His family never gave up hope that he'd fully recover, but what kind of charges would he face if he did survive?

Dalton watched Grandmother Tao give Nu a few drops of water, then dab his mouth with her apron. She sat next to him and stroked his hand with hers.

The devotion and love this family had for each other was heart-warming. Dalton knew that Soon Lee had been raised well, surrounded by love and family. It warmed his soul to picture her in such a wonderful environment. These people weren't wealthy—they barely had a roof over their heads and food to eat—but they were content as long as their family was safe, healthy, and together. Worldly possessions couldn't provide any of that.

Grandmother Tao looked up and saw Dalton watching her. She bowed her head and continued stroking Nu's arm. Then she stopped and looked up again.

Her voice soft, Grandmother Tao began to speak to Dalton. Dalton had no idea what she was saying, but he knew it was important.

Scooting closer, Dalton knelt on the other side of Nu. The flicker of candlelight played on their faces.

Grandmother Tao said the words again.

Dalton shook his head.

By the look in Grandmother Tao's eyes, she desperately wanted him to know what she was saying. Dalton hoped that perhaps in the morning they could find someone to help. Maybe he could find Kito to translate for him, although he didn't know whether to trust Kito or not. Of course, Anh seemed to believe Dalton had done the right thing by trying to help Paige and Sky escape. Still, Dalton had to wonder how the guards had managed to see the woman. It was almost as if they were waiting for her.

Dalton's thoughts were interrupted by a weak whisper escaping Nu's lips. He looked at Grandmother Tao, whose own eyes reflected amazement.

They both leaned closer.

"The elders . . ." Nu murmured.

Realizing that the message was for him since it was in English, Dalton put his ear next to Nu's mouth to hear him better.

"Visit the elders," Nu managed to whisper.

"Is that what Grandmother Tao is trying to tell me? To visit the elders in the village?"

"Yes," Nu answered, then started to cough.

Dalton raised Nu's head so Grandmother Tao could give him a sip of water to coat his dry throat.

"Hang in there, Nu," Dalton told him. "You're going to be okay."

Tears streamed down Grandmother Tao's cheeks as she gave him one last sip of water, then Dalton gently lowed Nu's head so he could rest.

"Thank you," Dalton told him.

Nu didn't respond, but it was obvious that he had turned the corner, somehow cheating death. As he rested comfortably, Nu's breathing came steady and strong.

Dalton looked at Grandmother Tao, who gave him a gentle smile. Her eyes and her smile reminded him of Soon Lee, and his heart grew warm. "Thank you," he told her and knew, somehow, that she understood.

The elders in the village were powerful. Dalton hoped that they would find it in their hearts to help him. Hopefully the gift to the school would show that their purpose in the village was purely to visit Soon Lee's family and bring supplies to the children.

Feeling hopeful, Dalton finally fell into an exhausted sleep, with a plan to go to the village early the next morning and find the men who could help him.

CHAPTER EIGHTEEN

Sky felt bile rise in her throat as she looked down at the bowl of rice in front of her. She was starving, yet eating bug-infested rice quelled her appetite.

She exchanged glances with Paige, who was also disgusted but famished.

They had to get out of there.

Last night's escape fiasco had set the whole camp abuzz. Paige and Sky couldn't understand what the other prisoners were saying, but they knew it had to be about Beatrice trying to escape and getting shot and killed.

Sky felt overcome with guilt. Warning dreams weren't exactly something she was used to, but this one had seemed so real, she knew in her heart it wasn't just her imagination.

With the failed escape attempt, Sky knew there would be tightened security. They were already being watched like hawks. Sky felt the guard's eyes on her every move. She hadn't said more than two words to Paige for fear that the guards would suspect they were up to something. Being beaten was one thing; being shot was another.

The one person who did seem to be treating them differently was the woman who had seemed to have it out for Sky. Had Sky earned her respect by not telling on her? Had the woman suspected them of trying to escape, and that act of defiance had gained her respect?

Sky didn't know, nor did she care. She just wanted the woman and her pack to leave her and Paige alone.

After eating as much of the rice as they could without gagging, Paige and Sky went out into the common area. The guards kept a close eye on them, and they refrained from speaking between themselves. At least before this happened, they could talk and help pass the time. But now they didn't even have that. Sky knew they'd both go nuts without conversation.

She thought about her father, wondering what he was doing and if he was safe. Was he being watched? And had Nu survived? She would never get the image of his lifeless, bloodstained body out of her mind. This whole experience seemed surreal—a living nightmare.

Yet, as bad as it was, Sky knew her father had suffered even worse conditions than they were in. He'd seen much worse than they had.

Tears stung Sky's eyes as her love and appreciation for all he'd been through grew to enormous proportions. She drew strength from the thought that he'd survived. Not only survived, but triumphed. He was her hero, and she missed him with all her heart.

She swallowed, fighting back the tears. When she looked over at Paige, she saw tears in her eyes also. Paige was thinking about the same things—Sky knew it. They'd come to Vietnam to gain an appreciation of Dalton's experience as a POW, and here they were in prison.

Vowing to stay strong, to be as valiant as her father, Sky swallowed the knot in her throat and took a deep breath. She would not let them break her. She believed that her own prayers, Paige's prayers, and, most assuredly, her father's prayers would be answered. She knew that her mother was watching over her. She knew that God had more in store for her than wasting away in a Vietnamese prison. Her patriarchal blessing was full of promises, and they wouldn't be fulfilled inside this place!

No! Sky straightened as the thoughts empowered her. This experience was not going to rob her of who she knew she was and what her purpose in life was.

She grabbed Paige's hand and gave it a reassuring squeeze. Paige sniffed, looking at her with a puzzled expression. Sky looked her straight in the eye and gave her a knowing wink. They would get through this together. More than anything, she was grateful she wasn't going through this alone. Her love for Paige knew no bounds.

The dark clouds overhead broke, and after a few warning droplets of rain fell, a torrent burst down upon them, drenching them as they ran for the cover of their cell.

* * *

It hadn't been easy, but Dalton managed to find someone who could translate and take him to see the elders in the village. As they visited hut after hut, they found none of the men home. The men were old but continued to work in the rice fields day after day. This was their way of life. It would never be easy for them, and it would never end.

With one last stop to make, Dalton felt his hopes weakening. The rain showed no signs of letting up, but the people of the village didn't seem to notice. They went about the daily business of trying to make enough money to feed their families.

As they approached the final hut, a small bamboo structure with a thatched roof like all the others, Dalton said a silent prayer. Someone had to help him. He couldn't wait one more day to get his wife and daughter released. The thought of them staying even another hour was almost more than he could bear.

A thin bamboo mat hung over the doorway, keeping out the rain, but Dalton could see through enough to make out the shape of a man sitting next to the dim glow of a fire.

Dalton's Vietnamese companion called out to the man inside. A weak reply told them to come in.

To Dalton's dismay, the man sitting on the floor near the fire was the elder who had shunned him earlier.

Feeling the rest of his hopes evaporate, Dalton joined his companion on the floor next to the elder. Out of respect, they didn't speak but waited for him to address them first.

All three of them sat in silence until Dalton decided he couldn't wait around for this guy to come to his rescue. When the elder showed no signs of communicating, Dalton nudged his companion and nodded toward the door.

The translator bowed his head, and they both began to stand. The elder finally spoke.

"He wants to know why you are here," Dalton's companion said.

"Tell him that my wife and my daughter and I came to his village in peace. My first wife died, and we came to visit her family so my daughter could learn about her ancestors."

The elder listened to the translation, then gave one slight nod of his head, allowing Dalton to continue.

"Let him know that my wife and daughter are in jail for something they didn't do, something they had no part of. They weren't aware of what was going on until the shooting started. I don't know where to go for help," Dalton said, feeling emotion clog his throat. "The American Embassy is trying to get someone down here, but it may take a few more days. My wife and daughter have done nothing wrong. They don't deserve to be in prison."

The elder listened to Dalton's words through the translator.

"I just can't bear the thought that my wife and daughter are in there. I can't imagine what kind of treatment they are receiving. I was here as a prisoner during the war," Dalton said, allowing the man to have time to translate. "I know how difficult prison life is. I lost my leg in prison."

Dalton noticed that as the elder listened to the other man speak, the elder's expression changed. Was it pain? Anger? He couldn't tell, but it was clear the old man was upset.

The old man lifted his hand and motioned toward the door.

"It is time for us to leave now," the translator said.

"But . . ."

"I am sorry. We must respect his wishes. Coming here has upset him."

The translator stood and went directly out the door. Dalton had no other choice. He pushed himself awkwardly to his feet and stood, his head nearly brushing the bamboo rafters above.

Then, without benefit of the translator, Dalton said, "Sir, if there's anything you can do—please, please," he begged, "help my family."

The man kept his head turned away, and Dalton left the house.

* * *

Early the next morning, the guard woke up Sky and grunted for her to follow.

Sky, along with several others, including the woman who had started the fight with her, stood in line at the door, waiting for instruction. Turning to look back, Sky lifted her eyebrows, trying to ask Paige what was going on.

Paige shrugged her shoulders, her expression worried.

The guard finally announced something to them that Sky didn't understand, and the door opened. The line of prisoners slowly followed the guard down the stairs and out into the courtyard, crossing to the other side to a building where a heavy door was opened. One of the prisoners gasped and stepped back, bumping into a guard. Sky watched in horror as the guard promptly whacked her on the arm with the club. Sky thought she heard the crack of bone underneath the solid blow of the club. The prisoner doubled over in pain but suffered in silence.

What was this place?

Sky soon found out.

The prisoners were herded into a black, empty room, void of windows or furniture. It was damp, dark, and without a doubt would turn into an oven during the heat of the day.

They were being punished.

Feeling the urge to cry out, Sky bit on her bottom lip to prevent any sound from escaping her mouth. She didn't want to be on the receiving end of that club.

Once the eleven prisoners were inside, the guards slammed the door shut, the sound reverberating through the blackness.

Falling back against the wall, Sky slid down until she sat on the floor. Resting her arms on her knees and her head on her arms, Sky let her tears fall silently. Why? Why was this happening?

* * *

What was he going to do? Dalton couldn't stay at his mother-in-law's hut any longer doing nothing but waiting and worrying. He went to the noodle shop, where he used the phone to call the American Embassy. He was told someone would call him within an hour's time, so he waited.

He felt like a zombie. Sleep had been difficult. His mind was busy dredging up old nightmares of his time in the jungle prison and in Hanoi. But he also saw images of Paige and Sky enduring horrible, painful things.

At the shop, Anh offered him food, but his appetite was gone. He sat, resting his head in his hands, praying constantly for help.

The feeling of being helpless to do anything for his wife and daughter was driving him insane. Thoughts of bursting into the prison to rescue them flashed through his mind. All sorts of plans and ideas formulated, but none of them made sense. He would be dead before he even found out where they were inside the prison.

The embassy was his last hope.

Nu's three children stayed at the noodle shop with their grandmother until it was time for the two oldest to go to school. The youngest stayed with Uncle Kiem while the women worked, but Uncle Kiem was so upset over Nu's situation and Paige and Sky being in jail that he seemed almost comatose at times.

The minutes seemed like hours as Dalton waited for the call. Finally, a little over an hour later, the phone rang, and Anh summoned Dalton to the phone.

"Hello, Mr. McNamara?" a woman's voice came over the phone.

"Yes," Dalton said anxiously.

"My name is Linda Green. I was told to call you. You are in need of assistance?"

"Yes, Ms. Green. I desperately need your help."

"Could you please explain the situation to me?"

Rolling his eyes, Dalton began the lengthy task of retelling his story to the woman. She said, "I see," several times, murmured "uh-huh" in a few places, but when he finished, her end of the line was silent. Finally she said, "And what exactly is it you would like us to do for you, Mr. McNamara?"

Dalton had reached the boiling point. "I want you to help me get my wife and daughter out of prison!"

"I'm sorry, Mr. McNamara, but we can't do that. Perhaps I should explain the purpose of the U.S. Consul. You see, when you are in a foreign country, you and anyone traveling with you are subject to its laws. We can provide you with a list of attorneys, we can visit your wife and daughter in prison, we can contact any family or friends for you, and if you suspect inhumane or unhealthful conditions, we can *try* and obtain relief for them."

Dalton noticed her emphasis on the word *try.*

"But we are not able to just come and escort them out of prison. I'm sorry if you were under the impression that we could."

"But they didn't do anything and are being charged with drug smuggling."

"Then I will be happy to get you the names of some attorneys in that area who can help you take care of this matter."

Deflated and hopeless, Dalton didn't even thank the woman. He just hung up the phone.

This couldn't be happening.

Feeling the strength in his legs leave him, Dalton quickly found a chair. His head throbbed as he tried to process the woman's words. The knot in his stomach tightened until he thought he would lose the few bites of noodles he'd eaten earlier.

Then he had a thought. Maybe Hai could help him. Maybe Hai knew someone they could trust, an attorney who would be fair.

With that thought, Dalton raced for the phone, knowing he would have to leave Anh a hefty sum of money to help pay for his calls. But right now, cost meant nothing to him. If he had it, he would gladly pay a million dollars to get his loved ones out of that prison.

Dialing the number to the phone in Quang's mother's shop, Dalton closed his eyes, praying that Quang and Hai had returned safely.

To his surprise, Quat answered the phone.

"Hello, Quat? This is Dalton McNamara."

"Mr. Dalton, hello. How are you?"

"I'm fine, thanks," Dalton lied. "Listen, Quat, have your brother and uncle come back yet?"

"Oh, yes. They are home. Quang is outside."

"Could you get him for me?"

Quat left the phone, and Dalton prayed like he'd never prayed before.

A moment later, Quang's voice came on the line.

"Mr. Dalton?"

"Hello, Quang."

"Is everything okay?"

"Actually no, it's not." Dalton told Quang what had happened to Nu, Sky, and Paige.

"Sky is in jail?" he said, his voice filled with concern. "That is very bad. They will not like her inside the prison."

Fear filled Dalton's heart. "What do you mean, Quang?"

"Because she is part American and part Vietnamese. This is not good."

Dalton shut his eyes, begging for strength from above to help him.

"I need help. Does your uncle know any attorneys? I need someone I can trust. Someone who doesn't hate Americans."

"Yes, of course. I am sure he does. I will go find him right now, and we will call you."

"Thank you, son, I appreciate it."

"Okay, Mr. Dalton. You wait right there."

Dalton hung up and felt his hopes grow. Finally there was a glimmer of light at the end of a very dark tunnel.

* * *

The hot, stifling air closed in on Sky until she felt like she was going to pass out. Her head throbbed from the intense heat. Sweat ran down her neck and back. They would die in here if it got much hotter.

"Why?" she whispered, not caring if the others heard her. "Why?"

From the darkness, a voice answered. "They think you are troublemaker."

"You speak English?" Sky sat up straighter, relieved to have someone talk to her.

"Yes."

"They think I'm a troublemaker, that's why I'm in here?"

"Yes. To teach lesson. To show others what will happen if they cause trouble."

"How long will they leave us in here?"

"Hours. Days. Who knows?"

"Will they feed us?"

"Yes, if there is food left over."

More than food, Sky needed water. Her skin was drenched with sweat, and her mouth was as dry as a desert. Her head throbbed so severely that she wondered how much longer it would be until she passed out.

"We could die in here," Sky said.

"Yes, many do."

"Would you mind if I ask why you are in prison?"

"Stealing," the woman replied.

"What did you steal?"

"Food. For my children. Just a few baguettes. They were so hungry." The woman's voice broke. "I do not know what has happened to them."

Sky's heart ached. A mother's desperate act to save her children had ended in this. Such a sad story.

"You have no husband?"

The woman made a noise in her throat that sounded like a groan and a sardonic chuckle.

"He left when I was pregnant."

"How many children do you have?"

"I had three, but my baby died soon after birth."

"How do you know English so well?"

"My parents made me learn so I could go to America to live with my uncle. They wanted me to have a better life. I met my husband there, and we had two children in America. Then when I got pregnant with my third child, we came to Vietnam to visit my family. My mother was very sick. She died soon after."

"I'm sorry," Sky said.

"It has been very difficult," the woman explained. "I felt I needed to take care of my father, but my husband was ready to go back to America. One morning, I woke up, and he was gone. I could not find him, and I had no money to go back, so I stayed with my father. But he has also died, so I am alone."

"And your baby?"

"The cord was wrapped around her neck. She died during delivery."

Again, all Sky could think to say was, "I'm sorry."

"Yes," the woman answered softly. "I am sorry, too."

"Sorry? Why?"

"For beating you up."

Sky straightened. "That was you?"

"Yes."

"But why?"

"Your people ruined our country. My husband ruined my family."

Sky saw her point. Many horrible things had happened in this woman's life as a result of Americans.

"Why are you being nice to me now?"

"You did not turn me in," the woman said. "They would beat me, maybe kill me."

Sky was grateful she hadn't turned in the woman. Those children needed their mother. She wished there was something she could do for her.

"If I ever get out of here," Sky said, "I will find your children and make sure they are safe. I promise."

"Why? Why would you do that?"

"Because not all Americans are like your husband."

"Thank you."

CHAPTER NINETEEN

Dalton's goal the next morning was to find an attorney. Hai knew a man in Ho Chi Minh City, but the man could not come all the way to the village for the case. Hai and Quang offered to come back to help, but Dalton told them to stay. He heard the anguish in Quang's voice, the concern for Paige and Sky. Dalton assured them he would call if he needed them.

Dalton had stopped into the noodle shop for breakfast, and now he stared at the steaming bowl in front of him. He would give everything he had to take his family and go home.

The door to the shop opened, and several more people came inside. Dalton continued holding his head in his hands, praying for help, guidance, inspiration. Something had to happen. Something soon.

A shuffle of feet next to his table caught his attention. Dalton looked up and was shocked at the person standing before him: it was the elder he'd visited yesterday. This time, the old man looked Dalton straight in the eye.

"Hello," Dalton said, wondering what was going on. "Uh, would you like to sit?" he spoke slowly, motioning toward the empty chair.

The man looked at the chair and nodded.

Dalton pointed to his food and asked, "Are you hungry? Would you like something to eat?" He made an eating motion with his hands.

The man shook his head and said, to Dalton's surprise, "No, thank you."

"Oh! You speak English."

"Yes."

"I'm very happy to see you. I need help. I will do anything, pay any amount of money, to help get my wife and daughter out of prison."

"You love them very much."

"Yes, sir. I do."

"Family is very important in Vietnam. We too will do anything to protect our family and our country. Sometimes we have to do things we don't want to do to protect our family."

Dalton nodded his head. He understood.

"It is a duty, an honor, to protect family and country."

"Yes," Dalton agreed.

"Sometimes it takes great courage," the man said.

"Yes." Dalton nodded.

"You have great courage."

The man's comment took Dalton by surprise. He looked at the man and studied his face. There was something familiar, something that pried at his memory. But he just couldn't put his finger on it. He just couldn't—

Then it hit him. Dalton clapped his hand to his heart and took several breaths to calm the erratic beating in his chest. "It's you. From the camp."

The man gave one nod of his head. "Godzilla."

Dalton's mouth dropped open. "You knew?"

"I knew everything."

Dalton didn't know what to say.

"You were a good soldier," the man said. "You had great courage."

A knot formed in Dalton's throat. This was too much of a shock for him.

"I will help you."

Dalton reeled from the shock of seeing the man who'd overseen his suffering during months of torture and deprivation. But here he was, offering to help. And Dalton was at his mercy.

"You will?" Dalton asked.

"Yes."

Dalton still couldn't believe he was talking to Godzilla.

"They are innocent?" the elder asked.

Dalton nodded.

"You are a man of honor. I believe you."

Wiping at his eyes, Dalton quickly gathered his composure. "Thank you."

* * *

Sky felt movement in her hair and the nip of rat's teeth on her scalp but was too weak to move. They had received no food or water since they'd been moved to the black chamber. She'd finally passed out from the heat the day before and had drifted in and out of sleep through the night. But it was a new day, and in a few hours when the sun was overhead, they would get cooked alive again. She doubted she would survive.

She received some comfort from the fact that her mother was in heaven and would be there to greet her. She was also grateful that she'd been trying her best to live a righteous life. She wasn't perfect, but she wasn't afraid to stand before the Lord and account for her life.

There wasn't much movement around her except for the rats waiting for them to die so they could begin their feast. They were already using Sky's hair for an appetizer.

The sound of movement outside the door caught Sky's attention. Was it real, or was it her imagination? She seemed to slip in and out of consciousness so much that she didn't know what was real anymore.

A crack of blinding light speared the darkness as the door inched open. Sky willed her eyes to open and her head to turn, but her body wasn't listening anymore. It was as if the separation of her spirit and body had already begun.

Voices surrounded her, but they drifted farther and farther away until they were gone. She waited for the other light, the one that welcomed her to heaven, where she would finally see her mother again.

* * *

Water. Nothing had ever tasted so sweet. Sky felt her swollen tongue absorb the moisture like a dry sponge. She licked her cracked and swollen lips. Then, a soothing, cool cloth on her forehead and face seemed to breathe life into her limbs, the blood flowing and strengthening her limp frame.

"I think she's coming around," a woman's voice said. "Sky, honey. We're here. You're going to be okay."

Sky didn't even have enough moisture in her body to squeeze out a tear, but she wanted to cry. She tried to whisper Paige's name but the *P* was all she could get out.

"We're safe now, sweetie. We're out of that horrible place."

Sky whimpered.

They gave her more water, the fluids filling her with life again.

"Hey, sweetie," her father's voice came through the clearing fog in her brain. "How ya doin'?"

Sky nodded her head a fraction of an inch. Slowly her strength began to return and, with great effort, she managed to lift her eyelids.

There in front of her, their faces only twelve inches away, were her father and stepmom.

"Hi," she whispered.

Both of them beamed with smiles of relief.

"We made it," she said to Paige.

"We sure did," Paige answered, stroking Sky's forehead.

"And as soon as you feel strong enough, we're heading to Hanoi and going home," Dalton said. "Are you still in the mood for a cheeseburger?"

Sky licked her dry lips. "And fries."

Paige helped her take another sip of water.

"And a chocolate shake."

Dalton and Paige chuckled.

"I think she's going to be okay," Dalton said to Paige. "Hopefully by tomorrow we'll be on our way to Hanoi."

Sky thought about going home to the life she'd always known. She would never—could never—be the same again. There were things now that she wouldn't take for granted again. Especially freedom.

Then she remembered. Like a bolt of lightning, she remembered her promise. And she knew they couldn't leave. Not yet.

"Wait!" Sky said with a start. "We can't go. I promised—"

"Shh, it's okay. You rest. We can talk later," Paige said.

"That's right, sweetie. Everything's going to be okay," her father assured her. "And Quang and Hai are here. Your grandmother, Uncle Kiem, and the rest of the family are all here."

"Nu?"

"He's here too. And he's doing better."

Sky wanted to tell them about the promise she'd made, but she was just too weak. Too tired.

* * *

There was much to celebrate, and Dalton's joy was so great he could barely hold it inside. Their new friend, Nang, or Godzilla as Dalton once knew him, was no monster at all. He proved to be the one person who finally had helped in the release of Paige and Sky, which had come not a minute too soon. Sky had suffered heat exhaustion and was dangerously dehydrated. The other women in the sweatbox had handled the intense heat better than Sky because their bodies were more accustomed to the heat and humidity. Still, they had all been released from the sweatbox and given rest and fluids at Nang's command. Appalled at the conditions inside the prison, Nang had conferred with the elders of the city, and all the guards were subsequently put on probation and given a list of improvements to make before their next inspection. He also appointed several men to review cases and find out which women had fulfilled their sentences and should be released.

But that wasn't all. Nang had been instrumental in saving Nu from having to serve jail time. Because of Nu's injury, he would never be able to return to work as a guard in the opium fields. Since he knew that Nu still had a family to support, Nang felt that Nu deserved a second chance.

Yes, there were many reasons to celebrate, and it was an even greater celebration having Hai and Quang there with them. After hearing the news of Paige and Sky being in prison, they'd traveled nonstop to get there, willing to do anything they could to help. They were also willing to accompany them to Hanoi, an offer which Dalton gladly accepted. In turn, he offered to pay for their flight back to Ho Chi Minh City. This was especially exciting for both of them, since neither had ever been on an airplane. Dalton was grateful for their loyalty and wished he knew some way he could repay them, even though he knew they expected no payment for their trouble.

Everything had finally worked out, and Dalton felt that it had all been in the Lord's hands. All of it.

"Dad," Sky said. "Are you sure Nang will take care of my friend?"

After several days of recovery, Sky had regained her strength and hadn't stopped talking about the woman in the prison.

"Yes, honey. He has promised to find her children and have her released so she can be with them. He's a very powerful man and a very good man. We can trust that he will take care of it." Dalton stroked his daughter's forehead as she rested her head on his knee. Everyone was eating and enjoying a day of celebration.

"Do you think I'll ever know what happens to her and her children?"

"Nu said he would find out and let us know," Dalton assured her. Sky seemed to be content with his answer.

"Are you sure you feel up to traveling tomorrow?" he asked. They were booked on a flight out of Hanoi. "I could check on the airport in Danang. It's only about eight hours away."

"Dad, I'm fine. I can sleep on the train. Besides, I don't want to miss Hanoi. That's one of the most important places we wanted to visit when we came."

"But after all we've been through, maybe we should just get home."

"Even Paige wants to go. We really want to see the place where you were in prison."

Dalton didn't tell her that the prison would probably be the hardest place for him to revisit. Part of him had hoped that his wife and daughter didn't feel up to the trip.

"I'm glad Quang and Hai get to come to Hanoi with us. I feel safer traveling with them," Sky said.

"So do I. And if everything goes well, Quang will be able to come to the States in a few months. He's serious about going to school so he can get a good job and help his family. Of course, you won't mind having him around, will you?" he teased.

Sky rolled her eyes. "Dad."

"I was starting to think we were going to have to extend our vacation longer."

"No," she exclaimed. "I'm ready to go home. This has been an amazing experience, and it will be hard to tell everyone good-bye, but if I don't get fast food soon, I'll die for sure. I need a cheeseburger."

Dalton chuckled. "You just read my mind. We'll be in Hanoi two days, and then we fly out. You'll be home before you know it. Who knows, maybe there's a McDonald's in Hanoi."

"They probably serve tofu burgers."

Dalton and Sky laughed, catching Paige's attention. She came over and sat down beside them. "What's so funny?"

"We're just fantasizing about fast food," Dalton explained.

"I would pay a million dollars for a cheeseburger," Paige said.

Dalton and Sky burst out laughing. It was definitely time to go home.

* * *

Sky wiped the tears from her cheeks as the train left the station. In her heart, she knew she would never see her grandmother again, and she was grateful for the time they had together. They would stay in touch, and that made it a little easier to say good-bye.

"Are you okay?" Quang asked as Sky gazed out the window, amazed at the life-changing experience they'd had since they arrived in Vietnam.

"I think so," she said, turning to look at him. His kind smile and the tender expression in his eyes warmed her heart. "I thought about you after you left."

His smile broadened. "You did?"

She returned his smile. "Yes."

Their gazes stayed locked for several seconds.

Then she said, "So?"

"So?" he echoed.

"So, did you think about me?" she asked.

He dipped his chin and looked deeper into her eyes. "Every minute that I was awake."

Feeling color rush to her cheeks, Sky looked away, but Quang reached up and gently turned her face back to look at him. "I missed you. I missed our talks. I missed the way you make me laugh."

Sky felt her heartbeat increase. "Same here." The train whistled loudly as they passed by a small village alongside the tracks. Children standing on a nearby dirt road jumped up and down and waved wildly at the passing train. Sky's eyes stung with tears at the sight. The children here were so precious. Even living in filth and poverty, they were happy. Somehow, someday, she hoped to find a way to help them, to provide them with more school supplies and other things they needed. These were her people. She was lucky to have freedom and opportunity to help them. She felt it her duty to do so.

Holding hands, Quang and Sky began talking. He wanted to know everything that had happened since they'd last seen each other, everything that had happened in the prison. And, just as before, Sky felt as if she were talking to her best friend, someone she'd known all her life.

* * *

The ride on the Unification Express took one and a half days. The train dated back to the time when the French had constructed the railroad nearly forty years earlier. It ran even slower now than it did originally. And Dalton felt every mile on his backside.

Finally, they arrived at their destination, the city of Hanoi.

Since the only part of Hanoi that Dalton had seen during the war was the inside of the prison and the inside of a military vehicle on the way out of town, there was nothing familiar to him. Still, he felt a connection to the city, and instead of feeling anxious about revisiting the site of his incarceration, he now looked forward to it. This was the point of final closure for him. This was the last step in his healing.

Paige and Sky nearly shouted for joy when they arrived at the hotel. By American standards their room was old, dirty, and disgusting. But after all they'd been through, they felt like they'd arrived at the Taj Mahal. Real mattresses, a real toilet, and a shower!

Nothing felt better than the good night's sleep they all had. The next morning, feeling like new, they met Quang and Hai for breakfast, then ventured out into the city.

Paige and Sky were in heaven when they realized that an entire section of the city was dedicated to shopping. Thirty streets were named after the products that were sold on that particular street— Music Street, Paper Street, Basket Street. Everything a person could imagine was found on one of those streets.

But no McDonald's.

They saw pigeon eggs, boiled snakes, spiced snails, stuffed intestines, everything but cheeseburgers. "It seems like all they eat is stuff that was crawling around in their garden the night before," Sky told her dad. "What did you eat when you were in prison?"

"I would have given anything for a few garden critters, honey," Dalton told her. "We didn't have much more than rice with a little pig fat in it, and occasionally there were a couple of pieces of vegetable in it. I lost sixty pounds on that diet."

"Are you nervous to go back to the prison, Dad?"

"Not anymore. With you and Paige here, and Hai and Quang, I feel as ready as I'll ever be to go back there."

"I know I will never understand what it was like for you, but after what Paige and I went through, I think I will have a better idea of it now."

"I think so too, hon. But having you in prison was worse than being there myself."

Sky returned her father's hug, then gave him a kiss on the cheek.

* * *

"So, this is it." Dalton stood in front of what was left of the Hanoi Hilton. Most of the prison had been torn down, and in its place was a tower of offices.

When they entered what was left of the prison, they were directed toward an area housing a museum that was dirty, run-down, and smelled like used cat litter. Dalton remembered that smell and felt his stomach turn.

The displays inside the museum were all propaganda. Black-and-white photographs showed the smiling victors and the beaten-down Americans. The English translations under the pictures were amusing. One caption read: "American soldiers flee Saigon in a plain." And one caption had spelled the word annihilation "annhilaten."

There was little mention of the American soldiers who were held inside the prison. Only two rooms of photos were provided to depict the soldiers' stay there. Ninety percent of what was presented gave the impression that the soldiers received good treatment. There was even a picture of two soldiers receiving packages from home. According to the displays, life at the Hanoi Hilton was the next best thing to being home.

"Dad," Sky said as they moved to the next area, "why don't they say how it really was?"

"Because the victors get to write the record, and that's how it's remembered in history," Dalton replied. He put his arm around his daughter and gave her a hug. "It's okay, honey. No one really won this war. America lost 58,000 soldiers, but the Vietnamese lost millions. It was horrible for both sides."

With Sky on one side and Paige on the other, Dalton walked toward the cells that had been preserved for the museum. Nothing had changed. It had been old and smelly when he was there, and it was still old and smelly.

They wandered in and out of several cells, listening to the guide explain uninteresting details about the prison. Dalton doubted they'd show the room where the soldiers were tortured, some to the point of death, all to the point of pain, and for some, to the point of permanent injury.

Lingering in one of the cells for a moment, Dalton told them about the time he sat inside his cell and saw a butterfly come through the small window.

"The Vietnamese believe that butterflies hold the spirits of those who've passed from this life," Quang told him.

Dalton liked that. "That butterfly offered a lot of hope for me that day," he said. "Just when I thought I couldn't go on, I saw that butterfly and knew one day I would be free again."

"What's this?" Sky said.

Dalton turned to see his daughter crouched down, peering at the wall.

"What?" Dalton asked, getting down on his one knee next to her.

"This. It looks like some sort of writing."

"I don't believe it," Dalton's voice came out a whisper. "It's still here."

"Dad?"

"Honey, what is it?" Paige asked with concern.

"This was my cell," he told them. "I thought it might be, but now I know for sure. I carved this into the wall."

"Let me see if I can read it," Sky said, peering closely at the scratches. "It says, 'Wait on the Lord.'"

Dalton squeezed his eyes shut as tears threatened. He nodded his head and drew in a long breath. When he could speak he said, "That's it. That's what I carved. It's from the twenty-seventh Psalm." He continued. "Deliver me not over unto the will of mine enemies: for false witnesses are risen up against me, and such as breathe out cruelty. I had fainted, unless I had believed to see the goodness of the Lord in the land of the living. Wait on the Lord: be of good courage, and he shall strengthen thine heart: wait, I say, on the Lord."

Tears ran down Paige's and Sky's cheeks. They joined in a hug, holding each other for a moment of silence, a collective prayer in their hearts filled with gratitude for deliverance and for the blessings of strength from heaven above.

And in that room, the final spot where the closure came, the healing began.

CHAPTER TWENTY

"Do you think I'll have any trouble getting these dog tags through customs?" Paige asked as she shut the lid on the suitcase containing their souvenirs.

"I think they'll be okay," Dalton said. "How many did you end up with?"

"Seventy-three. But I wish I'd found a thousand."

"Still, it's a good start," Dalton said. "Besides, who knows? You may get home and be able to find the rest on eBay."

Paige laughed.

Dalton pulled his wife into his arms and gave her a tender kiss and a long hug. "This has been some trip, hasn't it?"

"That's putting it mildly."

Dalton chuckled and squeezed her tighter, then stepped back and looked into her face. "I will never forget how close I came to losing you. I don't ever want to feel that way again."

Paige blinked several times. She was overcome with emotion whenever the mention of the prison came up. "Me either."

Giving her hand a squeeze and then lifting it to his lips, Dalton kissed his wife's knuckles. The memory of Paige and Sky in prison was one that would be painful to remember but one they could all work through together. "I knew it was going to take a miracle to get you and Sky out of there, and we got one."

Paige smiled. She felt there was no denying that God had held them in His hand and kept a watchful eye over them.

"This trip has changed our lives forever," Dalton said. "It gave me closure to my past and has enriched our future."

Nodding, Paige said, "We are connected to these people, Sky especially. For her sake we must help her stay in touch with them."

"I bet you would've thought twice about marrying me if you'd known what you were getting into."

Giving her husband a quick kiss, Paige answered, "I would go through you-know-what for you." Then she thought for a second. "Oh wait, I think I did!"

They were both laughing when Sky walked out of the bathroom, looking healthy and fully recovered. She was so excited for the trip home, she'd barely slept a wink the night before.

"What's so funny?"

"We were just talking about you and me in that prison."

"I don't remember anything happening worth laughing about," Sky said.

"That's for sure," Paige agreed. "You should have heard Jared on the phone when I called him. At first he was so upset he could hardly speak, but he finally settled down and we talked about it calmly. By the time we hung up, he was making plans to call *Oprah.*"

"That'd be cool!" Sky said.

"All that matters is that we're safe and together," Dalton said, scooping his wife and daughter into a hug. "And just think, we're only hours away from fast food."

"No more noodles and tofu," Sky said.

"And rice," Paige added. "It will be years before I have rice again."

"Not if Quang comes to stay with us for a while," Dalton reminded her. "We'll have to make rice for him."

"I'll make it, but I'm not eating it," Paige said.

"Paige, remember all the bugs in the rice at the prison?" Sky said.

Pulling a face, Paige answered, "I told you to not remind me of that." She shuddered at the thought and felt her stomach turn.

"Oh, I almost forgot," Dalton said, reaching into the pocket of his pants. "Before we left, Nu gave me something." He handed a small, tissue-wrapped item to Sky.

"What is it, Dad?"

"Open it. I think you'll be pleasantly surprised."

Unfolding the tissue, Sky exposed the contents and gasped. "My necklace! But how?"

"When Nu took both of you to get supplies, he did meet with one of his comrades, just like the police said. But it wasn't to make a delivery or exchange drugs. It was to get your necklace."

Sky's mouth dropped open. She didn't know what to say.

"He remembered the guard yanking it from your neck and was determined to get it back for you."

"He was willing to do that for me?"

"Yes. Because you're family."

"Here," Paige said. "Let me help you put it on."

Paige slipped the cool metal around Sky's neck and fastened the necklace. She then gave her stepdaughter a hug.

"I can't believe he did that. How can I ever thank him? I mean, look at all that happened."

"Sweetie, you don't need to worry about all of that," Dalton said. "Nu and your grandmother and the rest of the family believe that even though this has been a very difficult experience, it's also been a great blessing. This was the only way Nu could get out of guarding the opium fields. He has been spared going to prison. He has a chance for a new beginning, a new life. A better life. They are very grateful that all of this has happened."

"It's amazing when you think about it," Paige added. "The fact that Nang, the guard when you were in the jungle prison, was the one who helped set us free is a miracle. Almost like it has all been by design."

"Heavenly design," Dalton said.

"I wonder if Mom had anything to do with it," Sky mused.

"I wouldn't be surprised," Dalton answered, liking the thought that Soon Lee had been instrumental in this amazing experience that had brought closure in their lives and completed the circle that connected them all for eternity.

They all remained quiet as they stood together in a small circle, arm in arm.

Dalton finally spoke. "What do you say we have a family prayer before we leave?"

They knelt down on the floor of their hotel room, and Dalton offered a prayer filled with gratitude. By the time he was done, they were all crying. They ended the prayer with one last hug.

"I need to go fix my makeup," Sky said. "Then I'm ready to go."

"Have we got all the bags packed?" Dalton said, scanning the room one last time for any stray belongings.

"I checked several times," Paige told him. "I think I got—"

A scream from the bathroom interrupted her.

Paige and Dalton looked at each other and said in unison, "Gecko."

They laughed, and went to rescue Sky one last time.

* * *

Quang and Sky held hands as they walked down the concourse of the airport. Hai and Quang would leave for Ho Chi Minh City an hour after the others left for the United States.

"You are excited to go home?" Quang asked.

"Yeah," she answered. "I miss it a lot."

"Is America really so different?"

She stopped dead in her tracks. "Quang, America is different in almost every way. Compared to you and your people, Americans are very spoiled. We don't have to work hard all day long to get enough money to feed our family for just that day. We have cars, televisions, microwaves, and indoor plumbing. We can drink water out of the faucet if we want. We have carpet."

"What is that?"

"It's a soft cushion on our floors that feels good under your feet. Kind of like grass."

"What is grass?"

Nobody in Vietnam had grass in their yards—just chickens, pigs, and mud.

She didn't know how to answer. "You know what? I think this is all stuff you'll just have to see when you come to America."

Quang nodded.

"There's one other thing that is different," she said.

"What is that?"

"We have freedom."

They started walking again.

"What is it like?" he said. "I cannot imagine a life like you describe."

"Vietnam is your home, and it is an amazing place, but it is hard for me to see how much people struggle, how poor everyone is. Your government controls most of what you do and how you live your life. Uncle Hai can't work at a regular job because the government still punishes him for his part in the war over thirty years ago."

Quang nodded again.

"But you know what?" she said.

"What?"

"I have great admiration for you. Your lives are difficult yet you still find joy in the small things. Americans could learn a few things from you."

Quang smiled.

"I know that I will never, ever take freedom for granted again. I didn't understand how important it was until I didn't have it," she explained. "Our country went through so much so we could have freedom—so many people died fighting for it—yet we take it for granted. I wish I could help the people in my country understand how blessed we are. I wish everyone in my country could come here and see how other people live and struggle each day just to find enough food to eat."

"Maybe you can."

"Yeah, maybe," she said. "I hope so. I've learned so much while I've been here. I've learned who I am and who my mother was. I'm proud of this. I'm proud of my heritage. I'm also proud of my father and what he did as a soldier in the war. He fought so your country could have freedom like we have, and I'm proud of him for what he did and what he went through. I understand all of this so much better."

"I want to understand these things about my own father," Quang said.

"You will, when you come to America," she told him. "Knowing that you are coming makes it easier to tell you good-bye."

"For me too," he said.

"How does your mother feel about you leaving Vietnam?"

"She cried when I told her."

"I'm sorry," Sky said.

"No, her tears were not of sadness, but of joy. She is happy that I can go and make a better life for myself. And I promised her that I would take care of her and my brothers and sisters too. My father would want me to."

"What about Hai?"

"There is nothing for him in Vietnam. We are his only family. He would like to come to America before he dies. He wants to go to Disneyland."

Sky laughed. "Disneyland is very close to my house. He can go every day if he wants. The bus goes right down our street."

"He would like that very much." Quang gave her hand a squeeze and smiled. "You say that coming to Vietnam has changed your life, but having you come has changed my life. I am very grateful. And when I come to America, there is something else I would like to do."

"What's that?"

"I would like to visit your Mormon church. The book you gave me—I have read it."

"You read the Book of Mormon?"

"Yes. I liked it very much. I do not understand everything I read, but it made me feel very good inside. It made me feel happy. Those people had great struggles too. Many battles, just like our country. I would like people in my country to read this book. It would bring them happiness. It would help them understand the purpose of their lives better. I found one part in Alma that I really liked. It said, 'Whosoever shall put their trust in God shall be supported in their trials, and their troubles, and their afflictions, and shall be lifted up at the last day.' I like this very much. I told it to my mother, and she asked me to read more to her. It was hard to translate, but she also liked to hear about a Father in Heaven who loves us. This is a great thing to know. This is something I wish I could tell the people of my country."

Sky saw a great missionary appear before her eyes, and her whole body tingled with the thought of him bringing the gospel to his people. She wondered if that was one of the reasons they were supposed to come here—to meet Quang and his uncle and help bring the gospel to a land that so desperately needed its message.

"Thank you again for that book," Quang said.

"I will send it to you in Vietnamese as soon as I get home," she promised.

"No. I will come and get it," he said.

Sky smiled. "Yes, that's a much better idea."

Dalton and Paige called for her. It was time to say good-bye.

"I will see you soon, right?" Sky said, trying hard to keep from crying.

"Yes, as soon as Uncle Hai and I get our documents ready, we will come."

"Then this really isn't good-bye, is it?"

"No," Quang said. "I will see very you soon."

He gave her a hug and a kiss on her forehead. "Very soon," he said again.

Sky also hugged Hai, a gentle man with a gentle soul. He felt like a grandfather to her, kind and loving.

"We will see you very soon also?" she said.

"Yes," he answered. "I would very much like to see Mickey Mouse."

"He lives close by. We'll take you there the day you arrive in America."

Hai smiled broadly and bowed his head.

Their parting would only be for a brief period of time, and then they would meet again.

* * *

Sky checked her watch again, counting the hours until they were back in the States. Her mouth watered just thinking of the food. They'd all lost weight on their trip, and Sky's stomach had never really adjusted to the different diet. But she had no regrets. Any sacrifice they'd had to make on this trip was worth it. The course of her life had been altered. Not only had she gained an understanding of who she was and the great heritage she had, but she'd also come to understand how lucky she was to have Paige for a second mother.

A snore from her father broke her thoughts.

Sky and Paige looked at each other and giggled.

"I haven't seen him sleep so well since we got married," Paige told her.

"I haven't seen him sleep this well ever," Sky said.

"Maybe his nightmares are finally over," Paige said.

Sky nodded, hoping that her father was finally free from all the pain, guilt, and torment that had plagued him for so many years. Old memories had finally been replaced with new ones.

"How about you?" Paige asked her stepdaughter. "You're not going to start having nightmares now, are you?"

Sky shook her head. "No. I think that everything that happened was for a reason. And even though it was horrible, I know we were watched over. I really felt my mom close by. Especially in that dream I had. I don't think I've felt this close to her since she died."

"That's good," Paige said. "I thought a lot about Lou while we were in prison. I thought about how maybe she was looking down on us from heaven, helping to sustain us and keep us strong."

"Maybe she was with my mom."

Paige smiled. "They would be good friends."

"Yeah, I bet they would too."

Sky felt it was the right time to show her stepmom something. "Paige, I want to show you this." Lifting the locket off her neck, Sky opened it and tilted it so Paige could see inside. There, on one side, was the picture of Soon Lee, but on the other side, Sky had slipped in a picture of Paige. "This is so I can keep both of my moms close to my heart."

Tears welled up in Paige's eyes. Her chin quivered, and instead of saying anything, she wrapped her arms around Sky and gave her a hug.

After a moment, Paige let go, but she kept hold of Sky's hand. "Thank you."

"No, Paige, thank you. I know my mom's spirit was close to me in prison, but it was having you right by my side that helped me get through that. I couldn't have done it without you."

They hugged again, each of them sniffing and wiping at her eyes.

"Hey," Dalton said. "What's going on?"

Paige and Sky laughed. "Nothing. It's a girl thing."

Anyone interested in finding out more about POW or MIA soldiers from the Vietnam War can contact The National League of Families of American Prisoners and Missing in Southeast Asia, 1005 North Glebe Road, Suite 170, Arlington, Virginia, 22201, (703) 465-7432.

ABOUT THE AUTHOR

In the fourth grade, Michele Ashman Bell was considered a daydreamer by her teacher and was told on her report card that, "She has a vivid imagination and would probably do well with creative writing." Her imagination, combined with a passion for reading, has enabled Michele to live up to her teacher's prediction. She loves writing books, especially those that inspire and edify while entertaining.

Michele grew up in St. George, Utah, where she met her husband at Dixie College before they both served missions—his to Pennsylvania, and hers to Frankfurt, Germany. Seven months after they returned they were married, and are now the proud parents of four children: Weston, Kendyl, Andrea, and Rachel.

A favorite pastime of Michele's is supporting her children in all of their activities, traveling both in and outside the United States with her husband and family, and doing research for her books. She also recently became scuba certified. Aside from being a busy wife and mother, Michele is an aerobics instructor at the Life Centre Athletic Club near her home, and she currently teaches in the Relief Society.

Michele is the best-selling author of several books and a Christmas booklet and has also written children's stories for the *Friend* magazine.

If you would like to be updated on Michele's newest releases or correspond with her, please send an e-mail to info@covenant-lds.com. You may also write to her in care of Covenant Communications, P.O. Box 416, American Fork, UT 84003-0416.